MESSIN' WITH T

– A Dave Hunter novel –

Steve Bartington

FPP
Fulton Point Publishing

Fulton Point Publishing

Communications House

9 St. John's Street

Colchester

Essex CO2 7NN

www.fultonpoint.co.uk

ISBN 978-1-5272-5199-1

Also available by the author

Essex Man Blues

For Automatic Slim

Chapter 1

POW! Dave slugged the ugly bastard right in the kisser and split his lip, and hurt his hand doing it. His opponent didn't flinch, so Dave repeated the blow – BIFF! This time he caught the spot between the nose and the mouth where he knew it could really hurt. Yet it didn't seem to register.

Danny and Mick came out from behind the bar to try to contain the situation, and both of them hoped the club's policy on fighting – no weapons, keep it clean, shake hands after, etc. – would be adhered to. Lianda, Dave's saxophone-playing girlfriend, had done as he said and gone out back; he didn't want her near this sort of thing.

"Now get the fuck out of h —"

BAM! Dave never finished the sentence. He was cut off by a lumpy knuckle sandwich that crunched his nose and sent him crashing to the floor. He'd heard of people being downed in one punch before, but he hadn't seen it until now.

He got to his feet quickly enough to make him dizzy

but ultimately not fast enough, for no sooner was he standing once more when …

K-POW! Another devastating blow! This time Dave took down a passing waitress who had scurried behind him, mouse-like, in an attempt to flee the scene. She yelped as she lost her footing and her plates landed with a clatter.

Now you've done it.

The band stopped playing at the first sign of trouble, and the people on the dance floor hadn't really known what to do. A few of them winced and made that strange sucking noise some people make when they see something that looks painful, but that was about it.

Danny and Mick watched on nearby. They both found themselves in a similar predicament to Rocky in the fourth installment of the popular movie canon; they respected a man's wish that you don't throw the towel (or bar towel) and stop the fight, but they didn't want their friend to die horribly at the hands of a madman either.

But Dave Hunter was the way Dave Hunter was, and there was no chance of him backing out or breaking the rules and accepting help now. His mind was made up. This dickhead was going down – it was just a matter of how and when.

He got to his feet then helped the waitress get to hers. With her out of the way, he weighed up his adversary and stared him down, calm as you like.

He was shorter than Daves's five-feet-nine but made up for it with a wider frame. He had a bald, almost bullet-shaped head and a stocky build, and Dave reckoned he couldn't have had more than twenty-five birthdays. Dave checked his eyes, and they were calm but menacingly so; something was brewing in there, and it smelled like trouble.

The next thing Dave checked was the ears. His late father, Don Hunter, had been a boxing coach nearly all his life, and he had taught Dave to be wary of people with cauliflower ears. The old man told him this was a sign that someone had had a few fights over the years, so he would probably know how to handle himself. This young man's ears looked normal, so Dave moved on to his footwear. Adidas trainers. Not a breach of dress code *per se* but frowned upon nonetheless, and Dave was glad he wasn't wearing Dr. Martens or Bovver Boots.

Dave's nose was bust for sure, and his mouth and nasal cavities were filled with hot blood, much of which dripped on his dance floor. For some reason, this stoked his fire, and he jammed his fist into the mouth of the young thug again — ZOK! His enemy winced and drew breath, his first show of emotion since the dopey smile he'd worn as he'd groped Dave's girlfriend's ass just a moment earlier.

In fact, he reminded Dave of cricketer Ian Botham as he spat out a mixture of blood, teeth, and attitude, and this was when it hit the fan. He roared as he charged at Dave and heaved him high in the air before slamming him onto the wooden dance floor. '*Ooh, that's gotta hurt,*' thought Mick, standing close by. "Do you need some help, Dave?" Mick called out.

"Noooo!," Dave groaned, not wanting to lose face even though his poor chances of winning told him he probably should. He also knew he should get to his feet before this guy put the boot in, but he didn't have the strength. All he could do now was let the bastard wear himself out.

The blows rained down, and they rained down hard. BAM! He caught Dave's jaw with a quick left, then KRRRUNCH! He cut Dave's eyebrow with his right. WHAP! The same arm whiplashed back like an angry rattlesnake and caught Dave's mouth and nose with a brutal back-fist strike; Dave's head spun with the momentum of the backhanded blow, and he spilt a mouthful of blood, like Arnold Schwarzenegger in his final battle with his nemesis 'Predator' in the movie of the same name. Then, his nameless foe raised his fist for what was surely the final blow.

Only, he took a bit too long doing it, and as the death-blow came down, Dave tipped his head to one side. Nobody made the sucking sound as Dave's enemy punched the dance floor hard enough to send ripples along the nearby Thames Estuary. This was the bad guy, and he deserved no sympathy.

But didn't he just howl with pain, though? Danny, Mick, and to a lesser extent, Dave all had a little snigger while the crowd looked on with a mixture of horror, disgust, and fascination.

But everybody laughed when Dave's would-be aggressor, doubled-up with pain and hopping from side to side, came back half-a-dozen steps or so and slipped on a piece of banoffee pie from the tray of the toppled waitress a moment ago. He went arse-over-head and made a satisfying thud as he hit the ground.

The laughter stopped when he sprang to his feet,

seemingly unhurt, and drew a flick-knife, which made a sickening 'tchk' sound as he released the deadly five-inch blade. He held it out at Dave, focusing on his kill and forgetting to check the space behind him …

Certain skills never leave those who master them. As a soldier in the British Army, Daniel Blyth had learnt to move in total silence, and it was something he'd been teaching Mick Davies to do recently. Danny gave Mick a nod, which confirmed it was time for him to leave training school.

They crept up behind the menacing figure, with Mick to the left of him and Danny to his right, and he never heard them coming. Mick tapped the big guy's shoulder, and as he looked around — SMASH! Mick struck him so hard his head spun nearly a hundred-and-eighty degrees, setting him up correctly for Danny on the other side — BOOM!

Though he was still vertical, he dropped the knife, and Mick kicked it over to Dave, who picked it up and tucked it away in his sock.

"Can we please get this right?" Danny said to Mick.

Mick nodded. He was ready. This would be easy.

"We need you to turn around so we can have a look at you, sir," said Danny, and in his delirium, the thug did just as he was told (one of Danny's left-hooks left you that way).

Danny looked over at Mick: "One, two … *Three!*" On the last count, they brought their fists back, Mick his right, Danny his left, and with perfect timing they hit him hard enough that his feet left the ground before his weighty body landed on it; he was out for the count, and Danny and Mick's practice had paid off.

Danny and Mick took a leg each and dragged the unconscious oaf in the direction of the nearest fire door, over by the front of the building. He looked funny down there, arms splayed out behind him, his head bobbing as they pulled him along, but to Danny and Mick, this was no laughing matter: this was business. Danny, who walked ahead of Mick on account of his longer arms, had the serious look of a chief mourner as he made his way forward. He put his hand down on the iron bolt and threw the double doors open – now for the hard part.

With some difficulty, they got him off the ground and carried him out the building and over to a parked dumpster nearby. After another count to three, they slung him in the big trash can on wheels, where he could sleep off his hangover and think about what he'd done. As they re-entered the building, Mick slammed the fire doors shut. The applause started, and they each took a bow.

Dave got to his feet. He was a bit wobbly, a bit tattered and torn, but otherwise, he was okay. "You can come out now, honey!" he shouted, hoping Lianda would hear, though she had only gone as far as the staff cloakroom behind the bar. She was soon by his side with an ice-pack for his face, helping him along and actually quite turned on by it all.

Mick and Danny shook hands and retired to the bar, where pints of Estuary Lager with brandy chasers were waiting. Dave followed close behind, girlfriend in tow, but he stopped and called across the dance floor to the singer of the house band. "Hey Elvis, what do I pay you for? Playtime's over. Stone me, it's like a funeral parlour in 'ere."

The band started playing again, and normal service was resumed — or so it seemed.

As with any Friday night at Bobby's Bar and Grill, Southend-on-Sea, business was good. Diners, drinkers, dancers — they were all there. The place was packed, and the tills were ringing like Rickenbackers. Dave Hunter, Mick Davies, and Danny Blyth had handled their crisis well (even if it wasn't the first of its kind, sadly), and they deserved their celebration drinks.

What they didn't know was that this and two similar

incidents that month had been orchestrated by shadowy figures simply to test their vigilance and their resourcefulness.

Dave Hunter thought he had three bad habits: smoking, drinking, and staying up late. But in fact, he had one more: making powerful enemies.

Chapter 2

Everybody turned their heads when they heard the knock at the door, knowing it was either a customer who had lost his wallet, a pizza boy, or someone with a pair of tights over his head and a shotgun. A voice shouted "Pizza!" and Danny went to let him in, showing great trust for one who nearly lost his life after coming into contact with the Essex underworld only two years earlier.

It was a pizza delivery, but Dave couldn't help but shake his head at Danny's gullibility. He'd talk to him about that later.

For now, however, all Dave could think about was the hot, delicious slices of pepperoni pizza that he and his workforce (16 in total, including Lianda) would soon be making short work of. He shoved Danny out of the way, unbolted the door, and gave the delivery man his money in exchange for the goods.

Pedro Pezaro, a chirpy Spaniard and former golf

caddy, made good on his promise of selling the finest pizza in Southend-on-Sea, even if Pedro's Pizza Emporium was, in fact, a converted ice cream van with a wood-burning stove that could well be a fire hazard. As always, Peddy refused Dave's offer to join them.

Dave carried the pizzas over to the table where his friends and colleagues were sat. "We've got pepperoni, double pepperoni, plain, ham and pineapple, and anchovies for anyone with bad taste and bad breath," he said as he put the fast-food feast on the table. "Let battle commence."

It was an expensive hobby treating the staff to after-hours pizza and beer, but Dave Hunter wanted his workforce to feel like a family, so it was important to him that they hung out now and again. The eight-piece house band was there, at the far end of the large table that was actually several small tables pulled together, as was the much-loved janitor Winston.

Winston drank rum (and little else) and talked about

the old days (and nothing else). Growing up on 'de aylan' ('man it waz sweeeeet back den'), moving to England in the 1960s, dancing to all-night reggae showcases at Hammersmith Palais. He repeated himself, but it didn't matter; the guys in the house band, led by Dave's old friends Nicky and Ricky on bass guitar and drums respectively, always wanted to hear more.

There were the two barmen, Jeff and Rodger, who Dave had known since he first walked the boards, singing and blowing harp on the Southend gig circuit many years earlier. They were no-nonsense, hardworking men who Dave, Danny and Mick all had a lot of time for. They sat and chatted with …

Patsy and Sandra, the two waitresses. Sandra, the younger one of the two, was still upset about being sent flying while carrying a dessert tray a while ago; Patsy, on the other hand, had seen this kind of thing before. If anything, this place was a bit too posh for the old girl.

Tough as old boots, she was.

The only staff members who weren't there were the two short-order cooks Sam and Earl. The Harlem-born brothers were still new in the UK and had gone clubbing; they were as crazy about 'English babes' as the local girls were about them.

Dave took his place next to Lianda, and it didn't take long for Mick to start the banter. "Good job we were here to save your ass, eh Dave?"

Before Dave could prepare his comeback, Danny joined in. "Yeah, I reckon old Alley Oop was getting ready to teach you a lesson back there," he said.

"Whatchoo' talkin' about?" said Dave. "I had him right where I wanted him … Do you two know anything about the art of conflict? Or the pavement arena?" He took a bite of his pepperoni snack, followed by a hearty gulp of Estuary Lager. "I was letting him wear himself out, making him think he's got the upper hand. I was setting him up for a fall – a fuckin' big one an' all."

Another bite, another chug.

"Yeah, right," said Danny, grinning and looking at Mick to see if he was enjoying this wind-up/piss-take as much as he was (Mick was).

"Face it," said Mick. "You're just not badass anymore. You've got all this money, you've got your trophy girlfriend …"

Mick gave Lianda a wink as he said the last bit just in case she wasn't 'in on it' before getting stuck into Dave some more.

"It's not your fault, Dave," he said. "It's like Mickey Goldmill said: *y' got civilized*."

"Fuck off," said Dave, with a grin followed by a wink. "If anything, you saved him, you pair of old queens."

"*That's* enough of that," said Lianda. Her eyes met his, and Mick and Danny may as well have ceased to exist: he was somewhere else entirely.

“*I* think you did really well against that big nasty man.”

She kissed the corner of his mouth.

“Really well?”

“Really, really well.”

She kissed the other corner of his mouth.

“I suppose you could say I was …”

“A hero?” she asked.

“Well, I don’t know about a *hero* exactly …”

She kissed his lips, staying there long enough for him to taste sweet wine and cherry lip balm.

“*My* hero. Don’t go eating too much pizza, you. I’ve got plans for you later, David, and while you’ll need to keep your strength up, you might be hungry afterwards.”

Dave looked around the table and hoped this lot wouldn’t be too long with their food and drink.

In fact, he wished they could disappear right now.

One whole hour later, Nicky, Ricky, and their six bandmates went off in search of a poker game or a strip club; everyone else had gone bar Winston whose job it was to power everything down and secure the building. But not tonight. Dave gave him a twenty-pound note and told him to catch up with the band and join them for a drink or three.

Now they had the place to themselves.

Lianda got to her feet and said, "Let's tidy up in the morning," referring to the empty pizza boxes and beer glasses scattered across the makeshift table. "I want to dance."

"What a great idea," Dave said. "Fast or slow?"

"You decide," she said, tilting her head towards the record machine, a 1950s Wurlitzer loaded with rock'n'roll, soul, and R&B 45s. Recalling a tender movie scene with Harrison Ford and Kelly McGillis, Dave punched in a number from memory and called up the ghost of Sam Cooke.

Lianda was at the edge of the dance floor by now, and Dave wasn't far behind. "Good choice," she said. She swung her hips loosely in time with the music and put her hands behind her head, her elbows pointing at Dave until he moved in close enough for her to reach.

'Don't know much about history ... '

They pulled each other close and swayed in time with the song.

They did this often, their relationship still feeling very much like a new one, and sometimes they sweet-talked as they did so. But not tonight – there was no need.

Wonderful World wasn't the only cut Dave punched in. They also danced to The Everlys' *When Will I Be Loved,* Roy Orbison's *Blue Bayou*, The Skyliners' *Since I Don't Have You,* and one more.

They broke away from their embrace just once. Dave spun her around a couple of times, but they returned to their original position, cheek to cheek. The 'one more' song was, of course, *Unchained Melody*, at the end of which Lianda broke the silence by saying, "Take me to bed or lose me forever."

Their naked bodies lay still in a moment of post-coital bliss. He sweated, she glistened, and neither of them said a word. Yet there was nothing uncomfortable about the silence, and Dave was sure this was a sign that things were good with them; at other times, they had plenty to talk about.

Dave decided he had his breath back enough to go and smoke a cigarette over by the window.

"Must you?" she said, as he reached down his side of the bed for his boxer shorts.

"Come on, honey, you know the drill," he said, now standing and checking his jeans pockets for his fags and lighter.

Dave lived in the flat above the club, and although Lianda stayed over most nights, she had kept a place of her own back in Colchester since she and Dave graduated two years earlier.

It was mid-September, and as Dave threw the window open, Lianda shivered as the cool night air landed on her glistening skin.

"You know those things kill you, right?" she said.

"Well, at least I'll die for a worthy cause," he said between two particularly satisfying puffs on his Benson.

"You're *such* an asshole," she said with great affection before Dave finished his cigarette in cosy silence.

As he prepared to take the last, bittersweet drag on his cigarette and return to the arms of the woman he loved, Dave heard a rustling from the ground below followed by a groaning sound: it was the man he fought with earlier, and who Danny had christened ‘Alley Oop’.

Dave flicked his cigarette butt out the window, taking only reasonable care not to let it land on Alley Oop and burn him. Then he went back to bed, blissfully aware that tomorrow was Saturday.

Chapter 3

A nine-year-old boy woke up in the cold hard bed feeling colder than usual. He felt dampness down his crotch and his legs. It couldn't be sweat in winter, so he must have wet himself again.

How did that happen? He couldn't remember the last time he'd done that, and he was six weeks away from his tenth birthday.

He needed a plan. If one of the other boys found out, he would tell the others, and everyone would be mean to him. The name-calling, the taunts, and the practical jokes would all start again, and they would probably beat him up too.

His only hope was to swap blankets with one of the other boys, then creep through to the laundry room and look for a new pair of pyjamas. It was still dark, and he prayed that the other boys were all asleep.

There were six bunk beds on each side of the dorm,

his being the first on his side of the room. Luckily, he was nearest to the hallway door, with the laundry room door not far down the hall. He wished he hadn't asked to take top bunk last night.

Mr. Peterson was on duty that night, and the boy knew Mr. Peterson was a nice man. He wasn't a bad man like Mr Raskey, the scary man with the war wounds who used to hit the boys and touch them in bad places. If Mr. Peterson found out, he wouldn't make fun of him and get the other boys to join in.

The boy decided to get to work. Freddie Boylston always went to sleep first and got up last, so the boy guessed he would be the hardest one to wake up. He knew that making it look like Freddie had wet the bed would make the boys pick on *him*, but Freddie was horrible to almost everyone, so he deserved it. He wasn't as bad as Paul Hanscomb, who was the worst of them all, but he was still horrible most of the time.

In the dark, he put his foot on the first rung of the metal ladder, expecting it to creak or squeak. It didn't, so he put his next foot down, and there was no sound this time either.

There were only five rungs to get down, and he was relieved to feel his left foot touch the floor without a sound. His right foot came up at an angle, though, and lifted the ladder up by about an inch, and it clunked against the bed rail. The boy found himself taking a deep breath, afraid he had woken the whole place up, but nobody moved or made a sound.

He pulled the wet blanket off his bed. Freddie Boylston was three beds along. This might work, the boy thought.

He bundled the wet blanket up and walked over to Freddie Boylston's bed with it. He took Freddie's blanket in his hands and started gently pulling it away from him. It seemed to be going well, but then, Freddie Boylston's voice called out, "Woss goin' on 'ere?"

Freddie Boylston's bedside light came on, and so did several others. The boy prayed Mr. Peterson would come through and stop what was happening, but he didn't. Instead, the boy heard Freddie Boylston's voice once more.

"Look, everyone – Gobble-guts has pissed himself!'

The boy felt a sickly feeling in his belly, and he started shaking. The boys started laughing and calling him names, and one of them started singing a dirty song.

'When Gobble-guts pissed his pyjamas, he began to cry ...'

The boy was big, and that was why they called him 'Gobble-Guts,' but he wasn't a fighter. Freddie Boylston threw him to the floor, and he hit his head as he went down. Then a new boy there came over and spat in his hair and punched him in the nose, and his nose started bleeding.

The other boys went wild at the sight of blood, and they took it in turns to punch and kick the boy who was now in a ball on the dormitory floor.

The beating didn't last that long, but the worst bit was yet to come. Two of the boys pulled him onto his back, one taking his arms and one taking his legs. Then, Freddie Boylston and Paul Hanscomb took down their pyjama bottoms and took it in turns to piss on him.

He was determined not to cry, but this was too much, and tears filled the boy's eyes.

Then, the boy was aged thirteen, on the run from his adoptive parents and spending his first night down by the canal after his new dad split his lip. He'd learned to stand up for himself a bit by then, and he wasn't scared of the junkies and weirdos that went there at night. If anything, he felt at home there, and for the first time in his life, he felt as though he belonged somewhere.

But then he was in the back of a police car, and not long after that, he was down at the station. A burly desk sergeant demands that he gives him his real name despite the fact he that had a blank space on his birth certificate after being dumped outside a church in Middlesex a few hours after he was born. He speaks with a stammer, which seems to upset the sergeant and make him tell two younger policemen to take him for a drive.

They take him to an abandoned warehouse several miles from the station, where the two young officers teach him a lesson in respecting authority. More blood, more violence.

In a borstal, aged fourteen, the boy sees a chap get a cup of boiling water thrown in his face by one of the daddies for not giving them his cigarettes. The daddy and his friends come for him, too, and the boy has a deep gash cut across his chest for refusing to wank himself off in front of them for their amusement. The cut requires twenty-eight stitches, and he needs to have a clot removed from his brain and his jaw repaired after they put the boot in for an extra touch.

Then he was in a boxing gym in the East End trying

to reach one-hundred push-ups after going twelve rounds. He heard the voice of his old trainer: *"It's not the dog that's in the fight, it's the fight that's in the dog. You're the dog, so get in that ring and piss out your ground!"*

His coach believed that the only way to win was to know how it feels to lose, and he made sure everybody he trained did this many times.

The worst memory of all, however, was the time when, aged sixteen, he bumped into Freddie Boylston and Paul Hanscomb again.

They were walking down a back alley one Friday night, returning from a night out in Romford while he was out for a late-night run. What scared him most was that he didn't remember *deciding* to do the things he did to them. It was as though he had been taken over by an unknown force that made his mind and body work together as one.

Then the boy found himself in another dark space, scared, alone, and crying. He was no longer a boy, though.

He was a grown man, twenty-five years old, and known by those who know him well as 'Alley Oop'. He was battered and bruised, and while no morning that starts off in a dumpster outside an American-style bar and grill in Southend-on-Sea was going to be a good one, the fact that he was now the wrong side of a cocaine high didn't help.

He was cold, and he was dirty.

Chapter 4

The Kawasaki Ninja ZX-12 R was a serious bit of kit, make no mistake. With its top speed of 187 mph and awesome 178.5 hp at 9,500 rpm, it was a quarter-ton of sheer virility.

Dave thought the Japs were right, naming it after the deadly warriors of old. He even saw the logic in the patter of the uncouth salesman from Canvey Motors, who said that a young man who wants to start a family but can't because he's firing blanks could sort himself out by taking a ride on one of these.

Dave saddled her up and put the key in before hitting the start button. He kicked the stand away, got the revs up, and began to roll.

Deep down, Dave wished 'Kwackers' were still built with kick-starters. As a boy, he'd imagined that kicking down on one of those and hearing your engine roar like a lion would make you feel like you were knocking the whole world on its ass. If there was a man on earth who didn't like to feel like that, then his name wasn't Dave Hunter.

With a light trail of dust behind him, he wheeled his way out of the low-walled limestone car park outside Bobby's Bar and turned onto Western Esplanade, heading right at a steady thirty. He was a local boy with a love of his hometown, which was why he (mostly) paid attention to the speed limit here. Plus it was Saturday morning in a busy seaside town. It was late in the season now, but the sun was out and still doing it's best.

Where Western Esplanade met Marine Parade, Dave made a left turn and began a steady climb up Pier Hill. Pier Hill's steep incline made it necessary for him to use more of the bike's power. It seemed strange doing thirty on a motorcycle that could reach almost 200mph, but Dave, a musician by trade, was a master of economy; the best guitarist in the world can't play solos all the time, and you should always save the best till last. Don't shoot your load too soon.

Many of the houses here were three storeys high, and Dave saw one building with a little roof window behind which he pictured an old boy with a telescope, looking out to sea and perhaps checking out the crumpet on the seafront. A stop sign at the intersection with Royal Terrace made Dave do just this, and he turned his head left and looked out to sea. Dave saw a cargo ship drifting along the estuary, not too far out, loaded up, and heading towards Purfleet.

Dave imagined he could hear the vessel sound its horn, even though the rumble of the engine and his close-fitting helmet meant he couldn't hear this or anything else. But Dave Hunter was a firm believer in the power of imagination, making your own entertainment. He saluted the ship's captain and got on his way.

He crossed over onto Royal Terrace and thought it lived up to its regal-sounding street name. A leafy, tree-lined affair, the nicely re-pointed houses here had a harmonious symmetry with one another as did the stripes in the freshly mown lawns.

What said the most about the company you were in was the names of their houses. *Viscount Place* sounded nice enough, Dave thought, but *Windsors Cottage* made him wish he had matches and some lighter fuel. *The Bullrushes* was a pleasant name, as was *Foliage Cottage.* But anyone who called their house *Serendipity Rose* was taking the piss.

Dave respected other people's ways – when in Rome an' all that – but as he cruised along Royal Terrace, he did wish some new-money type could come along and knock up a giant ode to tastelessness and call it *Estuary Heights,* or *Saarfend Manor*, perhaps.

Or maybe he and Lianda could move here one day and call their new home *Chevy Chase*, or *Aston Villa …*

Steady on old boy ...

It took him just under a minute to tire of Royal Terrace's preened pretentiousness. Thankfully that was how long it took him to reach the junction with Southend High

Street. A quick right-turn (Clyde!) and Dave was back in the nitty-gritty world of casinos, spit-and-sawdust boozers, and high-rise flats: he was home. And not only was he home, but he was also allowed to go at 40mph when the high street became London Road.

In fact, he did fifty, turning the throttle and hearing the engine get louder as the revs got higher.

The Ninja wasn't a particularly noisy beast, and certainly not at this speed. Dave compared its low rumble to the pre-mauling growl of an attack dog – like the one he fought off a couple of years ago, like Indiana Jones but with a Korean lashing cane instead of a bullwhip.

The past didn't bother Dave Hunter much, even though his past contained violence and several instances where he, Danny and Mick had been in grave danger.

He had also killed two people – he'd committed two acts of murder. He reasoned with himself that the two men he sent to meet their makers had it coming. He couldn't prove they'd killed Bobby Fulton twenty-five years earlier, but one of them, Norman Layer, put several rounds in his best friend right before Dave's eyes. The other one, who Dave later found out was known as 'left-handed Pete,' brought a shotgun to his house with only one thing in mind. Dave gave him the slip, but Pete caught up with him the next day, and although he only had a revolver this time, Pete fired, and he didn't miss.

The bullet caught Dave in his upper chest. It left his heart and lungs alone and, as if by a miracle, it passed right through him, causing only minor tissue damage. There was no internal bleeding, and the bullet didn't bounce about inside his ribcage like a bull in a china shop.

The way he saw it, he was a lucky man. Not everybody got to strike a blow for justice, and those that do don't always live to tell the tale: Dave Hunter had done both.

Also, his payout from the Criminal Injury

Compensation Authority allowed him to buy the power bike he was now getting ready to leave London Road for Southend's Queensway on. Not everybody got to ride one of these, either.

Not everyone got to kill the bad guy and save the day, and not everyone got to share a bed with a beautiful brown-eyed girl like Lianda, either. He knew she was drawn to him as a result of his flashes of fame and hero-worship, and it didn't bother him in the slightest.

Dave Hunter put his ability to rationalise and to move on down to his dad, the late Don Hunter. Dad was a tough-love sort of guy, a fighter – a brawler – and he didn't go for that 'pain is just weakness leaving the body' rubbish they teach you in the Foreign Legion.

Don Hunter had his own mantras, and Dave remembered them well. "Fear is a voice that needs to be shut up if it talks too loudly," was a good one, although Dave liked his dad's ringside taunt best:

"Don't cuddle 'im ya' fanny – fakkin' hit 'im!"

Dad was quite a guy, and Dave missed him.

The three-mile section of Southend's Queensway that would take Dave to his first destination was in a sixty zone – National Speed Limit, but on a single carriageway. Dave figured that if *Piston Broke* magazine was anything to go by, he could be there in two minutes. He didn't do it, but it was nice to know he could if he needed to. He took her up to seventy – a compromise.

The road sunk into an underpass, and for a moment, the world became artificially lit as Dave and his fellow motorists' exhaust fumes became thicker. He thought of the late Bobby Fulton and his concrete burial chamber, trying to rest in peace amidst the noise of an endless stream of cars and lorries. Soon, thankfully, Dave emerged blinking into the light, flanked on his left by a small shopping arcade comprised of a bookmaker's, a Chinese takeaway, a Tesco Express, and a phone unlocking shop. To his right, just at the edge of his periphery, Dave saw a passenger jet beginning its skyward ascent, and for a second, he was a boy again.

He took a B-road turn-off on his right, and looked down at his digital dashboard and checked his clock: 10:56 am. He'd timed this well.

He came to a roundabout and turned right onto a bigger road, which took him up to the entrance of London Southend Airport. He rode past it and kept going for another mile and a half.

London Southend's grounds were also home to Southend Flying Club, and Dave was glad to find he wouldn't have to dismount, as his friend had left the wrought iron gate open for him.

Capt. Paul Addington, or 'Adders', wasn't a flight captain, or even a captain of industry, but it looked good next to his mugshot in the clubhouse.

He was, however, an excellent flight instructor, who

over the years had worked his way up to become SFC's chief instructor, and Dave knew him because he and his wife came to the bar to dance occasionally.

Adders had purchased his Golden Eagle at auction price just under a year ago, after her previous owner, criminal mastermind Norman Layer, died at the hands of Dave Hunter, and his empire collapsed. Layer's estate was seized and auctioned off piece by piece at low cost for a quick sale, and Adders nabbed a bargain.

Dave Hunter too had capitalised on Layer's demise – not long after he'd killed him, in fact. The late Norman Layer owned a number of licensed premises throughout Essex, and one of them was a popular Southend night spot called The Boardwalk Club. Dave, Danny and Mick had clubbed together to buy the place, and after a period of hard graft and a new name in honour of the late Bobby Fulton, Southend-on-Sea had a new nightspot where patrons could hear the best music, drink the best beer and eat the best burgers and hot dogs in town.

Dave rode up the gravel driveway at a steady speed, but he wasn't going to the clubhouse. After a time, he swung his bike off the driveway and onto the grass. He sped across half a mile of grasslands, hoping the club groundsman was away until finally, he came around the back of four fourteen-by-five metre Nissen huts. Dave wondered why the club's planes couldn't live together before he realised his ignorance: just as some kindly pig farmers felt their little porkers deserve their own places to bed down of a night, and a guitarist might sleep with his six-stringed mistress, aviation enthusiasts gave their wings human treatment.

And rightly so, Dave thought.

He came out in front of the row of hangars and saw that the doors to the furthest one along were open and bolted into the ground. This was where Adders kept his beloved Cessna 421B, and just like Dave recently emerged from the darkness to light out of an urban underpass, Adders' Golden

Eagle made its journey into daylight and trundled onto the tarmac outside the hangar. Dave gave a left-handed thumbs-up, and though the late morning sun on the cockpit window stopped him seeing in, he was sure Adders returned the gesture.

Dave slowed his Ninja to a stop just where the taxi runway met the main drag and waited for his friend. He wasn't far behind, and soon they were side by side, ready for takeoff. Adders gave his friend a wave, and although he was silhouetted by the high sun, Dave was sure his friend was wearing (cheap) sunglasses instead of his usual goggles. Sunglasses. Very cool, Dave thought as he waved back at Adders.

They picked up speed as they rode shotgun down the runway. When Dave saw the 300 ft marker, painted in yellow in the middle of the tarmac, they were travelling at 45mph – not fast for his bike, but a good start nonetheless. They were doing sixty when they passed the 750 ft marking, and now Dave was feeling the backdraft of the Cessna engine. His bike was designed to handle this sort of thing, of course, and in fact, he remembered the salesman telling him the ZX-12's design incorporated elements of airplane technology to aid its aerodynamics and wind resistance. But this didn't stop him feeling like he could be toppled at any time.

Dave saw the 900 ft marker: now for the wall of death moment …

Inside a wall of death, a stunt rider has to reach death-defying speeds to live, basically. To stay upright, the motorcyclist must increase speed as he makes the transition from vertical to horizontal. The build-up of momentum leads to better tyre traction, which means the rider can tell Isaac Newton to poke it. The higher you get, the faster you have to go. Easy.

Only it's not easy because preservation of all that we know and love is ingrained, genetic. The higher the rider climbs, the louder the messages from the old brain get. Also – this is where it gets hard – the more the human brain senses danger, the stronger the instinct to act safely becomes. The old brain knows that increasing speed is a dangerous act in itself, and it goes against our base instinct to do this when you are already putting your life on the line. It's like defying the instinct that makes you put up your hands and catch a ball that is thrown at your face (it's also why some would-be stunt riders end up with their necks in braces and their pride in tatters).

As per Adders' instruction, Dave veered off the runway when they passed the 1,200 ft marker, as he began the final leg of the takeoff escort. Even ten metres out, the blowback from a plane big enough to carry six passengers was strong.

Time to ignore those ancient reflexes and think what Dad would say …

Dave leaned forward and put his arms down so that

his elbows were lower than his clutch lever and his throttle.

Any moment now …

A second later, Dave felt the pressure against him drop by half. He felt light, as though the sudden change of pressure might be the thing to topple him, but he knew he'd made it. He looked up, and although the Golden Eagle was now off the ground, Adders and he were still side by side, and he gave his friend a left-handed salute, confident that his friend would do it back at him.

"Krrrsch," said Dave, into an imaginary headset, imitating the sound of static interference. "Ground to air force one. The president has taken off safely. Over."

He got back on the tarmac, and the runway ahead of him went as far as the horizon. It was a late summer day, and the hot air on the tarmac and the cooler air above created a mirage in which Dave could see the runway melting ahead of him.

Dave looked up and saw that the Adders' wheels

were up. He honked his horn and pumped his fist, and Adders wiggled his wings by way of a reply.

It wasn't even midday, and this was already looking like the perfect day.

Chapter 5

Danny and Mick squared up to one another for their final bout of early morning pugilism. They were in the centre of the hardwood dance floor in the bar, still an hour away from its midday opening time.

Mick, the student, had suggested they use a gymnasium, at least for the early stages of their training, where there would be crash mats and, if necessary, access to a first aid kit. Danny, the tutor, insisted they do it in an authentic environment; bad guys don't play by the rules, and they don't care much about health and safety either.

Danny was wearing police riot gear, kindly lent to him by a friend of his in the firearms department, and an oversized baseball mask. This made him feel indestructible as well as making him look very silly, not that his student would be wise to tell him this. In his right hand, Danny held a battered old polycarbonate riot shield, which he liked to believe had deflected its share of rocks, petrol bombs and other missiles over the years.

“Right then, *fairy godmother*, you’ve got three minutes. Give me your best shot.”

Mick did, too, first with his left hand, then with his right. Two straight, well-aimed jabs that made Danny neither flinch nor blink underneath his baseball mask.

“Now, Mick, you know those boys who come in here on Wednesday nights for karaoke? Well, they probably punch like you did just then. Now concentrate.”

Mick swung for him – big mistake.

Danny saw it coming as if in slow motion, which gave him time to plan his response at an almost leisurely pace. The only hand protection he and Mick wore was some light knuckle bandaging; this meant he still had the dexterity to catch his friend’s fist, which he did after tipping to his left to dodge the blow. Mick sighed as he saw his mistake, and Danny tightened his grip on his friend’s tightly-balled fist before hurling him in the direction of the intended punch.

Mick landed in a heap.

Danny began the count to three but, to take Mick by surprise, he spun around somewhere between one and two. He was pleasantly surprised to see his friend vertical again, dusting himself off and thirsty for more.

Danny Blyth didn't teach a particular discipline. As he saw it, the only rule was that there were no rules. He knew nice guys finish last for a reason, and he wanted Mick to learn this.

Danny didn't bother with ancient philosophies, either – he just made his student watch Van Damme's *Kickboxer* three times a week in the hope that the film's underlying theme of self-reliance would rub off on his protégé.

Along with their friend Dave Hunter, the two of them had fought dangerous criminals in the past.

Throughout their ordeal, it was Danny who handled himself best. He had known what to do at crucial moments, and Mick approached Danny soon after to teach him everything he knew.

“What did I tell you about going in wide?” the teacher now asked the student.

“Don’t swing while in close quarters with your opponent,” Mick answered, short of breath, “or better still, don’t swing your fists at all.”

Danny was right to teach Mick this. To bring down an opponent quickly, you had to learn to punch straight and incorporate upper body strength into your blows. Bringing a fist round in an arc cost you both time and momentum, and Danny was keen for his student to learn this.

What Mick didn’t know was that Danny was working towards showing him the one-inch punch.

To Mick, this was the stuff of lore and fantasy, but Danny intended to show him soon that it was as real as a number ten bus or a letter in a brown envelope.

“Excellent, Michael. Very good. But your hands are letting you down today. Why not show me what your feet can do?"

Mick nodded as if to say 'challenge accepted.'

For the time, he kept outside the kicking distance of his mentor, despite knowing he would have to enter the deadly circle to execute his plan.

Danny's voice boomed out at him: "Do something or get off the pot!"

This stirred his charge into action, and in an attempt to confuse his opponent Mick pitched forward on his left-side, and this seemed to work. He saw Danny's head move by a fraction of a degree in the direction of Mick's left foot, and the grille of his football mask seemed to tilt forward a little. In a split-second, Mick replanted the ball of his right foot, as his left leg came up in a sweep-kick motion aimed at the back of Danny's knee. It almost worked.

Displaying a near-telepathic reflex action, Danny caught Mick's foot, and Mick cursed his mistake.

"Now I *could* end it right here," said Danny, "but

I'm not going to. What do I always say to you, Michael?"

"Go down fighting."

"That's right – literally in your case since you're going to have to take both feet off the ground to stand a chance. Now come on, do this well, and I'll let you land softly."

Mick attempted something that was both risky and complicated, and both men knew it wouldn't work. With nothing to push away from for momentum, and his knee as his only pivot point, he tried to fly-kick his friend. It looked so easy in the movies …

His foot didn't connect, Danny having stepped out of the way well before it came in. Mick was in the air, upside-down and preparing for a crash-landing. Danny could have let gravity aid Mick's downwards descent, but he decided to speed the process up. He delivered a karate chop to Mick's lower back that sent him crashing to the wooden floor.

To some or perhaps many, Danny's harsh treatment

of Mick would have appeared cruel or sadistic, even. But Danny was absolutely right in what he taught his friend about fighting till the end.

In another life, Daniel Peter Blyth had trained as a soldier in the British Army. He only intended to complete basic training, but, as is so often the case, fate played its hand. Danny planned to buy his way out and return to civilian life and his first love of music, women and wine just as trouble flared up in Afghanistan. Danny found himself onboard a military charter flight, his plans on indefinite hold.

A key theme in all armed forces training is getting used to the idea that nothing is guaranteed. This gets the new recruit used to the idea of dying – which is a possibility in any theatre of conflict. Once a subject gets used to this, and comes to terms with the concept of death as an occupational hazard, then, and only then, can he make the transition from man to a warrior.

This is why Danny knew he could never let Mick win one of their sparring sessions; Mick had to learn to lose so that he could learn to fight to the death. But, and this was the clever part of Danny's philosophy, if Mick did turn the tables on Danny, and beat his master, then it would mean he had taught him well.

A spluttering Mick tried to use a push-up motion to get himself vertical again, but he felt Danny's foot push him to the floor once more.

"You have let yourself down, Mick. I could spit on your back and insult your family now, and there would be nothing you could do. I won't, but don't think a street thug on crack will be as considerate as me. Now get up – we've got thirty seconds left."

Danny lifted his foot, and as he did so, he had to use his quick reflexes again. Mick rolled to one side and aimed a punch at Danny's groin. Danny caught it, and he was wearing a groin shield in case his friend had the good sense to ditch the dated conduct that prohibited blows to this area.

"Nice try, Mick."

When Mick was standing again, Danny said, "What do you do when your hands and feet let you down?"

"Use your head," said Mick.

"That's right, let's have three in a row."

Danny put his hands behind his back; Mick didn't trust him to keep them there, and he was sure Danny was grinning underneath that silly mask of his.

Mick didn't know it, but Danny wore the oversized mask to training not for protection, or to preserve his handsome looks: he wore it so Mick wouldn't see him as a friend or even a person. It was part of the dehumanizing process, although he planned to unmask as Mick's training progressed.

There were several of Danny's training methods that Mick didn't understand – or even know about. At band practice recently, Danny had handed over the job of singing back-up to Mick. His reason for this: singers, backing singers especially, needed to control their breathing. If Mick learned to control his breath, he could increase stamina and stay vertical for longer. Simple.

He would eventually learn how to slow his heart rate, and if he ever caught a bullet, this might save himself dying as a result of going into shock despite surviving the gunshot wound. His friend and trainer, Danny, owed his life to the man who taught him this.

Mick got within a yard of Danny and delivered a 'Glasgow kiss' against the hard plastic helmet. This hurt him as much as if not more than his opponent – just like it was supposed to. He gritted his teeth and followed it up with another thud. Danny seemed to come off balance. Perhaps today would be the day.

Sensing his chance once more, Mick moved his head back to achieve maximum force as he delivered the best of the three – the final blow. This was another mistake, and it was too good for Danny to pass up. He put out his forearm, and the only thing Mick headbutted was Danny's elbow.

"You cunt," Mick said.

" 'Tis not I who is a cunt, dear boy, for you who failed to listen to your trainer *again*. I've told you several times that when you are in close, you *stay* close. You asked for that, so thank me for it."

"Thank you, Danny," Mick said.

"You're welcome. Now let me look at that."

Danny inspected the gash above Mick's eyebrow, and he was disappointed that Mick let him get close enough to do this.

"That'll need an ice pack – too bad I haven't got one. Now, you know that one-inch punch I promised to show you?"

Mick nodded.

"Watch and learn."

Before Mick realised what Danny meant, he was

hurtling backwards, feeling like a wrecking ball had hit his chest. He was back on the floor, and he resigned himself to the fact that today wouldn't be his day after all.

Chapter 6

Samuel Cleaver put the fifth bullet in his Smith & Wesson Model 29 and snapped the cylinder in. He was sitting behind his office desk, and with the weapon now cleaned and loaded, he sat and counted to three in his head. Then Samuel Cleaver sprang to his feet, spun ninety degrees, and pointed his gun at his reflection in the wall mirror now opposite him. “Freeze!” he told himself.

Alex Cleaver had seen this more than a dozen times since his brother bought his new toy yesterday, and he had grown tired of it. “Will you pack that in? You’re making me nervous.”

Sam didn’t take his eye off the target for a second, and he didn’t respond. Or at least he didn’t say anything to Alex: he mumbled Clint Eastwood’s famous ‘I know what you’re thinking’ skit word-perfect, before sitting down once he was satisfied that his target was ready to comply and would put down his weapon.

Alex tried again. “You haven’t forgotten we’re expecting a visitor, have you?” he asked.

Samuel Cleaver most definitely hadn’t forgotten this, and the reason he loaded five bullets instead of six like an old cowboy wasn’t a safety procedure: he was getting ready to play a trick on someone. He put the gun away in a brown leather holster that he wore on his left-hand side under a long black leather jacket.

Their subject was, in fact, fifteen minutes late, and they were disappointed in him. The sound of their office grandfather clock chiming the eleventh hour of the day hadn’t been followed by the sound of heavy steps coming up the stairs as they had expected.

Their office was above a boutique estate agency on Kensington High Street. A place over a jeweller’s seemed too obvious, as did somewhere above a bookie’s or a pub backroom (the Cleavers had no interest in the licensed trade since this seemed far too much like hard work to them). The lease was given to them for free after they came to an agreement with the owner, involving a gun like the one that Samuel Cleaver recently drew on himself (they didn't pay rates either).

Eventually, they heard a 'ding dong' from the shop below as the door to the street opened, and for a moment, the traffic got louder. When the sound of passing vehicles died down again, they heard the sound of boots coming up the stairs.

As always, the sound of booted feet coming up the staircase made the paranoid Samuel Cleaver wonder, just for a split second, if they were being raided. But he soon heard that they were clumsy, lumbering feet, and he knew exactly who they belonged to.

Samuel and his brother both stood up, and came around their desks and waited by the door, about two metres outside its opening span. The man who they too referred to as Alley Oop entered the room.

“Freeze!” Samuel yelled once more, as he drew his ‘Smith’ and pointed it a real person this time: Ally Oop did as he was told and stopped in his tracks. “I thought we told you to knock each time … What the fuck happened to you?” asked Samuel Cleaver, seeing the state of this lackey who had spent the night in a dumpster.

Alley Oop had obviously tried to shake off the worst of it, but he still had ketchup stains on his t-shirt and a film of grease covering him almost from head to toe.

Samuel put his gun away again, and for a moment, he stood there looking puzzled. Eventually, Alley Oop found the courage to speak.

“I had t-, t-t-t-, s-s-leep outs-s-s-s-ide, s-s-ir.”

“You slept outside?” asked Alex Cleaver.

“Well, n-n-not outs-s-s-side exactly – in a d-d-dumper truck, sir.”

A small smile crept onto Alex Cleaver’s face, then Sam’s – but not Alley Oop’s.

“Okay, let’s get you inside, and you can tell us how you messed up again.”

“ ‘Fank you, chief,” said Mr. Oop, and he passed the two brothers and sat down in the guest’s chair by the grandfather clock at the far end of the office. The brothers stood either side of him. Alley Oop took a deep breath and began his story.

“They b-b-beat me up, r-really b-b-bad, sir.”

“Go on …”

“I … I think this D-D-Dave Hunter must, must, r-r-r-really, erm, love his girlfriend.”

His voice cracked when he said the word ‘love,’ and even though the Cleaver brothers oppressed their oafish employee, often making him the butt of their wicked pranks, they heard the pain that was right there.

“I m-mean, he was w-willing to take me on when I touched ‘er bum an ‘all.”

“Yes,” said Samuel. “And by the look of it, he did a

good job, too."

"Oh no, sir," said Alley Oop having composed himself a bit. "There was three of them."

"Just as we suspected," said Alex. "Go on, tell us more."

"They crept up behind me. One of them was all g-g-girly … Long hair … Looked like a bit of a poof."

"*Danny*," said the two brothers in unison.

"And the other one, well, he was round like me and shorter than the p-p-poofy one."

"That'll be Mick," said Alex, as his brother nodded in agreement.

"Now, what can you tell us about their set-up?" asked Alex.

"Whaddaya mean, chief?"

"What do you mean, *what do I mean*?" asked Alex in return. "I told you to find out where their cameras are, who works on the door, who they pay protection to … Use your imagination! Come on, you've been with us long enough."

"I'm sorry, chief. I let you d-d-down, didn't I?" said Alley Oop, hanging his head.

Samuel leaned down to where his face was only inches from Alley Oop's and put a comforting hand on his employee's shoulder.

"Don't beat yourself up – sorry, bad choice of words there – you did your best," he said, and his brother was momentarily thrown by Samuel's compassion towards this modern-day Baldrick: then he realised what Alex's twin brother was up to.

Sensing his bosses' compassion, Alley Oop seized the moment: "Can I have a-a-another line then sir?" he asked, his head raised once more.

"No, I'm afraid not," said Sam, as he took his hand off Alley Oop's shoulder and pulled himself upright again. "I think you need more training. Alley, if I may call you Alley for short, it's time for you to take part in a team-building exercise. Climb up on my desk."

"Wossgoin' on chief?"

"You'll soon see you have nothing to fear. Now on the table, please."

Alley Oop looked around to Alex, who smiled and nodded in the direction of the table. Alley Oop got out of the chair and did indeed climb onto the table and get to his feet.

"Now turn away from us, close your eyes and move back an inch at a time," said Samuel. "When you feel your feet on the edge of the table, I want you to stop."

Alley Oop still did as he was told, and he inched backwards and stopped at the edge of the table.

"Like I said, Alley, this is a team-building exercise. For the whole to become greater than the sum of its parts, we need to function as a unit. This requires trust. Now, when you're ready, I want you to fall backwards, safe in the knowledge that your teammates will catch you."

Alex smirked as his brother said this, even though he

knew deep down that what they were doing was wrong. Funny, but wrong.

Alley Oop hit the floor with an almighty crash. The Cleavers' office was soft-carpeted, but Alley Oop still had the wind knocked out of him when he landed. While he got his breath back, the two brothers laughed so much that they seemed to lose theirs.

Their laughing made Alley Oop want to snap their necks, but he couldn't: they had him right where they wanted him. Long periods of homelessness and his burgeoning drug problem meant that he needed Samuel and Alex Cleaver far more than they needed him. If he killed them today, he would have nowhere to live, nobody to work for, and nobody to top him up with lines of coke now and again.

After a time, the brothers' laughter died down, and Alley Oop got to his feet again. Samuel Cleaver decided that this serf-like lackey had been through enough today, and he didn't draw his gun again. He'd left an empty round in his revolver so he could trick Alley Oop into thinking he was about to be severely punished for his amateurism but decided he'd save this prank for another day.

"Would you like a cup of tea, Alley? Alex asked him.

"Yes, p-p-p-please, sir."

"Well, there's a soup kitchen just opened near Stamford Bridge," Alex said. "I reckon they'll let you in, the state you're in. Go on, we'll be in touch if we need you. Alley Oop … You kill me!" he said, unaware that Alley Oop had often thought about doing this.

Alley Oop saw himself out.

Chapter 7

Dave heard sizzling and waited for the delicious smell of flame-grilled steak to blend in with French fries, hot dogs, and onions. Sam and Earl were hard at work behind the short-order counter, and Dave noted as he often did that the two brothers almost seemed to dance around their cooking space. It was a few minutes before ten on a Saturday night, and Bobby's Bar was virtually full to capacity. Dave was confident that by 10:00 pm, they would have their maximum of two-hundred guests, many of whom would drink and dance until closing time at 1:00 am.

As Dave walked the floor, he mingled with guests, chatted with his staff, and generally acted in a proprietorial fashion.

They had a plain-clothed doorman on duty, and Saturday was the only night of the week they used him. He was a friend of the barmen, and had a sunny demeanor and fists – and balls – of steel. He was tough, but he was decent, and Dave reckoned as long as he was both he could be an asset to the company.

Dave walked the length of the room twice, starting and therefore ending back at the bar, where Danny and Mick were helping the two overworked barmen Jeff and Rodger. Dave had been glad to see the dance floor full as guests made themselves thirsty dancing to the sweet soul sounds of Nicky and Ricky and the rest of the house band. Man, they were cooking, Dave thought as the brass players swayed in time and a guitar cried out. The band played *Louie Louie*, and no matter how many times Dave heard this sad drunkard's lament, it never failed to grab him by the balls.

He asked for a beer and got one quickly – he was the boss – and took a moment to smile at himself. It had been a good summer, he decided. No, make that a good year … Two years, in fact.

That afternoon, he and Lianda went for a long walk along the seafront. It was one of those hazy September afternoons that Dave loved almost as much as Lianda did. In what was surely a case of fate playing its hand, they passed a café where a tinny radio was tuned into an oldies station that just happened to be playing Rod Stewart's *Maggie May* as they walked by. Lianda was clinging to his arm as they walked, and he pulled her a little bit closer and shuddered.

Moments like this made Dave glad to be alive – and a bit scared.

As they walked on, they talked about the past and the future. The future featured most prominently in Dave and Lianda's conversation, but they were reminded of the days when their romance was young when they passed the beach hut they first used to consummate their feelings for each other about two years earlier. But they didn't make a return visit, partly because they both knew you can never go back, but mostly because it was afternoon, and Dave knew that if someone saw him bust a padlock in broad daylight, then it could ruin a magical moment.

One of the things they talked about was the club's house band. Or, more specifically, their saxophone player Reese Whitman. Reese was good, no doubt about it … But he wasn't great. Dave knew it, Lianda knew it, and they suspected Ricky and Nicky knew it, too.

This in itself wasn't a problem; anybody can improve with help and with guidance. But Mr. Whitman didn't seem to want to get better. Dave, having led his own band for many years, knew that this definitely *was* a problem.

Dave Hunter's philosophy was that a musician's life was nothing more than a work in progress, an open book, or an empty canvas if you will. The problem was that not all musicians could see this. The years went by. Disillusionment leads to burn out which, almost as an act of preservation on the part of the burnt-out pro, leads to fatigue and indifference. Then said musician becomes a drain on all of those around them.

So Lianda was quite right to suggest that Nicky and Ricky fire him and give his job to her. Dave was okay with that. He was okay with the fact that it would lead to accusations of favouritism as well as a minor bust-up with Nicky and Ricky, who would point out quite rightly that running the band was their job (he paid their wages, which gave him a power-to-veto, but it would take a lot to make him use it).

None of this bothered Dave, but there was still a problem here: if he gave Lianda a break performing at the club, it could hold her back professionally in the long run. Dave knew that to be taken seriously as a musician, she would be better off to make it on her own. If her first success was considered to be a product of nepotism, then she might struggle further down the line.

They'd turned and headed for home while a blazing orange-ish sun lit up the estuary, and soon they stopped talking about useless band members. Instead, Dave told

Lianda how, as he'd prepared to set off on his bike ride earlier, he'd walked through the club and seen Mick and Danny trying to wrestle each other off the dance floor, and she laughed.

"Those two need girlfriends," she said.

"I think they need to find a room."

As Dave recalled saying this, he was pulled back from the recent past into the present by Danny, who patted his shoulder and reminded him it was time for them to switch duties.

Dave looked at the clock behind the bar: 10:00 pm.

"There's one more thing I need to see to," he told Danny.

Dave caught the eye of Sam behind the short-order counter, who tapped the shoulder of his brother Earl as if to say 'we're on.'

Then he looked over to Eddie Jordan, lead singer in the house band, and gave him a wink.

Something special was about to happen.

Chapter 8

"Ladies and gentlemen … Please clear the dancefloor."

This could have sounded like a strange request from the singer in a band who had just spent the last hour working their asses off to get people *on* the dance floor. But everyone there knew what was happening, and they wasted no time in carrying out Eddie Jordan's request.

With the dance floor empty, Jordan turned to the band and shouted, "1-2-3 …"

Right on cue, the band delivered a chord that could have been cacophonous had it not been so in tune and so in time, and Mr. Jordan was delighted to do it again.

"1-2-3 …"

BAM! A killing horn stab, the parallel thirds of the brass section stacking up beautifully above the rumbling root note of the bass guitar, accented by a bass drum and a crash cymbal played right on time.

It could only mean one thing: they were going to do

Land of 1000 Dances – with a little help from some friends.

As the bassist got the song underway, playing the driving eighth-note pattern that steered the band in, Sam and Earl jumped across the short-order counter and made their way to the dance floor. A spotlight fell on them as they made their way through the throng, high-fiving regulars as they went and grinning from ear to ear.

They took their position on the dance floor, standing shoulder to shoulder about fifteen feet from the stage, facing the crowd and very much the centre of attention. Then, like a pair of Wild West gunslingers, they turned their backs on each other and walked twenty paces before stopping dead and waiting for Eddie Jordan's instructions. But before they could start, there was one more ritual that needed to be carried out …

It is said that white men can't jump, but there was one other thing they didn't do very well: clap to the beat of a song. Whiteys always seemed to clap on every beat, or worse still do it on the 'one' and the 'three'. So while Sam and Earl waited to do their skit, the brass section quit blowing their horns and showed the crowd when to put their hands together. The horn-blowers put their hands up and, in perfect sync with each other, clapped on the second and fourth beat of the bar. It didn't take long for them to get the crowd doing this correctly, and the stage was set.

Eddie Jordan took the mic and gave the two dancers their first instruction: *"Gotta know how to Pony ..."*

Sam and Earl faced their audience and, in time with the band and the crowd, both men executed a perfect left/right/left, right/left/right six-step routine. Then they switched to right/left/right, left/right/left before repeating the whole thing three times. As if this wasn't enough, both brothers executed a 90-degree spin at the end of each repetition, Sam on his right heel, Earl on his left, making them turn a full circle and end up right whey started.

Standing back-to-back once more, they repeated

their L/R/L, R/L/R mash-up before grabbing a three-beat rest. Then they did another heel-spin, and this time both men spun ninety degrees. They were face-to-face and side-on with both the band and the crowd.

Not wanting to repeat themselves, they decided to bring in something new. The brothers added a two-handed finger-and-thumb click to every second and fourth beat of the bar. Then they made another spin, this time turning 270 degrees and landing in a position where they were facing the crowd again. A few crowd members cheered, but most concentrated their two-and-four clap (they knew the best was yet to come).

Once more, Jordan addressed the crowd: "Like *Bony Moronie!"*

'The Bony Moronie' was a more straightforward dance and something of an imperfect science too. Because of this, several people down at the front of the crowd copied Sam and Earl's gyrations – or at least they tried to.

The trick to getting The Bony Moronie right was to remember that while the bottom half of the body must work with the top half, it only needs to do half the amount of work. If your foot moves once to each beat of the song, then the arm it shares its side of the body with has to move twice.

Before they got stuck into this, Sam and Earl gave a demonstration to those in the audience who wanted to dance along. Sam, standing stage-right, put up his right foot, Earl his left, and they wiggled their raised feet side-to-side, their elbows moving along in double-time. Then they kicked out quarter notes while their arms jogged along in straight eights.

There were several more combinations, all of which they performed with ease. A group of giggling hen night ladies tried to copy the moves with mixed results, and when The Bony Moronie was over Earl signalled for the audience to applaud the young ladies. As well as singling out the prettiest one and making the kind of eye contact that seemed to promise a more in-depth lesson later on.

The band was still cooking, and the extended version of this classic cut from the late, great Wilson Pickett wasn't over yet. But *The Alligator* wasn't for beginners, and it was time for the brass section to teach the audience a new rhythm. With their horns resting strapped to their bodies, they put their hands in the air and got to work.

Anyone who understands Morse code will know what LONG-LONG-SHORT-SHORT-LONG means. If not, try to clap a simple 1,2,3,4, rhythm, only with an extra clap between the 3 and the 4 – or just check out the tambourine in *(I Can't Get No) Satisfaction* by The Rolling Stones.

Soon the two-hundred-strong crowd was clapping this rhythm just right, and Eddie Jordan told his boys to *'Do the Alligator!'*

Before the words left his lips, Sam and Earl were down on all fours, slapping the floor to the beat of the new rhythm. This was the first of ten stages of The Alligator, and to keep the energy levels up, the two brothers did this for only one bar before moving on to the next phase. They stretched out onto their bellies, still slapping their hands on the floor, *1,2,3+4 ...*

Next, the dancer must roll onto their left-side and let their left foot take over where their hands just left off, kicking the air, still 1,2,3+4 … Sam And Earl did this for no longer than one bar before …

They rolled onto their backs and started kicking the air with both feet. In the hands (or feet) of mere mortals, this was usually where fatigue, dizziness, and sometimes disorientation set in. But not for Sam and Earl, and certainly not on a night when the music was good, the vibe was good, and the brothers felt like they had pogo springs in their heels.

They stayed on their backs for one bar before rolling onto their right sides and using their left feet to kick the air. By now, both men had sweat in their eyes, and this and the lights from the bandstand meant they could see little more than a multi-coloured blur. This did nothing to slow them down, though, since they practised their routines blindfolded with the house band playing at the same volume they were playing at now. Sam and Earl acted on feel, on muscle memory, and it never let them down.

Now they were on their right-hand sides, kicking the air with their left feet and loving every minute.

Dave and Lianda watched all of this from the side of the stage. Lianda was wearing a sexy, elegant cocktail dress as she usually did on Saturday nights at the club. It was a dipped-hem number, and Dave held her closely from behind and ran a finger along an exposed section of her shoulders. He kissed the same spot, and she looked around and gave him a dreamy smile.

It was the perfect time at the perfect place, he thought. I'm happy, Lianda's happy, we're having the times of our lives … And so is everybody else, by the look of things. The band's cooking, Sam and Earl were shaking it down, and the crowd was well up for it. They whooped and hollered, and some of them even attempted to mimic the moves of their new heroes. But Dave was wrong to think everyone was feeling the good vibes.

As Sam and Earl had begun their skit, two men in their late thirties and wearing long leather jackets over expensive black-and-whites had started working their way to the front of the crowd.

The one on the left had a shoulder holster, which was a mobile home for his favourite pistol, the make and model of which had been made famous by a Hollywood legend many years earlier. It made him feel lucky, punk, and he had been reliably informed it had a range of over a mile. He couldn't shoot that far, but the man it was for was standing a lot closer than that.

The one without a gun had tried to persuade his partner to leave it in the car, but his partner wouldn't listen.

Instead, he suggested a plan – a good one too.

The man with the concealed firearm had stood in front of the other as they'd queued to get in so that he would be patted down first. The plain-clothed doorman would have to turn his back on the unarmed man to carry out his search. If he found the weapon, he would probably experience some sort of meltdown and become prone to errors in judgement. The other chap would have to do nothing more than poke a finger in the base of the doorman's spine and say something like 'I've got one too,' to make him freeze like a statue while the bad guys made a quick exit. Easy.

Clint Eastwood junior was almost disappointed that they'd been allowed to walk right in. Now, having made his way to the front of the crowd along with his right-hand man, he watched the show, unimpressed. "It's like a bloody circus," he said to his partner in crime.

They were identical twins, which could have drawn attention to them had the club not been dimly lit, save for a few parcan beams that sometimes spilt over the edge of the stage and into the throng. Plus, the guests were gripped by the two crazy dancers and the pulsing music of the house band.

Sam and Earl finished the right-hand side/kicking the air section of The Alligator, and moved on to the next piece, which involved laying on their bellies while slapping the dance floor some more. Then they were crouching again and clapping their hands in time with the band and the crowd before jumping into the squat position for the next stage. They were free to clap their hands together now, and as they lost themselves in their act, they didn't see two audience members leave barely a minute after they arrived.

Dave saw the two men walk out, but he didn't think anything of it. One-hundred-and-ninety-eight guests were enjoying themselves, and that was enough for him.

The dancing chefs were approaching the end of The Alligator, and having completed the penultimate stage of the dance, they were standing and clapping while they waited for Eddie Jordan to call the next dance. Instead, he told the crowd to give it up for Sam and Earl, and the crowd cheered loud enough to drown out the band.

"And now ladies and gentlemen, the king of swing … Mister Fuzzy Lester!"

'Fuzzy' Lester was the guitarist in The Blue Lights Houseband. At twenty-six, he was the youngest member of the band, and although he did have a silly afro, his 'fuzzy' moniker had been handed to him on account of his penchant for guitar stomp-boxes. Nicky, Ricky, and Dave had worked long and hard to wean him off using these, but Dave eventually gave up trying to reason with him and threw Lester's pedalboard off Southend Pier.

Sam and Earl were now standing on opposite sides of the stage, using this chance to catch their breath, knowing that Eddie would soon call them back on, and Lester's solo got underway.

The men in the long leather jackets only heard a few bars of the guitar solo. Before long, they were out in the cool night air, making their way to the car. They'd seen everything they needed to see.

Chapter 9

Bass frequency sounds are better at travelling through walls than their trebly cousins. When Alex and Samuel Cleaver walked out of Bobby's Bar and Grill, 'Fuzzy' Lester's guitar solo seemed to stop the moment the door closed, yet the rhythm section could still be heard clearly.

Samuel Cleaver was disorientated by the sudden lack of stimulus, the strange feeling of having had a portion of one of his senses lopped off. Strangely, this happened just as his eyes experienced an overload from the nearby Southend Pier in all its neon glory. He didn't show his confusion, and he and his brother walked the fifty yards or so to the car in stony silence. Only when the doors of Alex Cleaver's BMW 7 series were closed and locked did the brothers do any talking. Sam went first.

"Southend it is, then?"

Alex Cleaver took a moment to respond to his brother's question. "Oh, I see. I make the decisions now, do

I? Okay, then – yes. Southend it is."

It was music to Samuel Cleavers ears, and he slumped back in his seat and lit a cigar in celebration.

"Just don't think it's gonna be easy," said Alex. "Look what he did to Alley Oop the other day. We should tread carefully."

"Tread carefully?" said Sam, sitting up from his passenger-side seat. "We've got *these*, remember?" he said as he opened his jacket and showed his brother his 'piece'.

Anyone who has seen the movie *Layer Cake* will remember Daniel Craig's advice for would-be coke dealers, a key piece of which was that you must never meet the end-user. Having watched this film more than a dozen times, the Cleaver brothers had followed this rule to the letter, and it had served them well. But there was one rule that the brothers hadn't followed …

Early on in their careers, they had vowed never to use their own product. But three years ago, high on life and full of piss and vinegar, they decided to give it a try. Funnily enough, it was Alex's idea. He suggested that since suppliers would often give clients a chance to sample their produce, they might appear inexperienced if they didn't take their associates up on this and therefore risk getting ripped off in the future.

It was a good plan, and the brothers soon learned to walk it like they talked it. The only trouble was, the Cleaver brothers were wealthy and powerful men by then, and wealthy and powerful men are the last people in the world who should use cocaine.

"Never mind Alley Oop," said Alex. "I'm talking about *this*," he said as he opened a two-year-old copy of FHM magazine and showed his brother the same thing he'd tried to show him that morning.

It was a double-page feature about Dave Hunter and his tussles with the late gangland boss Norman Layer. There was a nighttime picture of Dave Hunter outside a rundown-looking boxing gym, wearing boxing gloves and squaring up to an invisible opponent under the strapline 'IS THIS THE HARDEST MAN IN ESSEX?'

"We've talked about this," said Samuel. "Where do we want to end up?"

"Top of the table, *bruv*," said Alex.

"Right," said Samuel. "And the way to do that is?"

"Take out whoever's there already."

Theirs had been a steady climb to the top of the tree in their native London. With the help of their daredevil friend Phillip Howlens (who was a stooge and had been working for Norman Layer the whole time), they had put a large number of small-timers out of business before they took their shot at the title and won.

Now the brothers had Essex in their sights, and they agreed that they should start as they mean to go on. They reckoned the best way to get started was to run a tough guy out of town. Someone like Dave Hunter.

Southend it was.

Fuzzy Lester kept his guitar break to under a minute as per the instructions of Nicky and Ricky, Southend-on-Sea's very own Blues Brothers, who led the band if not from behind the scenes then certainly from the back of the stage. The crowd applauded Lester's Stratocaster antics, but really they wanted more from Sam and Earl.

They got more, too. Having smashed The Alligator, the brothers, as per the instructions of the recently deceased Mr. Pickett, put their hands on their hips and let their backbones slip before showing the good people of Southend how to do The Watusi as well as The Jerk and several others.

When the song and dance were over, Dave gave the signal for Jeff the barman to bring up the house lights just as the band hit its final note, and the crowd gave the loudest cheer of the night. Feeling a sense of occasion, Dave stepped up on the stage and took the mic, and urged the crowd to give it up for the dancing cooks once more. The crowd did, and Sam took Earl's hand like a referee at the end of a boxing match and held up his and his brother's hand. The band launched into a reprise that was almost drowned out by the roar of the crowd before ending with a tight staccato. As the band hit the final note, Sam and Earl both grabbed their crotches and thrust their hips towards the audience with a throaty grunt.

"Huh!"

If the band had been worried about following this, they needn't have been, and despite the early climax, they kept the crowd buzzing until closing time, when the drained yet happy customers gathered their belongings and made their way into the night.

As the last guest made his way to the door, Dave called everybody over for a quick debrief. He explained that while he was glad the night was a success, and the team had done themselves proud, he was tired and fancied an early night. There would be a quick tidy-up without beer or pizza afterwards. He took 100 pounds from the till and gave the used notes to Sam and Earl as a tip. "Spend it all at once," he said.

He wasn't lying about being tired, but that wasn't what stopped him from sinking a few after work. No, the randy old git wanted to take Lianda upstairs and finish what they had started at lunchtime, and he was delighted to find out she'd been thinking the same thing.

Chapter 10

The last time Danny had looked at his bedside clock, the red digits told him it was 3:25 am: that was when he'd decided to get up.

He could see the outline of the club from the window of his modest third-floor, two-bedroom flat, and he could see the coast just beyond it. Beyond that was a dark horizon, and this was what Danny now focused on.

It had been a productive day. He and Mick had had a productive sparring session, and the club's takings had been good or even great. He'd gone to bed alone that night, but he'd had more crumpet than his auntie's tearoom since buying the bar. Things were good, no mistake about it. But the million-dollar question remained: what was bothering him?

As he looked out to sea, it occurred to him that he was using open water in the same way that Inspector Morse used classical music.

Danny hoped that calming imagery and the resulting peaceful state of mind would stimulate the part of the brain that spoke less frequently than the conscious mind, often leaving only trails of breadcrumbs when it did. Danny scanned the coastline. Bobby's Bar and Grill was as dark as the night outside, which was very dark beneath a cloudy sky. The pier, a hundred yards west of the club, was bathed in blackness.

This unsettled Danny, for Southend Pier – like his bar – was one of those places that was lively enough that he sometimes thought it to be a living, breathing entity; the lights and the sounds were man-made, yet you could almost believe something like this had a heart.

After what could have been two minutes or an hour, he decided that no answers were going to come, and neither was sleep now. Danny was by nature a tidy person, and he could find his clothes and get dressed without switching the light on.

The nameless teenager lay sobbing on the cold, concrete floor of a police cell somewhere in London's East End.

The young officer had thrown him to the floor, and the boy had decided to just play dead – maybe, just maybe, he thought, they would see that he had had enough and leave him alone.

He sobbed quietly, hoping the officer who'd just beaten him up or his friends who'd watched, laughing, wouldn't hear: there was a chance that would make the copper madder than before.

He'd done a lot of crying lately – sometimes out of sheer misery, other times when the cold night air had gone right down to his bones. Now, he didn't even know why he was crying: he just knew he was. It could be that he hadn't eaten hot food in over a week, or the fact that he'd just taken a blow to the back so vicious he'd wondered if he'd stand up again.

The blood from when he'd bitten his tongue after being punched for stealing a packet of crisps had dried and was sticking his face to the cold floor. The café owner had done what the police told him to when he'd phoned them, holding him till they got there. Two coppers took the boy off the café owner's hands and had beaten him even more before throwing him in a cell.

He must have been drifting in and out of consciousness because he didn't hear the cell door opening. But he heard footsteps, thick leather soles squeezing down on the concrete and heading towards him.

He was already shaking, but now he felt his heart beating fast again, and he curled into a ball like a hedgehog.

At first, he felt nothing – he just heard quiet voices. One of them sounded familiar or almost friendly. Then he felt a hand slap his cold face, and he let out a cry. His eyes opened, and the boy was now a young man, although the cold, hard bed was as real as it had seemed in the dream.

Alley Oop saw the faces of Alex and Samuel Cleaver peering down at him from a squatting position above the bus shelter bench that he'd made his bed for the night. "I might've known we'd find you here," said Alex.

"We'd better get you cleaned up," said Samuel. "We've got a job for you."

Danny fastened the last button on his knee-length leather jacket and reached for his purple velvet fedora. He patted the hat down, then reached into the breast pocket of his jacket and took out a lighter, which he used to light the wick of his beloved pewter-and-glass oil lamp. A warm glow filled the room.

The oil lamp sat on Danny's window ledge, where it often kept him company as he composed music past the witching hour; now, it would lead him into the night.

Danny crept down the dimly lit hallway and down two flights of stairs, tip-toeing all the way. A minute later, he left the building.

He noticed the wind was up, and he heard dead leaves scattering along the street and a creaking sign that hung outside one of the many guesthouses in town. He walked to the end of the street and turned right. He was on the seafront, now, and despite it being only September, a blast of cold sea wind sent a shiver right through him.

He didn't turn back. Instead, he made his way towards the club.

He walked around the perimeter of the building twice with his shadow close behind him. His companion was twice his size thanks to the glow of the lamp, and Danny was grateful for the company. As he made his way around, Danny checked the entrance was locked, as well as making sure the fire exits and the kitchen door were secure.

With his inspection of the building over, he found himself walking around the car park. There were two cars there that he didn't recognise, but he soon found that no-one was in them. From the far edge of the car park, he looked back at Bobby's Bar.

It occurred to him he was performing a kind of sentry duty, brought on by (and perhaps in an attempt to ward off) the case of the blues that had visited him. At first, he wondered if he was crazy, feeling guardianship towards a pile of bricks. Yet it made perfect sense.

He ran the club as a co-operative with his two best friends, Dave and Mick. Although they'd bought it for a knock-down price, it had become his – and their – main focus. Dave Hunter, who Danny took a bullet for in the ordeal that led to them buying the club, lived there and Lianda all but lived there with him. But this wasn't all …

The place had the feel of a family business, despite there being no blood ties between Mick, Danny or Dave. As Danny looked at the place from a distance, he realised this was why he felt so attached to it; he didn't live there, but it gave him a feeling of home nonetheless.

He climbed over the stone wall surrounding the car park and walked along the street, past the pier and along the concrete promenade that took him almost to the water's edge. He sat at the point where he and Mick usually started their five-mile run at the end of every training session. He thought of Mick and the boot camp-style drill he'd put him through every day, and wondered: why was he bent on protecting his friend? Was it the same feeling of family that had him checking up on the bar in the dead of night?

He cast his mind back to long nights in the desert in Helmand Province. One of the older soldiers told him that the anticipation of battle was, in some ways, worse than combat itself. The same soldier also talked occasionally of his late father, another veteran of the British armed forces, and this was the part that stood out in Danny's mind.

Often, Danny and nineteen other soldiers lay in their camp beds wanting desperately to sleep but afraid that doing so might render them unprepared if they were suddenly called to action. It was during these times that his mysterious friend spoke of what his father had called 'the dark blues'.

Danny learnt that the dark blues was an otherworldly melancholy that came over men who were close to death, a haunted state in which they became fatigued and acceptant of their fate. Danny came back to England a changed man, knowing that seasoned soldiers believed a man's fate was governed by his ability to not give in to this, and to fight against the dying of the light.

Danny had never quite been able to dismiss this as soldiers' superstition even though he wanted to. In fact, he wondered more than ever now if this was true, and as he heard waves breaking, his mind brought to the fore a similar story involving the late Otis Redding.

Years after Otis's death, his producer and friend Steve Cropper recalled in an interview how a deep melancholy came over his friend the day they recorded the classic *(Sitting on the) Dock of the Bay*. Cropper claimed to remember his friend saying something about knowing something was coming to an end, which turned out to be chillingly prophetic: Redding died soon after, and he never heard his finished masterpiece.

What didn't add up here was that a dark weariness hadn't come over Danny on the day he was shot three times and at close range.

Danny sat and looked out to sea, his usual hawk's eye vision diminished by the gas lamp that he held with his right thumb and index finger. He wondered if the dark blues hadn't found him that day for no reason other than he hadn't been ready for it.

It was hard to believe lady luck had just smiled when you'd caught three bullets in the back, but there could be no doubt that it happened at the best – or least worst – time.

There had been twelve policemen already at the scene. Six of them were firearms officers, and this stopped the late Norman Layer from coming back to finish the job. This bought Danny some time, but the real credit went to a quick-thinking superintendent (now chief constable) from the Cambridgeshire police force. The Super knew just what to do, and he wasted no time in doing it …

The first thing he did was take out his baton and tap Danny's right knee, like a doctor checking a kid's reflexes. Danny's knee popped up an inch or so and allayed Danny's and the super's greatest fear: the bullet had missed his spine. Now the soon-to-be police chief could get to work.

This happened outside the lobby of a travel lodge on the outskirts of Cambridge. Two members of staff ran out right after the shots were fired. The super shouted to them to fetch an ironing board as well as several duvet cases and a blanket. The moment he gave this instruction, he heard the footsteps of someone running up behind him; one officer had reacted well and grabbed the trauma bag. 'Scissors,' demanded the super, opening his hand and holding it out behind his head. He took the scissors and cut Danny's blood-drenched shirt open, and revealed a sucking wound. 'You're gonna be alright,' he said as he called out for a vented chest seal.

By the time the hotel orderlies had brought out the ironing board-cum-stretcher, he had fixed the protective seal around the wound and soaked up enough blood to inspect the rest of Danny's torso. Danny knew what the super was doing, even if nobody else there did.

The superintendent was trying to find out how many bullets had passed through Danny's body. He'd been hit in the back – that much was obvious – and three shots were fired. Having rolled Danny onto his side, the superintendent found three entry wounds in his back and, as far as the superintendent could see, as he wiped away one lot of blood before a fresh coating appeared, only two exit holes. A bullet was still lodged somewhere in his abdomen.

The superintendent being quick to think and quick to

act may have played a big part in Danny's survival, but that didn't mean Danny didn't help himself too. The superintendent would have been gravely concerned at Danny's low pulse, had he taken it.

The reason Danny's pulse would have been slow for a man three times his age was that he'd been taught to slow his breathing and, therefore, his heart rate. Slowing his breathing reduced his chances of going into shock and possibly dying of the resulting fall in body temperature; getting his heart rate down allowed him to keep as much of his blood as possible.

The resourceful super, having been a military man himself, knew what his friend was up to, and he even winked at him and said 'Good lad.' Then, the super along with two other officers rolled Danny onto the improvised stretcher face-down, the superintendent knowing there was a chance of vomiting if Danny went into delayed shock. And he was bringing up blood, which put him at risk of suffocation.

Danny imagined he must have lost consciousness at this point, as he remembered nothing of his ride in an ambulance that was, in fact, a van belonging to the Cambridgeshire firearms unit. He remembered little of his stay at Cambridge City Hospital, although he did have a dreamlike recollection of coming to shortly after his arrival. He remembered feeling disorientated, as he was now facing upwards and had soft cushioning beneath him. There were white lights – not at the end of a tunnel, but several feet above his head. The strip lights over the corridor flew by like the broken sections of white line in the middle of the road.

He found out later that the smart superintendent who saved his life had called ahead and given a full description of Danny's injuries and condition to the doctor whose team would be treating him, before saving time and having a fellow officer drive them three miles to the city hospital.

Danny pulled himself from the past and back into the present, sitting in the dark with the whole of Southend seafront to himself. While he was deep in thought, his lamp had begun to burn less brightly. Then, just when his mind joined his body there in the present, the circumference of the glow from his lamp shrank around him until there was nothing more than a singed wick by his side.

The effect of this was similar to that of a squid firing a cloud of black ink in his eyes, and for a time, Danny could see nothing. Five minutes later, his night-vision returned, and he was reminded that he could see better – and further – without the lamp. He picked up a stone and pulled his arm back before swinging his arm in a lasso motion and throwing the missile towards the water. He looked out to sea, then around to the club, about fifty yards back, and then out to sea again. A broken patch of cloud allowed the moon to shine some light onto the estuary.

Danny shivered and pulled his knees up to his chest.

He guessed it was about 4 am, which meant there was an hour-and-a-half until daylight. He breathed out and breathed in again, and a thought entered his mind that he had been trying to keep out for some time.

Something was coming.

Chapter 11

"What's D-D-Dave Hunter ever done to you?"

Alley Oop was walking along an embankment by the Thames, not far from the Cleaver's HQ. The river – the whole of the UK, in fact – was bathed in an eerie half-light as the dawn prepared to break. He had a Cleaver either side of him.

"Well, Alley, it's not what he's done to us," said Samuel Cleaver, his brother Alex nodding in agreement, "it's what he's done *for* us."

"Yes," said Alex. "You see, Dave Hunter bought and did up a nightclub in a prime position."

Bobby's Bar was in a good spot – there was no denying that. It was close to a local tourist attraction, it was close to the town centre, and it was owned by someone who was a bit of a local celebrity. As if that wasn't enough, it was near the sea, *and* there was a private airfield just a short drive away.

"So you see," said Samuel Cleaver, not really sure why he was selling an idea to this modern-day Baldrick, "if we need to make a speedy exit we get a choice of air, sea or land. Is that good or what?" He gave his brother a wink, which went unnoticed by Alley Oop, who was staring at the floor as he always did when he walked. Alex took the chance to cut in.

"Just now and again, we – well, you – will have to receive a package. Certain people won't like us – you – doing this," Alex said. "Why not give yourself the best chance of an easy pickup."

It was Sam's turn again.

"Nice little walk along the beach, eh? Do you a world of good," he said, patting Alley Oop's back, confident that he wouldn't notice his hint of mockery.

"I suppose I always did like the seaside," said Alley Oop. "Mind you, it still don't seem right, though."

"Don't be so moral," said Samuel. "Was it right that

you were left to fend for yourself from an early age?"

Alley looked up at Sam and shook his head.

"No. Of course it wasn't. Here – have this," Sam said as he handed Alley Oop a little wrap of cocaine. "And remember there will be plenty more where this came from. Hey – we might even have a party for our grand opening?"

Alley's face became lit-up – as he soon would be.

The sky over London had also lit up in the time they were talking. There wasn't daylight yet, but the sky had turned a lighter shade of pale; before, it had been as murky as the river that ran beside them.

"I fancy some breakfast," said Alex. "Are you in?" he said, looking at Alley Oop, who nodded in agreement.

"Good," said Alex. "I know a lovely little café near here – you can go in the gents and put that stuff up your nose where it belongs. Then we'll talk business."

***

Half-a-mile from the spot where Samuel Cleaver made

Christmas come early for his hapless assistant, there was a charming little Parisian café, owned by a chap named Malcolm who was about as French as Jeremy Clarkson. Malcolm had just put the *Ouvert* sign up, and Alley Oop and the two Cleavers had the place to themselves.

"A job like this," said Alex to Alley Oop as Malcolm walked away from their table, having served them freshly-made croissants, jam and thick, black coffee, "is basically a repossession – banks do it all the time. We do it too, but we've never taken you with us before." He took a bite of croissant, slathered with delicious strawberry preserves.

He paused long enough to chew, then swallow his mouthful and said, "You must be excited, Alley – this is your chance to shine!"

Sam picked up as his brother ate more croissant.

"Here," he said, tapping Alley Oop's knee, "if this goes well, we might be in a position to give you a bit more responsibility."

Maybe it was the prospect of making a name for himself – and perhaps being taken a little bit more seriously – or maybe it was the cocaine he'd just hoovered up in the café toilets. Alley Oop's initial reservation had melted away, and now he was as keen as mustard.

In the past, the Cleavers had used a man named Phillip Howlens to do this. There was a difference between Howlens and Alley Oop – they respected Howlens, and they paid him well. He risked life and limb for them, but at least he knew this and acted – and was paid – accordingly.

Howlens was tough and clever; Alley Oop was the former but by no means the latter.

In fact, as it had turned out, Howlens was too bright – or at least, he thought he was. He'd tried to mug the Cleavers off – unsuccessfully, as it happened, and he was now in the nick where he would be for a long, long time.

Phillip Howlens had played a substantial part in making the Cleavers what they were today (even though he had conned his way in, they found out later). But the plan was all theirs.

The Cleaver family was from Deptford, South-East London, and this was where their story began – nearly. The nearest train station to them was Deptford Bridge, which wasn't quite the end of the line on the Docklands Light Railway (but the end of the line in the non-literal sense, the brothers always felt). That particular title went to Lewisham, and one night five years ago, Phillip Howlens went there with a bag of ecstasy tablets and nerves of steel.

He went into a grotty little bar-cum-nightclub, where he was able to deduce from the wild-eyes of the customers and the trance-like nature of the music playing in there that drugs were being used. He did some asking around to find out who was dealing, and when he was sure he was on somebody else's territory, he started trying to peddle his illegal wares. This soon caught the attention of the resident dealer, who objected strongly to a young upstart stealing his customers. This was the good bit …

Howlens was followed when he left the club, and he led his three tails down a blind alley. They cornered him and demanded to know who he was working for. They found out soon enough, as half-a-dozen of the Cleavers' heavies stepped in. They overpowered the three men from the club and instead demanded to know who *they* worked for.

It turned out they worked independently. The young men shared a flat not far from the nightclub they'd just left to follow Howlens. They were frogmarched to their flat by Howlens and his accomplices and relieved of two-hundred ecstasy tablets and a briefcase full of cocaine. And twenty-thousand pounds in cash. And their clothes.

Then Howlens gave them two choices: either they could be left alone with the six heavies – after they'd helped themselves to the goods on offer – or Howlens could order the six heavies to tie the three ex-dealers up and leave them with just enough of their supplies to suggest this stuff wasn't for personal use. And then call the police to report a burglary at that very address. Either way, they were finished, and they made the sensible decision to accept the second option.

Howlens was delighted they'd made a decision that would allow for a peaceful resolution. He and the Cleaver brothers were not prone to violence if it could be avoided – the threat was usually enough. The police were called to the flat in question – let's not forget that an act of theft had been committed – and the three small-time peddlers were never seen again. A gap in the market had been created, and the Cleavers wasted no time in filling it.

A few weeks later, they repeated this procedure at Elverson Road – the next stop along the Docklands Light Railway. Another run-down nightspot, another small-time operation closed down and swiftly replaced. Next, it was Deptford Bridge – their home patch – then Greenwich and Cutty Sark soon after.

Within three months, the gang had worked their way north to Stratford, putting one dealer after another out of business, often taking away their bulk supplies of illegal substances and selling it as their own. And, when they had worked their way from north-to-south of the docklands region of East London, they looped their way back and headed to Bank, and began their march from West to East. They came, they saw, and they conquered, choosing their targets carefully and disposing of them likewise.

"So, what will I do?" said Alley Oop.

"Well," said Alex, "hopefully, very little. Let me explain."

Alex outlined the details of the plan simply – because it was a simple plan.

A man they had never met – and wouldn't meet again once the transaction had taken place – would go down there one night in the not too distant future and start proceedings off. He'd make Dave Hunter an offer he couldn't refuse, and hopefully, it would be plain sailing from there. The two other chaps who worked there would be taken care of by a few of the Cleaver's less well-heeled employees, as would any staff members who fancied putting up a fight. The heavies would fortify the building in case of the unlikely event of Dave Hunter mustering a cavalry and retaliating, while the man-with-no-name would take Dave's girlfriend for a drive to Scotland or Newcastle.

"I still don't see where I come into th –"

"Patience, dear boy. I'm getting to it," said Alex. "You'll need to bring Dave to us – rough him up a bit, but nothing too serious. We need him alive and well for what comes next."

"Go on," said Alley Oop, his eyes wide like a child and his mouth hanging open like a blowfish.

"We'll need him to meet with our solicitor in the morning – just to go over a few formalities, make it all look legit … You know, just in case he tries to contest the terms of the contract."

Both brothers laughed at this, and they were right to. Being forced out of town would be quite a blow for the man who had been branded the hardest man in Essex by the biggest-selling lad's mag in the country.

"One more thing," said Sam. "The man who will make the offer that Dave Hunter can't refuse – you're his point of contact." Alley Oop's eyes went wide again.

"Here's his number," said Alex as he slid a piece of paper across the table to Alley Oop. "He charges a grand just to answer the phone. Memorise this number, and burn the piece of paper afterwards. Go and start communications with him, and make sure he's available on October 31st."

"Eh," said Alley, "that's Halloween! Good choice, sir – people get scared on Halloween!"

"Yes, they do," said Sam with a small sigh. "Now run along, and try not to get knocked down by a milk float."

Chapter 12

The phone rang three times at the other end before it was answered.

"That's a thousand pounds you owe me," said the voice at the other end. "I hope you can afford it. Who do you work for?"

"I-I-I … M-m-mustn't s-say, sir."

"No, you mustn't. Your name from now on is 'Orderly,' and you don't need to know mine. Got that?

"Yes, sir."

"You have permission to speak and a minute to do it. Go."

"I n-n-need somebody taken out … Not d-d-d-dead, like, just evicted. Oh, and then I need them brought to me." There was silence, and for a moment, Alley Oop wondered if he'd blown it.

"That will cost you sixteen grand. Fifteen for the job, and a thousand for talking to you. Do you wish to proceed?"

"Yes, s-s-sir, absolutely."

"Right. Tell me what I need to know."

Over the next sixty seconds, Alley Oop relayed all the essential details. Who Dave Hunter was, where he lived and worked, how many people worked for him at the bar, and, of course, the name of the bar and its location. He also told his contact about Dave's girlfriend and began to give a description of her – but was cut off as soon as the man revealed he would be able to identify her without his help.

"Tell me what I *need* to know," he said again, relieving Alley Oop from doing any more thinking than was absolutely necessary. Alley told him that the job was planned for the evening of October 31st, and the mysterious voice told him to be there well before ten.

"One more thing, p-p-please … Where will you meet me on the night? You know ... To hh-hand him over."

"Park up somewhere nearby and just wait. You'll know when I'm ready for you. Remember, no-one from your team comes in the building until I'm out. All you have to do for now is go to Chelsea Village Bus Station – it's about a mile from where you are now. Put half my fee in one of the lockers before midday. I'll know which one you've used. Then wait to hear from me."

The line went dead and, like someone in a film, Alley spun around when he realised the man he'd just spoken to knew his whereabouts. Alley Oop scanned his surroundings for a moment before he realised he didn't know who he was looking for.

What he did know was that he needed to track down his bosses and get hold of 7,500 pounds. It was more money than he'd had in his whole life.

It was nine o'clock, and Alley Oop was feeling pleased with himself. He'd made contact with the man who would put Dave Hunter out of business, and though his nervous stutter had returned (in spite of his cocaine-high, which usually made the problem vanish), Alley Oop had managed to send out the message that he and the Cleavers were worth working for.

As soon as he'd finished his conversation with the nameless agent, Alley – or 'Orderly' – had run back to the café and explained the situation to Alex and Samuel. He'd caught them just as they were leaving the pretentious establishment, and the three of them had gone on foot back to the Cleaver's office. 7,500 pounds was easy money for people like them – they kept more than this locked away in the base of the grandfather clock in their office.

They also had a backpack for Alley to carry the money in, as he now did while wearing a camera around his neck and clutching a book of London street maps as well as a timetable for the London Underground.

Alley found an empty locker – number 21 – and put the backpack containing the money in there. He knew he was being watched, but he also knew there was no point looking for a face he'd never seen. In fact, he avoided making eye contact with anyone at the bus terminal. There were lots of them, too, people from all walks of life.

He was able to look outside his tunnel-vision enough to see that his cover as a tourist was a good one; many of the people here carried tourist guides like his book of street maps and train timetables. But only one of them was the dangerous man he'd spoken to just hours ago.

Alley Oop left the bus depot and prepared for the two-mile walk back to Cleaver HQ on Kensington High Street. It was a Sunday, but it was hard to tell from the number of people and the volume of traffic: away from the sea of tourists at the bus station, the streets of Fulham were bustling just as they were on any day of the week. The roads were busy too. Cars, buses, vans, motorcycle couriers – they were all there, tearing around and trying to shave minutes or seconds off their journeys.

Until today, Alley Oop had often wondered why

everybody seemed to be in such a hurry these days; now, he could see why, and he quickened his pace accordingly.

He was walking up North End Road in the direction of Kensington. To his left, he saw the towering spectacle of Stamford Bridge Stadium, and although this wasn't the time, he took a moment to take in the view.

His bosses, Alex and Sam, had promised to take him there one day, and he couldn't help thinking that if he did a good job down in Southend, then maybe a trip to see a match could be on the cards. He'd heard the two brothers talk about a thing called a VIP box, and though Alley Oop had no idea what this was, he couldn't help thinking it sounded very important.

It was outside the sphere of his imagination, however, to consider going there by himself. He was born poor, he had lived poor, and he had grown accustomed to being treated poorly. The most money he'd ever carried was a 20-pound note, and the landlord of the pub he'd tried to spend it in had demanded to know where he got it from.

Alley Oop kept walking, passing antique shops, boutique estate agents and houses with half-a-dozen steps leading up to their front doors, wondering if he would ever get used to such a sight. About a mile into his journey, Alley Oop came to North End Road's intersection with the busier West Cromwell Road. He didn't want to risk his life that morning, so he went to press the button to activate the traffic lights that would help him get home safely.

There was a phone box next to the traffic control box, and Alley Oop heard ringing inside it just as he was about to press the button to make the green man appear on the other side. "I don't believe it," he said before he went inside and picked up the receiver.

"I've got my money – the first half, anyway. Now for phase two." It was the same voice he'd heard an hour ago, firm, sibilant, authoritative with little in the way of regional distinction.

The voice went on to tell Alley Oop to return to the same locker at seven o'clock that evening.

6:59 pm. Chelsea Village Bus Station was less busy than it had been that morning, which put Alley Oop at ease. He had the key for locker number 21, and he opened it and looked inside. There was a bag, like the one he left earlier but not the same one. There was also an iPod, and a small umbrella, which Alley Oop correctly assumed were to convince people he was a tourist.

With the bag on both shoulders and headphones in his ears, he walked out the bus station, turned left, and walked about a hundred yards before sitting down in a bus shelter to see what was in the bag.

It had been quite a day, and although his cocaine high from earlier had long since worn off, there hadn't been the usual low that followed. He'd been to see the Cleavers after his second telephone conversation with his nameless associate, and although they told him he was doing well, they hadn't given him another blast.

Inside the bag was a mobile phone: now he knew he'd made it. He'd only carried one once before, and although he'd soon had it confiscated when it became clear to Alex and Samuel that he didn't know how to use it (and earned himself a slap when this became apparent), he was sure he wouldn't mess up this time.

But he nearly did, for he almost dropped the fancy gadget when it rang in his hands. After a quick game of keep-it-up, he caught the expensive phone and pressed a button that was flashing green. He held it to his cheek.

"Lose this, and you lose your money," said the man at the other end.

"It's s-s-s-safe w-w-with me, ch-ch-chief."

"You can't make calls from this phone, and it can't be traced: it doesn't exist. I'll call you if I need to. See you on the night."

“Thanks, chief – I appr –”

The line was dead.

Chapter 13

Dave Hunter had long been vocal about his dislike of American culture seeping into the fabric of British life. Which made him a hypocrite since he was now the majority owner of an American-style bar and diner, slap bang in the middle of a town that was as synonymous with the British way of life as tea, scones and drizzle. In short, he was a sell-out.

He could argue that because Bobby's Bar and Grill was an American-style (but definitely not 'American themed') bar and grill, then at least he was honouring tradition by hosting a Halloween bash. But he didn't need to. Because he was the boss.

Tonight, he was busy warming up his own crowd. Danny, Mick and Dave – supported by the solid rhythm section of Nicky and Ricky – had taken to the stage to get things started. For the last hour they had been blowing up a storm on some Rock 'n' Soul floor fillers: *High Heel*

Sneakers, Barefootin, I'm a King Bee – they were all there. The capacity crowd was enjoying every minute, and the best was yet to come.

The house band minus Nicky and Ricky was in the flat above the bar, trowelling on white face paint having squeezed into Vincent Price vampire suits. They were getting ready to perform a supernatural-themed set that would take the crowd into the witching hour and beyond.

This was Dave's idea, and the members of The Blue Lights House Band had been pleasantly surprised by how many spooky songs from the world of popular music could be given a blues band makeover. Michael Jackson's *Thriller* was an obvious choice, with its opening synth stabs arranged for a three-part horn section. Anyone who has seen *Blues Brothers 2000* will know that Donovan's *Season of the Witch* works well as a raunchy soul limbo. There was *Devil In A Blue Dress* by Mitch Ryder, *I Ain't Superstitious* and *Evil*, both by the late Howlin' Wolf, and the god of hellfire would have his greatest hit played tonight. Fuzzy Lester was getting excited about using an FX pedal to mimic the sitar lick on The Stones' *Paint it Black,* and *Werewolves of London* was sure to get an airing later.

At five-to-ten, Dave looked out at the crowd and allowed himself to feel a little pride. The guests had gone to work on the Halloween theme. Not far from the stage, he saw four young men, possibly students, dressed up as ghostbusters, and a man dressed as the dark-robed executioner from the *Scream* movies weaved in and out of the crowd of vampires, vixens and werewolves.

Dave turned to the band. "Last one, boys," he said as he wiped his brow with a bar towel.

No-one needed to be told that *Tulane* by The Steve Gibbons Band was next – least of all Mick, who peeled off the intro lick with scalpel-like precision before the rhythm section came in, and Dave got to work soon after.

Dave always saved this Chuck Berry-penned tale of

love on the wrong side of the law until the end of the set because he didn't feel anything could follow it. He wanted the band that was on next to give 100%, and by saving his best till last, he gave them no choice.

"Go Tulane, he's lagging behind go head-on," he sang as the song hurtled towards the finish line. He repeated the line, and the band hit a staccato followed by a brief pause. The musicians on stage all watched Nicky bring his right arm up (they think it's all over!) then down again, and they hit the last note of the song just as his stick hit his cymbal (it is now!). The song was finished.

Dave dabbed his forehead again and made his way through the crowd receiving pats on the back from many members of the gruesome troupe, and he grinned as he passed a chap who had come to the party dressed as Simon Pegg in *Shaun of the Dead.* Dave was sorry to insist that Shaun hand over the cricket bat that he claimed was just a feature of his costume, but he took it off him anyway.

Dave had a man cave down a secret corridor behind the stage, and that was where he was going right now. The hidden room had a wooden office desk, a swivel chair, tea and coffee making facilities and a small fridge with an ice compartment if he fancied a taste from the bottle of Scotch he kept in the left drawer of his desk. He had a stereo on his desk and a selection of vinyl so that if the mood took him, he could dim the lights, pour a scotch, hear some blues and mellow down easy. There was one other thing.

Dave had a metal combination safe underneath his desk, about eighteen inches high, nine inches across, and about six inches deep. This was where he kept the small single-action revolver that he took off his friend the late Ted Maskell, the night he was shot dead on Dave's doorstep.

Dave Hunter didn't like guns, and he didn't like the fact that he had one in his office. He didn't like it that the only people who knew about it were Mick and Danny, which meant Lianda was kept in the dark (Dave especially disliked that).

But he didn't like gangland criminals either. He didn't sit quietly the first time they came into his life, and he had no intention of going down without a fight if ever they came back.

Dave reached for the keyring attached to his belt and found the key for the door marked PRIVATE, to the right of the stage. He turned the key in the lock and made his way along the short, bare corridor to his office, where peace and quiet and a quality malt were waiting for him.

The corridor was cold and bare, and so was his office. Yet he was fond of his man space at the back of the club, especially after a long set under the hot lights. The room was dark, but he'd made this trip enough times that he could feel his way to the lamp on his desk and flick the switch. Then he turned around and fumbled through his collection of keys like a prison warden and opened the lost property cupboard.

He felt a chill as he looked at the assortment of contraband. Two sets of brass knuckle-dusters. A pair of nunchakus that had been particularly difficult to confiscate. 'Alley Oop's' flick-knife.

Two small wraps of cocaine …

There was a set of police handcuffs in there that Dave hoped had been used for kinky recreation and not for brutal interrogation (although he knew that the two could overlap). He added the cricket bat to the weapons cache, saddened that people felt the need to tool up when they ought to be enjoying themselves.

Then again, he kept a gun in this room …

Wanting to put this thought out of his mind, Dave poured himself a measure of Scotch. Then, as was part of his ritual, he lifted the needle on the record deck he kept in his so-called office, and the turntable started spinning. He put the needle down and put his headphones on, and soon T-Bone Walker began showing Mick Davies, Fuzzy Lester, and every other damned wannabe how it was done. For a short time, Dave Hunter was in private heaven. Then he realised that Lianda was working while he had his feet up.

Ah, well ...

As soon as he thought of Lianda, he thought of the Catwoman suit he'd bought her in advance of tonight's party. She hadn't worn the tight, shiny outfit to work that evening, but there was a chance she would put it on later. Just for him.

"I'll drink to that," he said as he raised his glass.

Then, he realised he'd forgotten his cigarettes: now he had a problem. Either he could go and fetch them, in which case the magic of the moment would surely be lost, or he could drink whisky in his backroom, listening to blues and *not* watching smoke rise under his desk lamp.

He didn't want to get up, and so he shut his eyes and tried to find solace with blues and booze alone. It didn't work, of course, and after three minutes, he opened his eyes and began steeling himself for a walk through to the bar, where he could pinch a fag from Mick, Danny or one of his customers. It didn't go to plan, for he opened his eyes to find that he wasn't alone.

The man who had crept in while Dave was lost in his music looked about forty, sober, and businesslike in a grey suit and tie. He had a briefcase in his right hand.

Dave took his headphones off and looked him right in the eye. "Don't you know it's fancy dress tonight?"

The guest didn't get a chance to answer, and before his lips moved, Dave asked a more pressing question: "Who are you?"

"That's not important. I'm here to make you an offer."

"An offer? What kind of an offer? I've got to hear this," said Dave as he slid his headphones off and put them on his end of the desk.

"An offer for the club. My clients would like to buy

your business."

"This place isn't for sale."

The man didn't respond right away, which Dave thought was good because it gave him a chance to assess the situation. This was going to get ugly, no doubt about that. He had come into his office via a door clearly marked PRIVATE, so it was a no-brainer.

What Dave did have to think about was where Lianda was. And how many goons this potential buyer had brought with him – and where he kept his gun.

Dave hadn't told the uninvited guest to foxtrot-oscar right away because he wanted to keep him talking. This allowed him to make eye contact, which helped Dave establish that this wasn't a run-of-the-mill thug; they were fiery, emotionally-driven people, and you could see their eyes narrow as violence simmered.

No, this was a professional. This was good since they preferred to work alone. But this was why Dave reckoned his gatecrashing guest was carrying a piece: the psychos weren't allowed them. He also noted that the man carried his briefcase in his right hand, so he wasn't a southpaw. Dave reckoned it might come in handy to know that.

"Will you hear my offer?" said the dark-haired stranger.

"If you like," said Dave, still not 100% sure how he would deal with this, only sure that the time to stop thinking and start doing was only seconds away.

"I must say, I don't usually conduct business standing up," said the man who looked more liked an accountant than a professional killer (even though Dave knew or was at least prepared to wager everything based on the suspicion that he knew better).

"Well, I'm sure this won't take long, so it's best you don't get comfortable," said Dave. "Now, what have you got in that briefcase? On the table where I can see it, please."

Dave maintained eye contact with the mystery caller while pondering Lianda's whereabouts. Had she gone for her break, having seen him doing the same thing?

She usually went up to the flat for her breaks, and Dave could only hope and pray that this was the case tonight.

He regretted not hanging on to the cricket bat he'd confiscated a moment ago, but he couldn't dwell on it. Dave owned a gun, but it was out of his reach in a small, metal combination safe. He put that out of his mind too.

He was running short of ideas.

"Very well," said the mystery shopper, and he put the briefcase down on the desk in front of Dave.

Before he could show Dave what was inside, the mystery shopper turned the briefcase around so that the handle and the latches were facing Dave. "See for yourself," he said.

Dave opened it and saw a single crisp five-pound-note inside.

No more fucking around, then.

Chapter 14

"I'd say take the money and run. That or use it to pay for a bus ride out of town."

Dave acted dumb and said nothing.

"Well?"

"Gee," said Dave. "I don't know what to say … I've come over all stupid. Stupid, and a bit clumsy."

As the last word left his lips, Dave brushed his whisky glass off the side of his table, and it shattered as it hit the hard floor of his office. The trick worked. His would-be assailant broke off from the staredown battle-of-wills that he and Dave had been engaged in for the last minute. His eyes shifted towards the source of the noise. Dave seized the opportunity and picked up the whisky bottle and brought it down across the head of the intruder. He was dazed, cut, and likely to need stitches, but still conscious and vertical. At least he was until Dave took him by the hair and slammed his face against the desk, once, twice and then a third time.

Now, he was out cold.

Dave knew that a brute like this wouldn't stay down for long, so he would need to be quick. The first thing he did was reach inside the guy's suit jacket. Just as he suspected, his guest was carrying a pistol which Dave took from him and carelessly tossed onto the floor, kicking it away from his new buddy. Then he wheeled his swivel-chair around from behind his desk and parked it behind the man he'd just roughed up.

The man was bigger than him, but not by much – he was 6'2 to Dave's 5'9, and Dave didn't have too much trouble lifting the man's resting body onto the leather-backed chair. Then, he found the key to the lost property cupboard before opening it again and taking out the set of handcuffs, turning his back on his dazed visitor.

It took five seconds for Dave to unlock the cupboard and find the stainless steel cuffs. If his captive had stirred in this time, then David Ian Hunter would have been as dead as

Jimi Hendrix. Luckily he was still sleeping (if that was all he was doing, Dave thought grimly) when Dave turned to face him again. Once his wrists were secured around the back of Dave's office chair, Dave checked to see if his guest still had a pulse.

Dave reached around from behind the chair and unfastened the man's belt before removing it and using it to tie his heels together. As a final precautionary measure, Dave tilted the chair back so that the chair – and its occupier – was balanced precariously against his desk: Dave was satisfied that if his hostage tried to wriggle himself free, he'd risk a nasty fall and possibly a fatal landing.

The gun, thought Dave, as he rushed over and picked up the discarded weapon and put it in the inside pocket of his jacket. He stopped to catch his breath and think for a moment.

He was ninety percent sure there was no-one else in the corridor between his man cave and the bar. His office door was unlocked, and if the sound of glass breaking hadn't been enough to make any additional intruders show themselves, then the sound of their colleague involuntarily headbutting Dave's desk surely would have. Dave listened. He could hear the house band jamming away – that was all. To do what he needed to do, he had to believe the corridor was clear.

It was clear, but Dave stepped into the walkway with a heavy heart nonetheless. He took a deep breath and made his way along the corridor, back to the bar.

The door between the dark corridor and the club felt like a portal to another world. The music got a huge treble boost as Dave turned the handle and stepped into the throng. The band was loud, and the party atmosphere couldn't have been more at odds with Dave's mood. He scanned desperately through the crowd with the hope of seeing Lianda, but she was nowhere to be seen.

She's probably just gone upstairs ...

He saw Danny and Mick at a table not far from the stage, drinking champagne – thankfully, they were alone. Dave made his way over to them, resisting the temptation to break into a run, and Danny got up to greet him.

"Davey b …"

"Shut up. We're in trouble."

Danny's eyes narrowed. "How many?" he said.

"One," said Dave. "I took something off 'im."

"You've got it on you now?

"Yes, mate."

"Hold onto it. Where is he now?"

"Tied up out the back – he's sparko for now," said Dave, tilting his head in the direction of the office.

Mick listened intently, knowing that for now, at least, this was all that was required of him. If he felt left out, then he needn't have: he was about to get his big chance.

"Right," said Danny. "Lianda just went upstairs. Join her – I'll come for you when I'm ready." He scanned his eyes around the room before he caught Mick in a headlight stare.

"We've got work to do."

Chapter 15

As Mick and Danny had left their table, Danny had pointed to a table where a couple was leaving their seats to go and dance. Mick had clocked the five-litre stainless steel champagne bucket, which he removed as discreetly as possible, and Danny took one of the chairs with him.

"He can't tell us much like this, can he?" said Danny to his sidekick, who solved the problem of their subjects sleepiness by giving him the ice-bucket challenge.

It worked: their hostage came to. He shivered, drew his breath, and scanned the room as he took in his surroundings, no doubt weighing up the situation and looking for a way out. Danny kneeled down before his subject, and their eyes met.

"We meet again," Danny said.

He got up and lowered the swivel chair down from the precarious angle Dave had left it at, and wheeled the chair and its occupant around to the back wall of the office.

Mick watched the door with a sense of unease, and he soon voiced his concern.

" 'Ere, Danny, do you want me to prop that chair up under the 'andle?" he said.

Danny smiled at his guest and forgave Mick's 'Don't tell them your name Pike' gaff since Mick must have suspected the two had met before: at least he was paying attention.

"Chair underneath the handle, eh? You must forgive my colleague. He's new, and I think he watches too many films." Then he addressed Mick but maintained eye contact with the blood-splattered captive in the chair before him.

"For now, yes, we shall use the chair as a doorstop – but before the night is out, I may request that you break it over the head of our guest. But for now, there is something I am dying to know …"

The moment Dave came up to the flat, Lianda knew

something was wrong. He took the stairs faster than usual, his brow was furrowed, and his fists were clenched. If this wasn't enough to suggest a worried mind, then the fact that he dead-bolted the door – something he never did – was all Lianda needed. "What is it?" she asked.

Dave had no intention of keeping the truth from her, so he lifted the front of his shirt and showed her the semi-automatic pistol he'd confiscated from the tough guy downstairs. "Let's just say somebody is interested in buying the club, and his-slash-her representative thought I might need some persuading," he said.

Dave expected her to gasp or maybe clasp her hands, but instead, she looked disgustedly at the sight of a gun in what was practically her home.

"I assume he's with Danny and Mick?" she said.

"Yeah," said Dave. "Danny told me to come up here and make sure you're okay … I'd have done it anyway."

Lianda tried to smile when he said this, and she damn nearly did too.

“Get me out of this alive, Dave Hunter,” she said, and Dave that imagined that a kiss and a cuddle was coming his way. He was wrong, for it was time for them to get to work, and she said as much.

As luck would have it, the upstairs portion of the building would be easy to fortify. As well as the entrance to the flat, there was a door to the stairs from the private space behind the bar, where staff hung their coats and sometimes took their breaks. Dave told her he had locked this so that any intruders would have to force the lock before climbing the stairs, which would be akin to someone holding up a megaphone to announce their arrival.

“Which will allow me to scare them off with this,” he said, waving the confiscated firearm not far above his head before squinting and taking aim at the door. He imagined from the professional air of the man he took it from that it would be fitted with some kind of a silencer, but the sight and sound of wood splintering would be enough to make his point.

As Dave talked Lianda through all this, he saw another one of her smiles creeping through: she was proud of her man and not afraid to let it show.

"Now, let's get the couch over to the door, eh?" he said.

Alley Oop sat in the driver's seat of a stationary Ford Escort, down a street not far from the club. He was trying to be patient, playing it cool, and he drummed his fingers on the steering wheel.

Despite not having a driving licence or a car, the man known as Alley Oop was an excellent driver as well as an experienced car thief. Though he was an expert at the hot-wiring method of vehicle repossession, opportunity had knocked on his door this morning when he'd walked past a petrol station on London's Park Lane. The vehicle's previous owner, a hurried blue-collar guy in his late twenties, had run back in after paying for petrol – most likely for cigarettes or a lottery ticket – and left the engine of his sickly-orange 1993 Ford Escort running. Alley Oop was now the proud owner of one of Dagenham's finest, and this and the events of the evening unfolding left Alley Oop excited.

Excited, but also a bit anxious.

Yesterday, he finally got to meet the people with whom he would be working – or at least who he would be handing the job over too. And while Alley Oop was a tasty kind of fella, a seasoned boxer who'd had more black eyes than all the pandas in China, this lot scared him anyway.

They scared him because they lacked humanity; he could see no warmth in their eyes. There was also the fact that at the end of the meeting, in a deserted warehouse inside The World's End Trading Estate, Sam Cleaver had used a crowbar to jemmy open the wooden crate he'd been sitting on for the duration of the meeting. He'd taken out two sniper rifles and two machine guns, which he'd handed out to the four heavies whose job was to guard the building in case Dave Hunter had an extra card up his sleeve. Alley Oop's heart had skipped a beat at the sight of the guns; he'd never been around them before, and he'd never wanted to either.

Another thing that bothered Alley Oop about this four-strong team of hired muscle was the fact that one of them was a girl. Her head was shaved, and her nose was pierced, and she answered to the name of Spike, but that didn't change anything. Sending a lady into battle was just plain wrong to him even though she swore as much as the fellas and was just as muscular.

He wouldn't have felt so bad if he'd been allowed a little white line (he hadn't had any for ages), and the combination of crippling depression and finding himself surrounded by guns had knocked him off guard. But it was too late to back out now, and he would lose face if he did.

He'd found a spot along Pier Hill where he could sit in darkness, and he'd been there nearly twenty minutes. In that time, he'd seen several lights flick on behind windows along the pleasant, leafy suburban street. These little bursts of light seemed to give off warmth, a warmth that he couldn't feel from his position out in the street and in the cold, even though he longed to.

The cold and the dark were no strangers to Alley Oop. The only times he'd had a fixed address had been either in that horrible orphanage back in London or, later on, a borstal. He'd slept in police cells a few times, but they always let him go in the morning.

None of these places offered the warmth of a family home, something he had never known. For that reason, he had been happier sleeping in abandoned warehouses or underneath railway bridges, living off food that others had thrown away (long before the middle-classes rebranded this practice as 'freeganism').

Since hooking up with the Cleaver brothers a few years back, they'd sometimes let him have a spare room or a chance to kip in their janitor's cupboard. He'd been grateful for this, but it seemed a long way away from the cosy scenes that surrounded him now yet seemed so far away.

An upstairs light went off, and Alley Oop imagined some lucky bleeder curling up beside his lovely wife in a cosy bed. The thought of this made his big hands ball into fists as he pondered the injustice of one man being up there while he was down here.

Alley Oop often used this to justify his actions (and the Cleaver's encouraged him to think this way), but it didn't psyche him up as much as usual. He exhaled slowly, and his frame became less taught, and his hands opened out until they were no longer balled as fists.

It occurred to him that what he was about to do would mean taking an extra step away from the kind of warm light that spilt from the homes on either side of him. Where he was now was cold and dark, but it seemed to him that, once the night was over, he could be like this for the rest of his life. If it went wrong, the police would be after him, and he would have to go on the run. He didn't think this would be much fun, for at least when he slept in bus shelters or on the floors of houses that were still being built, he only had to worry about being moved on.

He wasn't enjoying this, so Alley Oop decided to think about what it would be like if it all went well.

He would have proved his worth to the Cleavers, so they would surely make him a fully paid-up member of the gang. He would have money, respect (maybe), and he might get to move into a house or flat of his own – perhaps in an area like this.

But would he be out of the dark? He'd know that

he'd taken something precious from someone, and he'd have to live with that. And how did he know that this tough cookie called Dave Hunter wasn't going to come after him one day?

If he was still capable of it ...

The other unpleasant thought that went through Alley Oop's mind was that he would still be by himself. He didn't have any friends, and the only time any woman looked at him twice was to see if she was being followed.

So Alley Oop was forced to wonder if he would ever really be like the people around here.

He slapped himself hard across his face for thinking this at the worst possible time.

Don't get cold feet now ... This is your chance.

Chapter 16

Mick jammed the chair under the door handle, then went and stood next to Danny. The room was wider than it was long, and the dark-haired prisoner was backed up against the north-facing wall of the makeshift office. The prisoner didn't seem to notice Mick, as he was locked in a battle of wills with Danny.

Danny opened the lost property cupboard and chose his weapon: the knife he took off Alley Oop several weeks earlier. When he flicked the blade, Mick drew his breath, but their prisoner didn't show a flicker of emotion. Danny grabbed the captive by his left collar, jamming his forearm underneath his chin to force his jaws shut: he knew you needed to watch this sort.

With the prisoner's head secure, Danny used the knife to make a tear in both layers of the prisoner's clothing over his upper arm. He threw the knife to Mick, whose reflexes were quick enough that he caught the handle and not the blade.

With both his hands now free, Danny reached inside the three-inch tear and pulled the left arm of the suit jacket and the shirt underneath it wide open, revealing a muscly arm with a tattoo of the Grim Reaper just below the shoulder.

"The best of the best, eh?" said Danny. "These guys are the stuff of army myth and legend," he said to Mick, who was briefly mesmerised by the detailed illustration of The Angel of Death, wielding his scythe with two sets of cold, bony fingers.

"Only, you're not the best, are you?" said Danny, turning his back on the ex-special forces operative who had taken his eye off the ball for a fraction of a second longer than he'd been trained to. "Because, if you were the best, you wouldn't be tied up here, would you?"

"Fuck you," said the Angel of Death, the first thing they'd heard him say.

"Excellent!" said Danny, turning his back to him. "The first rule of surviving interrogation: maintain the role of aggressor."

Danny turned to Mick, who was beginning to wonder if someone had spiked his drink with an acid tab that night.

"You see, Michael, special forces operatives are taught to keep in mind that they have something their captors want, thus maintaining the upper hand. That's what old 'Death' here is doing right now."

As Danny said this, he turned to his captive and asked him, "Are we allowed to call you Death by the way? We both know there's no point asking you your real name, and while I was looking forward to issuing you with the temporary codename 'Daisy,' I have absolute respect for you – being a Reaper and all."

"You can call me what you like, and you can do what you like," said Death. "Just don't expect me to tell you anything." Death relished the chance to make eye contact with Danny once more. "Fuck. You."

Danny ignored this and showed Death the knife. "I took this off a man we call 'Alley Oop'. I suspected he was checking us out, sizing us up, etc., and it looks as though I was right. Now, who do you both work for, and where's Alley Oop now?"

Death started to whistle *Onwards Christian Soldiers,* and Danny turned to Mick and said, "Go for his head and body, Michael. No weapons – just try to wear yourself out."

Dave and Lianda finished moving the three-person sofa over to the door of his/their flat.

"That should keep them out of our home," he said, and she smiled, noting his use of the word 'our'.

What was happening to them took some believing, but she felt safe as long as he was around. Traditionally it was his job to keep her safe, but Dave took comfort from her being there too. He wanted to pull her close to him, feel her breathing against his chest, but they both knew this wasn't the time: they had a home to defend.

The building was brick-shaped, and from Prince's Esplanade, it was longer than it was wide. The sides of the building that faced the street on one side and the sea on the other were one-hundred feet long; the east wall and the west wall were just under half of that.

The flat upstairs was divided roughly into three sections: the living space (lounge and kitchen combined), a bedroom, and a bathroom. The west-facing living space took up half of the upper part of the building, whereas Dave's bathroom and his bedroom each got a rectangular quarter of the east side. The bedroom faced out to sea, and the bathroom would have offered a view of the street had it had a window. The bedroom had a skylight that had been installed by the previous owner, who Dave had killed two years earlier.

The living space had windows that looked out of the north and the south sides of the building. "You check the front, I'll watch the back," he said before he flicked the lights and sent the living room into darkness.

Five minutes went by, and neither Dave or Lianda saw anything suspicious. On her side, there was the usual mix of drunks and hen party crowds clogging the pavements while classic cars and various blue-light vehicles filled the roads; Dave saw nothing more than a few people cooling off on the decking area that Mick had recently put up outside. "Nothing," Dave said, as he lowered the binoculars for a moment.

"That's good, isn't it?" she said, not quite sure if she believed it.

"Not really," said Dave, as he put down his binoculars and switched to observing his post through the cheap, portable telescope he kept in his living room. "They – whoever they are – will wonder why their friend's taking so long. They'll send someone else eventually, and frankly, I'd rather they just got on with it."

After a brief silence, Lianda had an unpleasant thought: the bedroom skylight. For some reason, she felt silly for thinking of this, and she didn't mention it. One minute later, another unpleasant thought entered her head, and she wasn't prepared to keep this to herself.

"What about the staff, Dave? Or the band?"

"It's me they want," he said, hoping to God that he was right.

"Fuck," he said when he saw it was starting to rain.

Chapter 17

"You can make this easy or very difficult – it's your choice. Where's the bloke we took the knife off?"

This clichéd spiel was the best Mick Davies could come up with. Unsurprisingly, it was followed by a period of silence. "Very well," he said, as he lunged forward and caught 'Death' with a forearm smash across his left cheekbone – BASH! Silence followed, and so Mick repeated the blow – BOOM! Still, nothing.

"You'll have to do better than that," said Danny, his arms folded as he watched the interrogation from across the room. "Just remember he brought a gun into the club, eh?"

This was the kind of encouragement Mick needed, and he brought both fists up underneath his chin and delivered a dozen blows that would have made a normal man sing like a canary. But Death was no normal man, and as Danny expected, he remained tight-lipped.

"Try a backhand slap," he said to Mick, who did this

three times with his left hand and then three more with his right. Death spoke, but not in the way Mick had hoped he would.

"He's not very good at this, is he?"

"There's room for improvement," said Danny. "I'll give you that."

Running out of ideas, Mick tried an open hand slap, and Death didn't even blink. Mick realised he was short of breath, but he fought it and struck Death three more times, this time with a closed fist: now he needed to catch his breath.

Like most people on civvy-street, Mick didn't know that showing signs of fatigue was a mistake; Danny – and Death – knew what was going on and understood the psychology at play here.

Any boxer, be it pro, semi-pro or amateur will be familiar with the rope-a-dope technique, the tactic of letting your opponent tire himself out while you use the ropes around the ring to absorb the force of their blows. The canny fighter does this before launching an offensive against their now-weary opponent who usually sees their big chance disappear right before their eyes.

The man they called Death was doing this right now – the first part anyway – not that Mick knew or even suspected it. Death had had it drummed into him, years earlier – and had subsequently drummed it into many outstanding recruits, including one Private Daniel Blyth – that the key to keeping schtum was to keep it in your mind that you are still in combat here. You have something they want, and if they don't get it – you win.

Only, not many people could feel like an aggressor while they are tied to a chair with a mouthful of broken teeth. But Death could, and Mick Davies was on a hiding to nothing here. He managed one more straight, solid punch to Death's chin before slumping against the desk in the middle of the room: Mick, not Death, was beaten.

“You did your best,” said Danny, although his portly chum was too out of breath to reply. “Go and see Dave. Tell him I’ve almost got this under control

Mick tried to say, ‘What do you mean?’ but he only got as far as ‘Wha–’, before Danny reminded him he’d used the word ‘almost.’

“Just stay there and wait for me – I’ve got something up my sleeve.”

The rain wasn’t heavy enough to dampen visibility, but Dave found himself peering more intently into his binoculars nonetheless. He saw nothing out of the ordinary, even though he kind of wished he did. Quite sensibly, he’d put the gun under his right foot, for though he had his nerves reasonably under control, his heightened state of alert could make him prone to sudden movements.

The sound of his intercom crackling didn’t make him jump, but it did give Lianda a little start. There was an intercom button outside the club and another one next to the telephone in the small office/staff cloakroom behind the bar. It didn't take Dave long to work out that it was friend rather than foe, as whoever it was at the other end keyed in a monotone rendition of the intro to Dr. Feelgood's *Milk and Alcohol.* Dave pressed the button to open the door to the stairs.

Dave heard a pair of feet coming up the stairs, and his expertly-tuned ears told him the heavy steps could only belong to Mick: Dave and Lianda moved the couch back to let their friend in. They barely recognised him.

"What the f –"

"You should see the other guy," he said, catching his breath once more. "Gis' a fag, Dave."

Dave reached into his left jeans pocket and took a crumpled 'Benson' out of an equally crumpled box. He gave it to Mick, and Mick brought Dave and Lianda up to speed on what had gone down in the backroom. He told them that most of the blood on him belonged to the man that he and Danny had nicknamed 'Death,' and he explained how they came up with the moniker.

"And then I went *SMACK,* right across the chin," said Mick, finishing his blow-by-blow account of the interrogation. He held up his fist to provide a visual demonstration and revealed a set of knuckles that looked like they'd been mauled by an attack dog and a little finger that was already turning purple.

"That'll hurt in the morning," said Dave, shooting a concerned-yet-amused glance at Lianda.

"Not as much as that fucker will," said Mick with an unlit cigarette dangling from his mouth.

"I never thought you were going to tell my friend anything. Let's just say it was work experience for him. You know the game too well: let the other guy wear himself out, or see if you pass out first. It's a waiting game. You told me that, remember?”

Death said nothing: he just stared at Danny with cold, blue eyes.

“But you didn’t tell me everything, did you? I’m assuming that’s because you see yourself as a kind of modern-day Samurai, who as a final test for their student leaves him to figure out the last bit for himself to see if he too has the warrior spirit?”

Danny had been standing in front of his opponent, but now he lowered himself into a position where their eyes were level.

“Well, congratulations, Mr. Death – it worked. I came up with the next part all by myself. And it’s worse than anything you can imagine.”

Chapter 18

Survival instinct is essential in men who may be required to put their lives on the line. But the will to live to fight another day wasn't the only quality men like Death, and to a lesser extent, Danny Blyth had needed when they'd tried to make the grade and show they were up there with the big boys.

Most people would shield their eyes if they were in a car and the windscreen shattered, and they would claw the air if they were thrown from a greater height than their chin. This was because they had a fear of dying; men like Death didn't. Danny Blyth feared death, but he had a better understanding of this mindset than most.

This was why he knew Death wouldn't speak when Mick knocked several bells out of him: it was, as he said, a kind of on-the-job training exercise for his friend who had acted of his own free will when he'd asked Danny to train him after their last run-in with representatives of the criminal underworld. It was also why he knew he would have to try a different tactic: Death wasn't afraid of pain, either.

But he might just be afraid of himself, Danny thought as he knelt down before his guest and put his hand on his guest's knee.

The move caught Death off guard, and his eyes went wide as he looked at his captor in surprise.

"Well," said Danny. "That's got your attention. I bet you're wondering what I'm doing."

Danny let his hand linger on Death's knee for a time before he slowly slid it up Death's thigh, up to where his hand lay parallel with Death's groin. Danny used his right hand at first, teasing Death's left thigh, before using his left hand to make a similar movement along Death's right upper leg. He stopped for a moment before running both hands down and then back up Death's thigh.

"You'll die for this."

"Maybe I will," said Danny. "But you'll have to live with it."

Danny ran his hands along Death's femoris muscle, using his fingertips on the way down, then the warm flats of his hands on the way back up. Danny noticed Death's breathing speeding up slightly, and the parts of Death's face that weren't caked in drying blood seemed to be going red underneath the skin.

"Now I know you act the tough guy, but deep down, I think you crave affection like everyone else. Tell you what – let's find out, shall we?"

He reached down and touched Death's penis – and felt some movement there.

"You love it," said Danny as he fondled Death's genitals, wondering if Death was the only one who wouldn't be able to look in the mirror once this was all over.

Paul Addington – Adders – stepped out into the night air and unwrapped an expensive cigar. The cold didn't bother him since he had been dancing for nigh on an hour after a three-course meal. And he was wearing a dinner jacket. Bloody dinner and dance, he thought – couldn't they do it the other way round? That would make sense, he thought as he held a flame to his Havana Regal.

It was the annual chairman's dinner at Southend Flying Club, a fundraising bash that raised money for local causes and gave middle-aged and upwards men like Adders the chance to let down their hair and their wives the opportunity to show off their wardrobes.

Tonight there had been a choice of Game Pie or Lamb and Mashed Potato followed by dancing to a Dixieland swing band, and Adders had thought about inviting his friends Dave and Lianda along before remembering that they were hosting a party that night.

After a few slow pulls on his cigar, Adders, suddenly feeling the lack of company out in the car park, took his mobile out of his jacket pocket, and thought of his friend Dave Hunter once more when he saw that he had a missed call from him.

Danny's plan appeared to be working: the grim reaper's assistant seemed to be entering a state of arousal as a result of Danny's interference. Danny reckoned that all he needed to do was tease and fondle Death until he could stand it no longer, and he would surely reveal some, if not all, of the details of his plan.

"Don't pretend you don't like it," Danny said, having sucked his finger and putting it inside Death's right ear and then his left.

Danny sucked his finger again and reached under Death's shirt, circling his finger around Death's belly button, before withdrawing his hand and repeating this process, this time flicking at each of Death's nipples. He wondered how he would tell the others he had got information from a man who had been willing to take his secrets to the grave.

Worry about that later, and stop trying to put this off …

What Danny needed to do was bring his captive to the point of near-climax, the crudely-named 'vinegar stroke'. Surely the thought of being wanked off by another man would be unbearable to someone from a world so steeped in machismo, thought Danny. Yes, nobody would know – except for him. But that was what mattered, right?

Danny decided there was only one way to find out. He unzipped Death's fly, and, after much fidgeting, he freed the beast from the cage. Danny put Death's manhood on display, and though he wasn't flying the flag fully, he was at half-mast.

If looks could kill, then Daniel Blyth would be on his way to the morgue by now. Death's eyes were open wide, yet his pupils were just little pinpricks, and this made his eyes seem to burn with a special kind of hatred towards his captor. Death's breathing was like that of a man going into shock, and through clenched teeth and with spittle bubbling around his lips, he repeated his threat from a moment ago, albeit in a wheezing, raspy fashion.

"You'll ffffucking DIE fffor thissh!"

Danny ignored the threat and carried on with the business at hand. He threw off his leather jacket and rolled back his long paisley sleeves as he prepared for the grand, grim finale.

He put his hands inside Death's fly and cradled his balls once more. Danny ran his forefinger and thumb up and then down Death's shaft, slowly and smoothly. Death couldn't help reacting to the stimulus, and his penis began to throb against Danny's softly-pinched finger and thumb.

Death's legs kicked wildly but helplessly underneath the belt that Dave had wrapped them together with minutes earlier, and he tugged frantically at the handcuffs that held his arms together behind the chair.

Death's frenzied attempts to escape the back-stack position Dave Hunter had left him in made a series of 'chk-chk-chk' sounds that reminded Danny of the fencing duals of his youth; he'd been in control then, and he was in control now.

Danny took his hand away as he prepared for the endgame. Death looked on in horror as Danny sucked on his own thumb, and he knew the battle was as good as lost.

Having soaked his thumb with saliva, Danny reached for Death's crotch once more, and he circled the stumpy moistened digit over the tip of Death's penis: Death grew hard as a rock.

"Tell me, Death. What would your special forces friends think of you now, eh? Receiving stimulation from another chap? I think they'd be most amused. How about we take a picture for posterity."

With his free hand, Danny reached into one of the

pockets in his long leather jacket and took out a mobile phone. “Now, it could be hard – pardon the pun – but I’d like you to smile, please?”

Death didn’t smile, and probably never would again.

“Very well,” said Danny as held up the camera and took a selfie-style shot of him and Death.

“Now, where’s the man we call Alley Oop, who do you work for, and who else is coming here tonight?”

“Fuck off.”

“Oh dear,” said Danny as he began tugging back and forth at Death’s pole-like member. “You can fight it all you want,” said Danny as his rhythm got faster, “but sooner or later, you are going reach the point of no return. Think about that for a moment.”

By now, Death was breathing in a semi-quaver rhythm, but he remained defiant and said nothing. You’ll soon talk, Danny thought, as he gave Death’s balls a squeeze before going back to a tugging motion only this time slightly faster. After three minutes, Death's toes were about to curl, and he decided it was more than he could take.

"Alright!" he said. "I'll tell you everything – but kill me afterwards."

Chapter 19

"Where is he?"

"If you mean 'Alley Oop,' then he's parked up in an old Ford Escort along Pier Hill, registration number Kilo-Eight-Two-Zero-India-Tango-Bravo. He's outside number 147. I saw him on the way in. The silly fucker looked half asleep."

"Thank you," said Danny. "Hardly worth getting felt-up for, was it?"

Death offered no reply. He just shook his head and rolled his eyes.

"I need more than that, I'm afraid," said Danny. "Like who do you work for, to start with?"

"I work alone," said the wounded prisoner.

Danny half-believed him. There was no time to waste, so he decided to act on the information he'd been given. But before he got to work, there was something he needed to do: make contact with the rest of his unit. He took out his mobile phone and keyed in Dave's landline number.

Dave didn't answer. Good. Danny turned around to pace the length of the room as he waited for Dave to call back, having checked the number first. Thirty seconds later, his mobile rang, and he took the call.

"David," Danny said as he prepared to fill his friend in on what had gone down, minus the bit about the hand-job. "If I told you I'd have to kill you," was all he'd said when Dave asked how he got the information from this 'Death' chap.

Danny told Dave where Alley Oop was, and the make, model and registration of the car he was in. There was one more thing.

"I'm going to get Alley Oop now. I'll bring him down here, and we'll find out everything he knows. He should talk easily enough." As Danny said this, he turned around to take in the grim spectacle of the man he'd just violated. He noticed that Death's head was hung low, his chin touching his chest.

Danny imagined that Death had probably gone into a deep depression after his interrogation – partly a result of being broken, but also a result of having received sexual stimulation from a member of the same gender group.

"You're not going alone, are you?" said Dave, his voice mixed with static interference from the rain outside. "At least take the gun, eh?"

"Guns are for wimps," said Danny. "That's why I gave it to you. Like I said, Dave, when the going gets tough, the posh get going. You and Mick just sit tight and hold hands. If you get scared, Lianda can give you both a cuddle."

"You cheeky cunt," said Dave.

"That's the spirit," said Danny, confident that his friends were ready for action.

It occurred to Danny that although Death appeared subdued for now, he could still shout for help once he was gone. Especially if he had colleagues already in the building and his whole 'I work alone' schtick had been a lie. Danny also considered the possibility that Death's broken man thing was an act, a further part of his training.

He decided it would be better if he left Death there unconscious. He went to the lost property cupboard and took out the confiscated set of brass knuckles. He got the weapon in position on his right hand, with a finger slotted through each of the four rings and his thumb steadying the frame and his palm against the cold, hard grip. He walked over to Death and said, "Chin up, old boy."

In a film, it might have worked, but this bad guy didn't raise his head for the good guy to knock him out and tell him to 'sleep on it.'

"Oh, come on – I was looking forward to my line," said Danny.

There was no response from Death whatsoever, and Danny looked at him more closely. He was blue in the face.

Danny had heard about men who could hold their breath long enough to cause their own death: now he'd seen it for himself.

Danny knew this required superhuman willpower and discipline since it went against our human instincts. But so did killing one human being on the command of another.

Unless you were someone who didn't value human life much – like the late Mr. Death, for example.

Perhaps out of respect for the dead but more likely because he didn't want his friends to know what he'd done, Danny tucked Death's now flaccid member away and zipped him up again.

He left the room and made his way through the oblivious, drunken throng and towards the door and the cold, wet night. Before leaving the building, he took his hand – the one adorned with brass knuckles – out of the pocket of his leather jacket and punched a fire alarm. Two-hundred-odd revellers rushed towards the door at the same time he did, and he left the building anonymously.

Underneath Southend Pier, a hundred yards to the west of Bobby's Bar lurked four shadowy figures.

Only one of them – Spike – was under six-feet tall. At five-foot-nine, you could say she was the runt of the litter – but only if you fancied a trip to A and E. There were four of them, all wearing black from head to toe. In addition to Spike, the group comprised:

Max Cane, 47-

Unlike many underworld marksmen, the tall, sandy-haired Max Cane had never done military service. Some said he lacked the discipline, others said he wasn't a team-player, but neither was the truth. No, this self-taught rifleman – this expert rifleman – was criminal through and through, and he had had no illusions about 'serving Queen and country,' that tired old line that certain villains still reeled off from time to time. He was a professional, and he was all about the money.

Karim 'Nine Lives' Haswell, 31 (aka 'The Cat')-

'The Cat' had never climbed a drainpipe to burgle a property in his life. He was given these nicknames on account of his ability to cheat death. Although he was christened 'The Cat', or 'Nine Lives' when he was shot at for the sixth time, he'd survived four more attempts on his life since then. He was something of a trailblazer, having done a great deal to alter the traditional vision of the whites-only, football-hooligan style of British gangster.

Paul 'Parky' Walsall, 53-

In keeping with tradition, Parky was a military man – till he got thrown out for attacking his sergeant, beating him so severely that the sarge had to spend some time in an army medical facility and a coma. Parky had been given his moniker because he had something in common with the veteran TV presenter with whom he shared his nickname: he made people feel like talking. There were differences in their methods, of course – Michael Parkinson didn't use pliers to remove his celebrity guests' fingernails – but the fact remained that they could both get people to open up.

"Anybody see what I see?" said Parky.

It would be hard not to see two-hundred people legging it from a building you had been watching for over an hour, and The Cat said so. "Be hard to miss it," he said.

Spike watched in silence. Max Cane had been looking in the other direction at the time of the near-stampede from the club. He turned around to face the action. "Something's wrong," he said. "I'm going in."

He took one step forwards before Spike stopped him in his tracks with an H & K machine gun. She didn't point the weapon at him, she just pulled it up from its downwards fifty-degree angle to ninety degrees and held it like a barrier across his path. "I say when we go, remember?"

His silence said all it needed to. He wasn't going to break ranks even though he didn't like being told what to do.

The fact that Spike was a woman had nothing to do with it; he'd seen her fight, and he knew she could hit harder than any man he'd ever known. Plus, with her bald, rose-tattooed head and her equally decorated fists (she was so hard she had the word 'hate' on both sides), she was often mistaken for a bloke anyway. No, Max Cane disliked any form of authority, and he was there purely for the money. Quite frankly, he'd be glad when this was all over.

He knew that it would be bloody stupid to challenge Spike's authority. Samuel and Alex had put her in charge –

that was why she had been given a mobile phone, the only means of communication available to the group.

"What do we do, then?" asked 'Nine Lives' Haswell.

"Exactly what I say," said Spike. "And right now, I say stick to the plan."

Chapter 20

Dave had just finished his phone conversation with Danny when his mobile rang again – it was Adders, his friend from the flying club. "Thanks for calling back," Dave said. "I need your help."

The line wasn't clear, and much of the conversation was marred by static interference caused by the worsening weather conditions. This didn't stop Dave briefing Adders on what had gone down so far, and what he feared could happen next. "I'll need you to get one of us to safety by air," he told Adders.

As Dave said this, he turned to face Lianda, and she knew exactly who he was talking about. She mouthed the words 'I'm not leaving you' so quietly Dave almost had to lip-read; he turned away and returned to his looking post. He listened intently for two minutes, then terminated the call.

Lianda rushed over and put her hand on his shoulder and spun him around to face her. "Listen to me, Dave

Hunter. I am *not* leaving y –"

She was cut off by the sound of the fire alarm, and she and Dave returned to their posts and saw people gathering on both sides of the building. "*Danny*," they said in unison.

Alley Oop was getting impatient. He'd been sat there nearly twenty minutes now, and he was sure that the mobile phone he'd taken from the locker at Chelsea bus station would have rung by now. He wondered if the people he'd met the other night – the ones Alex and Sam had given guns to – would be getting angry. Alley Oop knew they were waiting for him to call them on the other mobile phone, the one he'd been given at the meeting when the guns were given out.

Alley Oop tried to block the guns out of his mind because he was making himself nervous just thinking about them. He was good at putting stuff out of his mind: the bullies in the orphanage, the carers who did bad things to him, the beatings he'd taken from policemen as a younger man … He'd had plenty of practice. He was beginning to settle, and was thinking about the lines of cocaine that Alex and Samuel would reward him with when …

SMASH! One of the windows shattered!

Alley Oop headbutted the steering wheel as he tried to dive for cover from his sitting position. He balled up in his seat and threw his hands over his head.

In the time it took Alley Oop to realise he was still alive, Danny put his hand through the space where the window used to be, pulled up the lock and jumped in the rear of the vehicle on the driver's side. He pushed the headrest up and put his brass-knuckled fist against the cervical region of Alley Oop's spine. Alley's whole body stiffened as the cold metal made contact with his skin. He knew better than to make any movements, but he managed to look in the rearview mirror to see who it was. It was Dave's friend – the poofy one.

"It won't take much for me to see that you never walk again," said Danny. "I'm going to ask you a few questions. You're going to answer them. Then we're going to get out of the car nice and slowly and go for a walk – I think you know where to."

Danny didn't ask Alley Oop if he understood since this would have suggested he was asking him rather than telling him.

"How many people are on this job? Just a one-word answer, please."

Alley Oop paused for a second, which was all it took him to work out that, while Sam and Alex would be mad at him for talking, they couldn't put him in a wheelchair this very second. The man behind him in the long leather coat and the silly hat could.

"F-f-four," he said.

"Have they got guns?"

"Y-y-y … Yes. All of th-th-them."

"Right," said Danny. "What kind of guns."

"Erm … Long ones – like you s-s-see in f-f-films, sir."

"And where are they, these four men?"

"I d-don't know chief. S-s-s … Swear to G-G-God I don't know."

Danny suspected that Alley Oop's stutter was faked in a bid to win his sympathy. If it was, then this didn't work: Danny dragged his brass-knuckled fist further up Alley Oop's spine, then levered his forearm horizontally so that the deadly weapon was pointed horizontally at the base of Alley Oop's skull.

"You may be stupid," Danny said, "but that doesn't mean you can't receive brain damage." As he said this, he pushed the rim of the brass knuckles into Alley Oop's head, softly, enough to cause minor discomfort and encourage the conversation to flow. "Where are they?"

"I don't know … Honest, ch-ch … Chief – the

bosses only tell me what I need to know. I'm j-j-j … Just a driver."

Danny was enthused by Alley Oop's mentioning of 'the bosses'. If Alley Oop were prepared to name them, then it would mean he was ready to spill his guts. If he was prepared to do this, then it would mean he was telling the truth about the number of extra visitors to expect that night and that he didn't know where they were.

"The bosses," said Danny. "Who are they? Who are you working for?

"The Cleaver brothers … Alex and Samuel … A couple o' b-b-b … Brothers f-f-from London … Out west."

Danny couldn't help notice the big man's voice crack as he said their names, and in the rearview mirror, Danny could see that Alley Oop had teary eyes.

Something told Danny this wasn't an act, and Danny considered that perhaps the stutter wasn't either.

He fought any inclination he had to pity Alley Oop,

and reminded himself that he'd taken a flick knife off this seemingly gentle giant only a few weeks earlier and that that he – Alley Oop – had been working in tandem with a man who carried a gun.

"I see," said Danny. "And what do they want with us?"

"They want the club," said Alley Oop. "They want to set up here in Essex – they sell c-c-c… Cocaine, y' see … They need a base."

"Go on," said Danny, not oblivious to the fact that Alley Oop was stuttering less frequently but paying more attention to what was being revealed.

"They know all about you lot – that business with Norman Layer and what 'ave ya'. They fink that if they run Dave Hunter out of town, they'll get a reputation for being in charge of the manor, like."

Danny could see the logic here. In fact, it put him in mind of the late Ted Maskell, regaling the lads with his tales of law enforcement. Maskell was old school, and he'd said that whenever he'd broken up a pub fight, he'd always gone to the biggest guy first – and decked him for all his mates to see.

"They can try," said Danny. "They can try."

Danny couldn't believe his ears when he heard Alley Oop take a sniff, and nor could he when he heard Alley Oop's voice crack with what he said next.

"They'll kill me for giving away secrets like this."

"Come on, big guy," said Danny, resting his hand on Alley Oop's shoulder. "They won't kill you."

"You don't think so?" said Alley Oop.

"No," said Danny, before taking his metal-gloved fist away from Alley Oop's head and jamming it against his ribcage instead. "We might beat them to it."

Confident that Alley Oop was suitably broken, Danny decided it was time to call base again. He took his spare hand off of Alley Oop's shoulder and used it to fish his mobile phone out from the left pocket of his leather jacket. As he listened while Dave's mobile rang, Danny, became wary of the bright LED display of his own device.

Pick it up, Dave.

For God's sake, pick it up!

Chapter 21

Adders dialled another number as soon as he finished talking to Dave. It was the mobile number of his eldest son, Reese Addington.

Adders junior worked for the South Essex Coast Guard Association. Adders – senior – remembered Reese saying he was on duty that night, but that he'd have his mobile on him.

Reese answered after three rings.

"Another quiet night for the Southend river police, I see?" said Dad. "No damsels in distress for you to rescue?"

"It's been about as exciting as your flying club dinner and dance, old man."

Dad chuckled despite the serious circumstances.

Paul Addington was a suave, smooth operator, and keeping his cool was as important to him as getting his friends out of trouble.

"I didn't hear you up there tonight, but you might get

it up before the night's out," he said to his semi-amused son on the other end.

Reese sat up in his chair, behind the brightly-lit control panel in his otherwise dimly-lit control station. He knew his dad valued humour above most things, but the fact that Dad forgot to put on his Kenneth Williams voice as he made the double-entendre was enough to make him suspect that this was something serious. "What's the matter, Dad?"

"Nothing yet – but it could be soon. Keep your mobile on, and if you get a distress call, be sure to call me before you spin your blades, okay?"

"Can't you tell me more than tha –"

Adders hung up, satisfied that his son knew he meant business. He took a pull on his cigar and turned around to go back inside. He looked across the dark foyer to the door to The Admiral's Suite, about twenty feet from where he stood. The door had been wedged open to keep the guests cool, and Adders heard the merry sound of big band jazz.

The party was in full swing. Adders looked around the room and saw a dark-haired lady in a medium-length red dress with black-and-white polka-dots. She was being spun in mid-air by a chap with jet-black hair who, appropriately, was dressed in a WW2 Flight Captain's uniform. It was a Navy-blue number that the handsome devil wore, with matching jacket, trousers, and visor-style cap, with three wing-shaped stripes on each of his shoulder-height epaulettes. But it was an RAF uniform, and Adders reminded himself that if the war were still on, then the lady in red would have copped off with a Yank hours ago.

Oh well, Adders had bigger fish to fry now, and he crunched his cigar into the car park's tarmac with his right foot. He went back to the party, preparing his excuse as he walked.

Dave answered Danny's call after four rings.

"This is no time for playing hard to get," said Danny.

"Any news?"

"Nothing much," said Dave. "All quiet on both sides – this rains not gonna help, mind."

"Listen, I've found Alley Oop. So far, he's been pretty good, haven't you, Alley?"

As Danny said this, he jabbed Alley Oop in the ribs with his brass knuckles, and Alley Oop said hello by way of a "Yeoww!"

"See? We're getting on great," said Danny. "Now, David, do exactly as I say. The first thing you need to do is put your phone on speaker. You all need to listen to me, got that?" he said.

Dave must have set the phone to speaker mode in an instant, for his answer came from three voices: Dave, Lianda, and Mick said, "Yes, Danny," in unison.

"Good," said Danny. "Four more men are coming – all armed. I'm going to ask Alley Oop here some questions. Pay attention, but don't look away from your posts. No need to confirm message received."

For a few seconds, there was quiet, and Dave – and quite possibly Mick and Lianda – assumed Danny was thinking what to do next. Then they heard Danny giving Alley Oop a detailed set of instructions. Danny asked Mr. Oop how he – Alley – could get in touch with the four gunmen out there in the dark Southend night, before reminding Alley Oop that he would need around the clock care if he messed him about.

They heard Alley Oop saying that there was a mobile phone in the glove compartment and that his point of contact was someone called Spike, and they also heard him swear this was the only name he knew.

Then they heard Danny open the glove box before asking Alley Oop, "Is this it?" Alley Oop confirmed it was and that it had been set up so that all he had to do was press 9 to get Spike. "I'll take that," they heard Danny say.

Then they heard Danny telling Alley Oop that, when

he said so, he would have to call this Spike chap and tell him something had gone wrong and that Dave, Lianda, Mick, and he – Danny – were still in the building. Danny told Alley Oop exactly what to say and made him rehearse it several times in case Alley Oop and his friends had prepared a coded warning.

After four attempts at rehearsing the message that Alley Oop would relay to his colleagues, Danny told Alley Oop he was ready to deliver the red herring – when the time was right, that was. Danny reminded Alley Oop that he was still on probation here and that if he made one wrong move, he would smash his skull and/or his ribcage to pieces. Then he needed to speak to Dave again. "Dave?" he said.

"Yes, mate," said the man in question.

"One of you needs to go and talk to the staff outside. The fire alarm should stop in about … Three, two one – now,"

It stopped on Danny's count, and Mick, Dave, and

Lianda had to marvel at his accuracy.

"Tell them to go home. Tell them everything's okay, but they must leave immediately. Think of something. Then go back up to the flat and wait for me to call. If I haven't called you back in five minutes, call me. If I don't answer, then remember to play *Whiter Shade of Pale* at my funeral."

Chapter 22

An idea was forming in Danny's mind. He'd heard American cops – in films, mainly – refer to 'having a hunch,' and he guessed that's what this was.

His hunch concerned the whereabouts of Alley Oop's armed colleagues – the four men who had agreed to play a part in his and his friends' downfall. He couldn't shake off the suspicion that the gunmen were hiding out under the pier. It was dark, secluded and near the club. On a miserable night like this, they would have the place to themselves, and they could monitor all comings and goings at the club and move in at a time of their convenience.

Because Danny's recent premonition – that ill-fortune would soon be visited upon him and his friends – had turned out to be chillingly accurate, he decided to act on his hunch.

"Right, you," he said, to Alley Oop. "Change of plan: we're going for a drive. Start the engine."

Alley did what he was told and started the engine.

"Stick to the speed limit and no funny business," Danny said. "If I even think you're trying to get a signal to your friends, I'll smash your ribcage like a set of china. Make a turn in the road, go back, then take the first left. I'll tell you when to stop."

They were going to Danny's flat, on a quiet side street just off Royal Terrace. Danny didn't want strangers in his home, and he wanted strangers of the criminal kind to come in least of all. But, his third-storey flat was almost 50 feet above sea level and offered a clear view of the club – and the pier.

It was a minutes' drive, tops, but Danny made Alley Oop rehearse his spiel for when he called Spike in a few minutes. He got it right on his first attempt – but Danny didn't compliment him.

***

Getting Alley Oop from the car, across the yard and up two

sets of stairs could have been difficult. Charlbury Crescent was in a respectable area, with many elderly and retired residents who weren't used to seeing hostages being marched along by people brandishing deadly weapons.

They weren't used to seeing single male residents bringing other chaps back to their houses late at night, either, and Danny's girly hair and bohemian appearance had made some of them suspicious when he first moved in.

They didn't pass a soul though, and soon they were in Danny's bedroom, with his beloved sea-facing window. With his free hand, Danny reached for a pair of binoculars on top of his wardrobe, picking them up by the strap and putting it around his neck. He marched Alley Oop over to the sea-facing window.

"In a moment, I'm going to give your the phone back. You know what to say, right?"

Alley Oop nodded his head, and Danny kept his knuckle duster pressed against the base of Alley Oop's spine. "There's something I need to do first," he said.

Danny held the binoculars up to his eyes and scanned the scene. His window was streaked, but he was pleased to see the that the rain was starting to hold off. The revellers had given up and gone home, and Danny was relieved to see Mick talking to the staff – band members included – and telling all 14 of them to do the same. Danny knew it was a risky business sending one of his friends out there like this, but if anyone was unaccounted for, it could lead to the authorities becoming involved.

For all of one second, Danny considered that this may solve the problem. He kept this in mind for a short time because this would only have been a temporary solution. They were dealing with ruthless people here, and though the police would deal with Alley Oop and the four horsemen of the apocalypse quickly enough, this would be akin to chopping one head off the hydra. The Cleavers would still be out there. And what was it Ted Maskell said?

Go for the biggest one first …

Danny saw Mick go back inside as the staff and the last of the stragglers left the area. Once Danny was satisfied that all guests, staff and musicians were out of harm's way, he let his binoculars rest against his belly and reached down into his pocket. He took out Alley Oop's phone, pressed 9, and gave the confiscated device back to its owner, telling him to hold the device with his left hand and keep his other hand in contact with the windowsill.

"Say it word for word, or you'll die."

As soon as he handed the phone to Alley Oop, Danny looked into his binoculars once more. Sure enough, he saw a yellow-green glow under the pier.

Got you, you bastards.

Danny needed no further proof that he was right in his prediction, but he got it anyway. The yellow-green glow from the LED display on Spike's phone died at precisely the same time as he heard Alley Oop greet his assistant.

“I messed up,” Danny heard him say, and Alley Oop’s voice cracked as he said it.

Adders was breaking every rule in the book and loving every minute of it.

He worked in the city by day, and his job – like his lifestyle – was as dull as it got. The money was fantastic, but he’d come to realise that if you look at figures on a piece of paper long enough, then they eventually blur into one as did the days of Adders’ working life.

So he felt no guilt about what he was doing – until he got to the hangar.

As he climbed the stepladder beside his glorious winged beast and pulled off the musty tarpaulin, he realised he would not get to carry out the full pre-flight check. This flight needed to look like it never happened, so there was no need to update the flight log. Neither was there any need to test the radio since that would leave prima facie evidence of his night-flight, or plan his navigation. He'd had a port not long ago too.

No responsible pilot would do what he was about to do.

But a young lady needed saving, and there was no way Adders was missing out on that. He got on with his off-the-books pre-flight essentials: his fuel levels were good, his flaps were parallel, and his circuits were glowing like he was.

At your service, ma'am.

Chapter 23

Not everything Alley Oop told Spike was a lie. He *had* messed up, the mysterious chap who Alley Oop had spoken to only by phone *was* dead, and Dave Hunter *had* taken his gun. It was also true that he – Alley Oop – was being held captive by 'the poofy one', aka Danny, and that he had told Danny who he worked for.

To make the whole thing sound more convincing, Danny had instructed Alley Oop to slap himself hard across the face a split-second after he'd referred to Danny as 'the poofy one'. Alley Oop did this with surprising force, and Danny issued a stern instruction to use his proper name from now on.

It was almost painful for Danny to watch Alley Oop tell Spike that he'd revealed the number of people that were on their way. Danny heard Spike launch a torrent of abuse at Alley Oop, and he hoped this wouldn't wreck his nerves for the last and hardest part: the lie.

"I'm in the c-c-club. Yeah, I'm … Erm … I'm here with Dave and his bird … And a b-b-bloke called Mick ... And *Danny*." Alley went quiet for a moment, but he got a chance to talk soon enough.

"I dunno why they let me keep the pho –"

Danny snatched the handset from Alley Oop's hand and answered the question for him.

"Because the bad guy's always allowed a phone call, just like in the movies. Now listen to me. Your man didn't just break – he snapped like a twig. And the Angel of Death didn't fare too well either."

Danny listened – he wanted to hear the bad guys voice and commit his timbre to memory – but no reply came. But the line didn't go dead, so he carried on.

"Your side isn't doing very well so far, so I suggest you listen.

"I know you don't give a shit about Alley Oop. He hasn't got the brains he was born with, and he was none too clever then. But you know what? He's good for us since he's easy to talk to. We're the good guys, so we're not going to let you kill him either. As I see it, your only hope is to take him off us. And to do that, you'll have to kill us all.

"There is another option. You can go back to London and tell Alex and Samuel Cleaver that you messed up – that's if we haven't got to them first. But we *might* alert the authorities to their drugs and their guns, so I don't suppose that option sounds appealing.

"So, your only option is to try to finish what you've started."

Danny wasn't surprised to be called a 'fucking c**t' by the person at the other end, but he was surprised to hear a female voice say it. The line went dead, and Danny had another call to make, this time from his own phone. He put Alley's mobile phone in his pocket, but he didn't take his own mobile out straight away. First, he needed to implement specific measures to make sure his guest behaved himself.

"Right, Alley, take three steps back from the window," said Danny. He and Ally Oop both took three steps backward, then Danny said, "Put your feet apart wider than your waist, and lean on the window sill."

Danny didn't copy the second action. Instead, he hooked his foot around Alley Oop's heel, and he didn't need to explain what would happen to Alley Oop if he moved another muscle.

Danny did all of this because he knew that what he was about to do next needed two hands; he was still wearing the brass knuckles, but they were no longer in contact with Alley Oop – who might not be as daft as he looked.

Danny fished his mobile phone out of one of his jacket's pockets. Holding his binoculars up to his face with his left hand, and his mobile with his right, Danny used his thumb to speed-dial Dave, grateful for this feature since the knuckle dusters could have limited his dexterity. Dave answered on the first ring.

"Wassup, Danny?"

"There's four of them – all armed. They're going to come any moment, and I *think* they're going to come one at a time. They're hiding out under the pier, and I'm going to talk to you in real-time. Get kitted up, then make your way downstairs. Make sure the entrance is unlocked, then get in position and wait. Stay on the line and listen carefully. Godspeed, and may you always shoot straight and shoot first."

"That silly cunt's enjoying this," said Mick, as Dave prepared to lead the gang downstairs. And he may have had a point.

Just over two years earlier, Danny had taken several bullets for Dave Hunter, and Mick had witnessed this awful spectacle. Danny survived thanks to a fast-thinking police superintendent and a faster-acting trauma surgeon.

Mick and Dave had cried tears of joy when they'd learnt that their friend would live to tell the tale over a sherbert or ten. But throughout Danny's speedy recovery, Dave became concerned that Danny may have been softened by his brush with death. So, being the true friend that he was, Dave put together a plan to ensure that his friend wouldn't take up embroidery or flower arranging.

The day that Danny was released from hospital – ten days after his admission – Dave arranged to pick him up not outside the hospital grounds, but from a pub half a mile away. This, Dave thought, should help Danny get back on the horse. He also told Danny that once he'd made it, he could have a sherry or two before they began the slow drive back to Essex.

Perhaps it was the allure of a free drink, or maybe it was Danny's military blood. Either way, it worked, and Danny resisted the temptation to throw in the towel and call Dave up and tell him to bring his Impreza around to him.

Danny made it to the pub, breathless yet defiant, exhausted but thirsty.

This wasn't the only proof that Mick and Dave had needed to see that their friend hadn't gone soft while nurses had fussed over him.

That day, Danny only had one more road to cross to get to The Forresters Inn, a lovely 16th-century hostelry just outside the city of Cambridge. A funeral procession was working its way along the stretch of road that was all that stood between Danny and liquid refreshment and a hero's welcome. Danny waited patiently, which was more than could be said for the bad-tempered chap in a black Mercedes and an expensive suit that sat behind the procession. The moneyed-up lout hit his horn – twice. Danny didn't like this, and he liked it even less when the newly-rich yob wound his window down and shouted at the chief mourner to 'get a fucking move on.'

So Danny did what had only seemed right. He

opened the door of the Merc, unclipped the impatient salesman's seatbelt and dragged him out of his seat, then headbutted him three times in the face, breaking his nose and glasses. Then Danny slugged him in the gut and threw him to the curb.

After this, Danny looked up to see Mick and Dave on a bench outside the pub across the street, grinning and raising their glasses.

"Yeah, you could be right," said Dave, remembering this incident more than two years later. "Here – take this," he said as he tossed the handgun to Mick rather carelessly.

Dave knew there was no point in asking Lianda to stay in the flat. She had already made it clear she wouldn't be separated from him, and he knew that she, like someone else he could think of, was someone who knew their own mind. He also didn't want her to feel left out, and for that reason, he promised she could have the baseball bat he kept hidden behind the bar.

With Mick now holding the gun, and Lianda about to take centrefield, Dave realised that he was unarmed, save for him being in charge of communications with their outside intelligence. Knowledge was power, he reasoned, so he wasn't unarmed at all.

Once more into the breach, he thought but didn't say, and he led the group down the stairs and into the arena.

Chapter 24

With the aid of binoculars, Danny's eyes roved across the hundred yards of beach between the bar and the pier. He watched for two minutes and saw nothing – then he saw a shadowy figure crawl out from behind a wooden pillar. Danny used his chin and his right shoulder to wedge his mobile in place, freeing up his hands to squeeze his binoculars closer together, thus allowing him to focus on his subject better.

Danny imagined there was something reptilian about the man, and the effortless manner in which he half-crawled and half-slithered across the sand towards the club supported this belief. He was wearing black, but with the help of the moon peeking through a break in the clouds, Danny was able to see that he had light-coloured or perhaps blonde hair.

There was also a leather strap across his back, which confirmed what Danny had feared.

"One of them's coming now!" said Danny to Dave, who had been smart enough to switch his phone off its speakerphone setting. "Male, caucasian, fair-haired. He's got a gun, and it's not a water pistol."

Dave acted quickly and got his troops into place. He told Mick, armed with Death's semi-automatic pistol and, God willing, nerves of steel, to wait on the left-hand side of the alcove. He told Lianda, baseball bat primed like a Millwall supporter of old, to stand on the right-hand side.

Dave crouched down behind the bar, where he could peer through a crack underneath the counter flap. The bar was wider than it was long, and Dave could see the entrance from his watchpoint. The club was dimly lit, unchanged from the low-level lighting they had used when they were open for business half-an-hour and a lifetime ago.

As Dave, Mick and Lianda had made their way down the stairs and into the bar, Dave had worked out a plan. He told Mick that he would clap his hands if he wanted him to deal with the intruder; if Dave felt Lianda would do a better job with her baseball bat, then he would drop a glass. He would make his decision based on which hand their would-be assailant used as his trigger hand despite the possibility that the intruder might be ambidextrous.

Dave considered this because the situation reminded him of the time when two gunmen came to his old house in Colchester. The first of these two men was called 'Left-Handed' Pete, Dave later found out as did Mick and Danny, who had also been there that night. Mick and Danny fought with 'Left-Handed' Pete, and despite his southpaw moniker, they found he could use a gun – and fight – with ruthless efficiency on both sides (they nailed him, but only just).

So Dave knew his plan wasn't perfect, but it was better than having no plan at all. Everyone was in position, and they began the hardest part of all: the waiting.

They didn't have to wait long. After what could have been a minute, Dave heard Danny speak. "He's right outside. He should be with you in … Three, two one."

"Any second," whispered Dave to Mick and Lianda, who couldn't hear Danny now that Dave's phone wasn't set to loudspeaker mode.

As Danny counted the intruder's footsteps, Dave saw a silhouetted figure appear behind the frosted glass double doors. With his heart-thumping like a drunk driver who's just seen a blue light, Dave took a slow deep breath, knowing he was about to see the face of a killer.

You've seen it all before.

The door handle twisted downwards, and the left-hand side of the door budged by an inch then stopped fast; the intruder must have expected the door to be locked, Dave thought. Then both doors flew open and the darkly-dressed intruder fired three shots that sounded more like a zippo lighter being sparked thanks to an added silencer.

The shots were fired quietly, but there was nothing quiet about splintering wood and breaking glass. Dave heard something fall to the ground, followed by more glass breaking, and he just knew it was the picture of him and his late father with Snail's Pace Slim and Wilko Johnson.

*You'll pay for that, you c**t.*

But only when the time was right, Dave thought, emboldened by his provocation but still able to think with his head rather than his heart.

The dust soon settled, and the smoke cleared, and the unwelcome punter got his gun up – a long-barrelled beast that he held right-handed – and took three steps forward. Then he stopped and kicked the door shut behind him, and Dave decided there was no time like the present – he dropped a glass.

Lianda didn't waste a second, and just as the gunman turned his weapon in the direction of the sound of the breaking glass, she pulled her baseball bat up and brought it down on the back of his head.

"He's down," said Dave into the mouthpiece he'd

clasped against his face as he'd watched events unfold. "That's my girl," he said.

It was no time for celebration, though, and Danny managed to ram this point home right after telling Dave to switch his phone back to loudspeaker mode.

"I reckon you've got two minutes. But that could change at any moment. Dave?"

"Yes, mate?"

"Stay where you are. You're doing fine. No need to reply. Mick?"

"Yeah?"

"Take him out back and tie him up. Use your shirt, use his shirt, or anything you can get your hands on. Improvise. Oh, and get the gun off him, too. You might want to turn it around and make sure he's out cold too.

"Lianda?"

"Yes, Danny?"

"You've put the boys to shame. Good work"

This compliment didn't bring out a smile since Lianda realised she'd seriously hurt a fellow human being – if you could call him that. It didn't help that she saw Mick prize the rifle off of him and chin the bastard with it.

Dave was up from his position behind the bar, and Mick wanted to throw the confiscated weapon over to him, but his sensible nature stopped him. Instead, he handed it to him sideways, and Dave put it above the bar and out of harm's way. Mick dragged the unconscious bad guy across the dancefloor towards Dave's secret man cave, not knowing there was a dead body in there.

Chapter 25

Danny used the lull before the storm to assess the situation. Things seemed to be going well: the first bad guy never got a chance to be a bad guy at all, Lianda had shown herself to be made of the right stuff, and Mick had laid into two villains without hesitation.

There was more. A chain of command seemed to have formed. Danny was at the top, Dave was under him, and Mick and Lianda were able footsoldiers. Better still, Danny thought, this hierarchy had formed organically: he hadn't had to call rank.

Best of all, the bad guys seemed to be behaving themselves.

They had fallen hook, line, and sinker for the lie that the good guys were all inside the club, which meant they had no idea they were being watched almost casually from afar. The chap who had just chanced his arm had fitted his rifle with a silencer, which meant his accomplices wouldn't have heard the shots that were fired inside the club.

This was a good thing, Danny thought. If Spike or either of her leftover henchmen had heard shots, they most certainly would have responded impulsively: the sound of gunfire did that to people, and armed criminals especially.

Danny had been right so far in predicting that the bad guys would come one by one. This was precisely what he wanted since they had been – and still would be – easier to deal with one at a time.

There was no guarantee that the rest of the gang would play ball, but it felt good for him to know that Spike and co. probably wouldn't storm the building all at once. They were treading carefully, and Danny liked that.

If alarm bells rang, and Spike's gang came up in convoy… Mick, Dave or Lianda would not survive a firefight.

But for now, things seemed to be going to go to plan. Danny saw a hunched figure emerge from under the pier.

Alone.

The people of Southend-on-Sea were a generous bunch. They supported a vibrant, homegrown music scene, they bought overpriced hotdogs and milkshakes down at The Kursaal, and this wasn't all.

They'd made no fuss whatsoever when, a few years ago, they'd found out their tax money was being spent on a state-of-the-art coastal search and rescue facility that was as much a tourist attraction as it was a public service facility.

It was just around the corner from The Cliffs Pavilion, on Station Road. The lower half of the building was 50 feet long on each side and ten feet tall. It was built from concrete masonry units that were painted blue on the outside to represent the sea and the sky that the building served.

The top half was 40 feet on each side and ten feet tall. Because the top half was smaller than the lower half, there was a five-foot-wide walkway on all sides. This was where the designers had got a bit showy.

On the south-east corner of the building, there was a life-size painted statue of Sir Francis Drake, staring out to sea in all his Blackadder finery. To his right, on the south-west corner, was Admiral Nelson, again, looking out at God's great sea with respect and awe. But it wasn't just seafarers of old that got a look in.

On the north-east corner of the building, there was Douglas Bader, looking dapper with RAF wings on his jacket and a pipe hanging from his mouth.

Any surviving relatives of the late Mr. Bader would be glad to know that his sculptor had been tasteful enough to let him pose for his statue before the poor fellow had lost his legs.

The north-west quadrant was guarded by the wonderfully-named Marmaduke St John Thomas Pattle, with RAF bomber jacket, Biggles goggles and all.

The east-facing side of the upper-building was glass-fronted like a car showroom. This allowed the public to look in and marvel at the half-size lighthouse that ran up the centre of the building. The lookout turret at the top of the scaled-down tower was inside the building to keep the roof flat for …

A Sikorsky SA-92 search and rescue helicopter! This American-built beauty had cost millions in public money, but it was such a sight to behold that not one local resident had called Taxpayers' Alliance to voice their disapproval.

The building had to be secure, of course, but the outer perimeter was secured only by eight-foot wire-fencing; no-one could get in, but no-one was stopped from admiring the spectacle, either.

The SARF (Southend Air Rescue Facility) was the workplace of Reese Addington – Adders junior!

Over at the club, Mick was returning from his grueling trip

to the backroom office. He returned lighter but troubled by something other than the heavy load he'd just had to drag.

He hadn't expected to see a dead body, but he remained tight-lipped and indifferent. Mick suspected Danny had his reasons for not warning him about the bruised, bloodied cadaver he encountered in the man cave, and Mick decided he too would let Dave and/or Lianda discover this for themselves without warning.

It had been a grim spectacle, mind, and Mick had half-expected the former special forces operative to come back to life and say 'hi' or 'boo' or something, but thankfully, it never happened. Instead, the man known as Death gurned and rictus grinned his way through the early stages of rigor mortis.

Mick was lucky he hadn't gone there ten minutes earlier when a series of post-mortem spasms and muscle contractions had caused Death to sit bolt upright in his chair and his head to pull itself up from its slump. Then, Mick would have had something to complain about.

Mick imagined there would be little time for celebration, and he was right. By the time he was close enough to Dave to talk – and attempt to explain why he was stripped to the waist – Mick noticed Dave was holding his mobile phone close to his ear, furrowing his brow and listening intently. Dave covered his mouthpiece for just long enough to tell Mick to get back in position, on the left-hand (but his right) side of the entrance alcove. Mick carried out the instruction.

Mick noticed that Lianda was holding her beloved baseball bat aloft as she waited on the opposite side of the entrance to him. Mick took this as a cue to draw his gun from under his belt.

Mick remembered Danny saying that there was no safety catch on this thing and that the red dot at the back was there to remind users that this thing is always live. Mick was glad of this now but could have kicked himself for having stuffed it under his belt, pointing at his lunchbox when Danny had first issued it to him.

Danny trained Mick mostly in unarmed forms of combat because self-sufficiency and survival were the cruces of Danny's teaching and philosophy. I A O was what Danny called it: Improvise, Adapt, Overcome. Hence the near-total lack of firearms in his training programme.

Legitimately acquired firearms always arrived with manuals, and Danny didn't think anything that came with instructions could be used to help someone think on their feet. Too ordered, he thought. Too rooted in the classroom-based, controlled-environment style of teaching.

Mick was still puzzled as to why Danny was keen to avoid the subject of guns. He wondered if Danny was building up to it when he felt the time was right, or if Danny believed he wasn't smart or sensible enough.

But Danny had given him one piece of advice on the subject of handguns: if the bad guy is close enough that you can bring your pistol up as a cosh while holding it in the firing position, then you probably should.

Danny sounded utterly convincing in his argument that an inexperienced shooter stood a better chance of incapacitating his opponent in this manner. Well bollocks to that now, Mick thought as he stood beside the club's entrance, his pistol held out horizontally as he waited for the next set of instructions to pass down the line of command.

Chapter 26

"The second one's coming up the coast now. The subject is male, non-caucasian, carrying a machine gun."

Mick wondered why Dave was describing their new arrival's ethnicity until it occurred to him that Dave was simply repeating what Danny said to him. Plus, Mick thought, it reduced the chance of them getting the wrong man if a stray drunk wandered in hoping for a late one.

A two-minute silence followed Dave's announcement. In this time, it occurred to Mick that there could be a macho war of words when he shoved the cold steel in the intruder's back and told him to drop it. There was a chance the other guy would test Mick by insulting him – what would he say or do?

Ah yes, Mick thought. I'll say 'you shot yourself in the foot there,' before blasting his big toe off.

Now you're thinking like a pro …

Mick's rather bizarre train of thought was silenced

when Dave announced that their subject was about to enter the building. Once more, the door handle turned, and someone entered the club without invitation.

Mick didn't wait for Dave to clap his hands. He waited for gunman number two to take half-a-dozen steps before creeping up behind him and putting the snub at the base of his spine. "Don't move. Don't say a word, and don't scream for help either," Mick said. "Drop it. If it goes off, it goes off. Drop it."

"And if I don't?" said the man with a big gun but little chance of using it.

Mick wasn't about to let control of the situation slip away from him.

"Well, you'll never dance again. You like music, eh? You like dancing?", Mick said, prodding the intruder's spine.

Mick didn't wait for an answer. "I like James Brown," he said. What's that song of his that always gets people up?"

Mick paused in false ponderance before saying, "That's the one – *Get on the Good Foot*!"

As Mick said this, he fired a near-silent no-range shot into the intruder's left foot, forcing him to carry out Mick's instruction via James Brown. With one foot shot to ribbons, he had to get on the good one to stay up, but his reflexes were torn between keeping hold of his weapon or instinctively clasping the damaged weight-bearing portion of his left limb.

The bad guy dropped his weapon, and it didn't go off. Mick put his right foot on it as if to say, 'it's mine now.'

"Hey, Dave," Mick said, not wanting to turn his back on the assassin with the knackered foot. "Did you tell Danny what happened and what I said?"

"No need, Mick. He heard everything"

"And?" said Mick, speaking louder than necessary as

people do when they can't see the person they are talking to. "What did he say."

"He said stop being a fucking twat and finish him off."

Mick didn't need telling twice. He moved within an arm's length of his new best friend and shot his other foot. The guy collapsed face down and writhed around on the spot where he fell. He must have had a high pain threshold for he didn't pass out straight away.

Satisfied that the bad guy was out cold, Mick turned to Lianda. "You wanted equal rights, well now you got 'em. Take him out back and tie him up with the rest of 'em," he said.

She went to do it without hesitation, and Mick was almost as proud as Dave was.

"One more thing," said Mick, stopping her in her tracks.

He picked up the bulky machine gun that the second

intruder had brought with him and handed it to her butt first.

"You might want to make sure he stays out for a little while longer."

She did an' all.

Danny put his mobile back in his jacket pocket with Dave still on the line. He did this after Dave had confirmed that the second intruder had been dealt with and was being put in storage by Lianda, which gave Danny an idea of everyone's whereabouts.

Two things were bothering Danny. Firstly, things were going a bit too well; Danny knew that lady luck didn't smile for too long too often. Could their luck soon run out? Danny reckoned there was a good chance it could and soon would.

The other thing was that although he had this oik called Alley Oop just where he wanted him, Danny couldn't see Alley Oop while he had binoculars pressed to his face.

While Mr. Oop was splayed out in front of him like a prison bitch, he could make a sudden movement, and there was a chance Danny wouldn't see it until it was too late.

Fortunately, these two problems wouldn't bother him for long. Thirty seconds after he last talked to Dave, another, bigger problem came along and demanded his attention: two more shadowy figures emerged from Southend Pier's cover of darkness.

They were running towards the club carrying carbine-length weapons, one of which Danny could see was a machine gun that could loose off more than thirty rounds per minute. The person who held this weapon appeared to have breasts as well, and Danny decided this must be Spike; her running partner seemed to have a sawn-off shotgun. Danny fished out his mobile and prepared to tell Dave that the party was just about to start.

Lianda wasn't about to admit defeat and ask for help, but

she had found out the hard way that moving a body – albeit not a dead one (she hoped) – was perhaps a job for the boys after all. But Mick's equal rights quip had made her determined to see it through, and she nearly had – nearly.

With both her arms in talon-shaped grips under the dozing bad guy's arms and around his shoulders, she had dragged him the length of the dancefloor then along the hidden corridor behind the bandstand. She came to the door to the man cave and let the resting body flop down as she reached for the handle.

She was out of breath from dragging a body that was a good deal heavier than her slender – though not quite petite – frame. She told herself this was no time to rest, and she pushed down on the handle and entered Dave's office for only the second time in her life.

She barely managed to stifle a scream when she saw two inanimate bodies in there, and not just one as she had expected. The air from her first near-scream was still in her throat as luck would have it when it dawned on the poor girl that one of the men was dead.

He was tied to a chair, and his face had been beaten to a pulp before death came as what Lianda imagined was a relief. Appropriately, he had a tattoo of the grim reaper on his right arm, and the skin around his upwards-looking face was stretched tight.

It was this taut, sinewy pose that conveyed the message he was no longer of this world. Lianda had never seen a dead body before, although she had wondered from time to time throughout her twenty-two years how she would react when she did.

Badly was how she reacted. Her imagination ran away with her, and she imagined that the man with the dark tattoo had turned his head skywards at his time of dying as a peacemaking gesture. It seemed to her he had believed that by turning turn his head towards God and the heavens, he might buy some time to explain himself and perhaps be spared from laying down to eternal rest on a bed of fiery coals.

Good luck with that ...

Lianda remembered she had a job to do, and she pulled herself together by getting on with it. The clicking of her high-heels along the corridor had been a nagging reminder that she wasn't dressed for this kind of business, so she kicked them off and wedged the tip of one of them under the door. She retook her victim's feet and pulled him into the office.

Lianda laid the unconscious body out flat at the opposite end of the room to Death and the tallish chap with sandy hair who she had taken out with the baseball bat earlier. Impressed at Mick's resourcefulness in using items of clothing to restrain the other, darker-skinned chap earlier (who was unconscious and tied up near to the dead body across the room), Lianda decided she would do something similar, albeit not with her own clothing. If she used the black cocktail dress she was wearing that did a remarkable job of being sexy and tasteful at the same time, then Dave (and quite possibly Mick) would become too distracted to get any work done. No, she would strip her prisoner part-way bare and use his clothing.

First, she took off his black pullover, which she put over his head using the arms to tie the jumper into a bag. Not tight enough to suffocate him, but if he came to during his operation, the blackness and resulting disorientation would buy her enough time to hold a stiletto heel to his ear or temple and remind him who's boss.

Then she pulled one of his leather combat boots off and unthreaded the long set of laces, using them to lash his hands together high above his head. She took his other boot off and tossed it aside as his hands were already secure.

The man whose name she didn't know – like the other two, actually – was wearing black running trousers. This meant he wouldn't be wearing a belt, which would have been excellent for lashing his feet together. Not a problem, she thought as she closed her fists around the hems of his running trousers and, with a heave and a sigh, pulled them out from under him.

She wasted no time in lassoing them around the ankles of his bare legs and pulling his feet together tightly as she had done his hands a moment ago. As she knelt down to roll him onto his front, it occurred to her that she was alone with a mostly naked man who wasn't Dave Hunter. She giggled as she toyed with the idea of taking a look under his boxers to see how this one measured up. Then she told herself off and reminded herself that this was no time for silliness.

She did it anyway, though, and she thumbed his underwear elastic and peeked in. Then she sighed and shook her head. "You've got nothing on my Dave," she said as she snapped the lining shut and retired to Dave's office chair to catch her breath.

She let her bare feet swing about the leg-space underneath the desk for a while, trying not to think about the key safe that was also underneath the desk. Then she heard a gunshot.

Chapter 27

It is said that great minds think alike. Yet people with limited intelligence sometimes tune in to the wavelengths of their bright counterparts.

This must have been what happened when Alley Oop, tired of being humiliated by Daniel Blyth, thought the same thing as his captor. Alley Oop managed to work out that if Danny was upright while he – Alley – was bent over in front of him, then perhaps Danny wouldn't see him move. If he moved quickly enough, he could stun Danny before putting the boot in a few times and breaking free and saving his friends – who seemed to be in serious trouble.

So Alley decided to take his chance. In a fraction of a second, he brought his right foot up stamped on Danny's, putting all of his weight into it and breaking three of Danny's toes. Alley Oop didn't give Danny, who felt like a bank's safe had been dropped on his right foot, poor bugger, time to react. Alley Oop did the same thing only this time on the left side. His size fourteen shoe crunched down hard on Danny's girly size-eleven foot, and Danny felt his big toe turn into splinters.

Danny's ordeal wasn't over. He collapsed in pain, and he would have stayed down had Alley Oop not pulled him up by the hair. Alley Oop delivered a death-chop to where Danny's neck and shoulder met, which downed him again. But Alley Oop wasn't done yet, and he pulled Danny up once more. He slugged Danny hard in the guts from his right side, before doing the same with his left. Danny went down onto one knee, and Alley Oop delivered a forearm crunch to his right cheekbone. Then, like a premiership footballer taking a free-kick, Alley Oop aimed the foot that had just mashed several of Danny's toes at his chin. Danny went down, conscious but perhaps wishing he wasn't.

For a short time, Alley Oop stood over his prey, relieved that he had shut the lanky bastard up but still concerned that the mission was fucked. But he wouldn't be called any more names or have to answer to this long-haired piss-streak of a man anymore, and that was something. He stooped down beside Danny's dazed yet semi-conscious body and took both the mobile phones out of the left pocket of Danny's leather jacket. Then, Alley Oop worked the set of brass knuckles out of Danny's hand, before fitting them onto his own bigger fist. With the lethal device fitted, he held his new, improved right fist against one of Danny's cheekbones.

For some reason, this was all he did: something stopped Alley Oop from delivering the blow that would shut Danny up for good. Confused by this, Mr. Oop told himself that he was messing about here and that saving the mission was a better use of his time.

Get a move on, big guy. It's your time.

Back at the bar, the last thing Dave heard Danny say was that the next – and hopefully last – attackers were in the car park; before then, Danny told him that one of them, the female, had a machine gun, the other a pump-action shotgun. Danny had been cut off just when he'd said that the two gunmen had entered the outer perimeter of the property, and much to Dave's horror, the last thing he'd heard from his friend was a cry of pain followed by a loud curse. He made the difficult decision not to tell Mick that Danny was either dead or in serious trouble. Instead, he prepared for the coming attack.

He reached for the confiscated shotgun up in the glasses rack above the bar. Then, with a sharp eye on the entrance door, he lifted the hatch and came out from behind the bar: time to change position and tactics.

Dave took Lianda's old lookout to the right (his left) of the alcove doorway that their next guest would surely enter by; Mick did likewise, albeit to the left side of the entrance. Dave decided that his chances of shooting straight with a weapon like this were somewhere between little and none, with the odds leaning towards the latter. So, he turned the hefty chunk of metal back to front so he could swing it like a baseball bat.

As Dave waited to strike, he thought of Lianda, the woman of his and no doubt many other men's dreams, out back in the man cave tying up the latest addition to their collection of bodies. She was safe there, he reckoned, but would she stay there as long as it took him and Mick to sort out the last two aggressors? What if he and Mick failed in their attempts to bring the last two gang members down?

They'll get to her, that's what.

"Mick?" Dave whispered.

"Yes, mate?"

"You shot the last one in the leg, right?

"Yeah," said Mick, not quite believing what he had done.

"Go for the head this time."

Spike and her assistant, one Paul Walsall, split up just after they jumped the wall into the car park outside the club. She imagined the previous two – Max Cane and Karim Haswell – had met sticky ends, and she didn't fancy Walsall's chances either. This didn't matter at all since she was faster than them as well as a better shot. This wasn't all.

She was quieter and more efficient than any of the men involved in the job; she was able to not leave footprints, to not be seen or heard, and to adapt to her surroundings. She'd also checked the venue out a few nights earlier to get a feel for the place, make a few mental notes, discovering as she'd expected that there was a rooftop entrance, in this case, a glass skylight that would give her access to the bedroom in the flat upstairs.

She'd been mildly amused, upon her visit to Bobby's Bar, to see a man sat a few hundred yards along the beach with a gaslight, deep in thought and staring out to sea. She'd suspected this character was in some way involved with the running of the club and that they would meet again. How right she was.

As her assistant took the front entrance, Spike moved around to the sea-facing wall of the building. She shimmied up the drainpipe unhindered by her body weight or the heavy rucksack she carried: the loaded machine gun strapped across her back was like a feather to her.

Her employers didn't want her to use her gun. But for all of her professionalism, she was going to do it anyway. Tonight she was going to break all the rules, in fact …

In the fine American tradition, Bobby's Bar and Grill had a flat roof. Having made her way swiftly up the overflow, exposed to the rising wind and cold autumn rain, Spike pulled the leather glove off her right hand with her teeth while still clinging to the drainpipe with her right arm. She threw the glove onto the roof with her left hand, before removing her left glove and throwing that onto the roof too.

She reached over her head with her open right hand and shaped her fingers around the edge of the asphalt roof, feeling the abrasive material against her skin as she did so. Getting the other hand across would have seemed tricky to some since it meant the would-be cat burglar would be left hanging on one with hand.

Spike didn't give this a moment's thought, and soon she had both hands on the edge of the flat roof. This put her in a position to pull her elbows up onto the rooftop like a swimmer climbing out of a pool. Using the deep tread of her combat boots to aid her ascent, Spike pulled herself onto her belly, then hooked her right leg over the edge of the roof, followed by her left, and then pulled herself into a standing position.

She found the gloves she'd removed a moment ago and put them back on. Then she walked across to the skylight, on the west-facing portion of the building. When she'd been here the other night, Spike had caught a dimly-lit glimpse of this Dave Hunter chap and his girlfriend bollock-naked on the bed beneath this rooftop window. Now, the lights were on, but nobody was home. Perfect, thought Spike, as she put her rucksack down by her feet.

Among the accessories that Spike had in her rucksack, there was one non-essential item: a black, 12-inch strap-on dildo and leather harness.

Spike brought this after seeing Dave Hunter with his picture-perfect girlfriend the other night. Spike loved and hated the likes of her in equal measure, and had done since she was at school. Her sort got all the breaks, got all the attention – and looked at people who weren't born perfect with a mixture of scorn and amusement.

But Spike still fancied women like her and, deep down, wanted to be like them – at least she did in part. It was a vicious cycle that, throughout Spike's life, had been building up to what she had planned tonight.

With Dave and his friends all taken care of, Spike

was going to violate little miss perfect here, was going to slip into the adult device and plunge and thrust into Dave’s girlfriend with all the energy and hatred she had. Either Dave’s bird would feel pain – something she’d probably never felt before – or she would love every bit of it and see that she was a dirty little bitch like the rest of them.

Her supposedly heroic boyfriend would be crippled and unable to intervene. And she planned to make him watch all of the things she had planned for his bird. Then she’d kill him and his missus, if she was lucky.

Dave Hunter had done nothing to Spike, but he had done something to her world when he’d killed the late Norman Layer. And in underworld circles, killing the man who killed a legend would make her infamous: no-one would fuck with her again.

Spike knew the authorities would come after her, but they were looking for her anyway, so her chances of going to prison would be no greater or worse. But if she was taken into the slammer, then she'd get a hero's welcome from the other lags and slags, and it would be her, and not not the prison governor, that ran the place.

But her diabolical plans were for later on. Spike had work to do.

She reached into her rucksack to fetch her pistol-grip glass cutter. This would be no use with toughened glass, but this was where Spike's professionalism had come into play. When she was here the other night, she pushed her luck a little and gave the pane a little tap with the knuckle of her right index finger. The hollow sound wasn't enough to wake the two love birds, but it was enough to tell Spike that the piece of glass between her and them wasn't tempered, and as such, she would have an easy entry.

Using the cutter, Spike scored a grid-like series of lines into the 30 x 30-inch pane. Twenty seconds later, she had what looked like an empty crossword puzzle, and she drew/cut a border about an inch-wide around the crisscrossed lines. The sound of the diamond tip of her small DIY tool engraving the surface of the inch-thick piece of glass was similar to the sound of a wind-up clock or toy, and it was a sound Spike liked but didn't know why.

Spike knew that there were easier ways to break a piece of glass – like shooting it – but this would attract the attention of the people inside; Spike wanted to enter the building as quietly as possible.

Just as she was wondering whether or not to coat the glass with strips of duct tape, a reel of which she had in her carry bag (along with an ammunition magazine and several other breaking and entry tools among other things), she heard the sonic boom of a shotgun firing somewhere down below. Perfect, Spike thought; their ears will close up for a few seconds, which means nobody would hear her break the skylight's glass, and she would enter the building undetected even though she had primed the glass to break rather than shatter.

The gun going off a second before she raised her boot to break the rooftop pane seemed like a stroke of luck, no doubt about it. But this wasn't Spike's only piece of good fortune today, as she heard another shot discharged downstairs at the precise moment that her booted foot stamped down on the pre-cut slice of glass. Nobody could have heard what little noise it made.

This didn't stop her pausing for five full seconds out on the rooftop in case anybody was foolish enough to come in and greet her. With the five-second grace period over, she slung her rucksack back onto her shoulders and lowered herself through the skylight, lowering herself onto the bed.

Chapter 28

Spike pulled herself off the bed and got to her feet. She slid her gun around to her front even though she wasn't necessarily planning on firing it. Not yet, anyway. The room was dark, and she waited a moment for her eyes to adjust. She'd just had a birdseye view of the most light-polluted town in Great Britain, and it would take more than a minute for her eyes to fully adjust to the transition, but time was of the essence.

There was also the fact that the next room along, which she reckoned would probably be the living room, could be well lit, so she couldn't be too concerned about this. On a deeper level, Spike believed that having a chameleon-like ability to adapt to your surroundings was part of what separated the men from the boys.

The bedroom door didn't have a lock, which meant Spike wouldn't be slowed down by having to force an entry. On the flip-side, there was no keyhole for her to peer through to see if there was anyone in the next room.

Not wanting to take chances, she arched her back and let her rucksack slip from her shoulders, catching the left shoulder strap before the bag hit the floor. With her free right arm she twisted the door handle down then waited and listened. Nothing. Then she pulled the door open just a few inches and used her left hand to throw her rucksack into the shaft of light that spilled through the partially opened door.

Nobody pounced or shot at the bag having thought it to be the intruder, but Spike still wasn't satisfied that the adjacent room was empty. She peeked through the narrow crack in the doorway as best as she could and didn't see anyone waiting on the other side, playing it cool and thinking they could beat her at her own game.

She pulled the door open wide enough to pass through, before simultaneously putting her right foot down to jam the door open and bringing her gun up, putting the sights level with her eyes. Nobody. Just as she expected.

Mick would have shot this chap in the head without Dave's instruction, but he'd missed his chance. The man known – but not to them – as Paul Walsall had fired three rounds. One from a few feet outside the club, breaking several panes in the frosted glass entrance, and two more when he'd planted his feet just inside the building, having kicked both doors open with a single right-footed bash.

Mick had counted three footsteps between Walsall's first and second shots and had worked out that, if he kept to this pattern of fire and movement, then he would move into view from the alcove at any second allowing Mick to put him out of his misery.

It nearly worked out that way. Mick, being an utterly inexperienced marksman, had wanted there to be no space between him and their final intruder. Mick didn't trust luck much and had decided he wouldn't the trigger until the barrel was resting against his enemy's head. This was where he'd slipped up.

Neither Paul Walsall or Spike had fitted silencers to their weapons of choice. Walsall had the ears of a bat and, despite having broken the sound barrier and several of Dave's optic bottles doing it, he'd still heard Mick coming up behind him.

Walsall's reflexes had served him well, and just before the tip of the barrel of Mick's gun tickled his ear, he'd managed to flip his shotgun back-to-front and swing it like an axe at Mick's wrist. Mick's wristbone shattered on impact, and he dropped the gun and dropped to his knees.

Walsall wasn't in the mood to take prisoners, but he wasn't in the mood to take chances either. To grant this foolish young man his wish of becoming a hero by dying like one, he needed to pump a new round into his 'Heckler'. To allow himself the time and the space to do this, Paul Walsall brought his right leg backwards in a giant stride and …

Not many people feel lucky after they've felt a size 12 army boot connect with their face, but in fact, Mick had been fortunate: the kick missed the spot it was aimed for. Had it landed on the underside of his chin, then his neck would have snapped like a pencil, killing him instantly. Instead, it caught his jaw side-on, and he was now semi-conscious as opposed to stone dead.

Paul Walsall turned his shotgun the right way around and the pushed the three-parts of his gun – the barrel, the chamber, and the stock – together before aiming them as one glorious whole at the man who looked to be thirty years his junior.

Dave Hunter tip-toed out from the other side of the alcove, behind Walsall, holding his gun like a baseball bat. He would only get one chance at this.

After ten seconds, Spike was satisfied that there was nobody in the living room, and in fact, she was sure the whole flat was empty. If there was anybody there, then they would have come out by now and tried something.

She wanted to sneak up on her target – or targets – unawares. Get right under their noses.

Spike had done time in a women's prison in her early twenties, and if there was one thing she had learnt in there, it was how to make yourself unseen and unheard. At first, this taught her how to keep out of trouble and keep away from the shaven-headed lesbian gang that ran the place. Then, after a time, she learnt that this was a way to gain an advantage and assume the role of an attacker – she could be the hunter rather than the hunted. Soon, she pretty much ran HP Bronzefield and was sad when her parole came through early.

Previous to this, she'd done a short spell in the British Army hence her knowledge of firearms. She'd thrived during training and could have been a great soldier if not for one small problem: she wasn't a team player. She didn't mind people telling her what to do, but she couldn't tolerate people holding her back. And the British Army, what its modest-at-best salary, crummy pension, and obsession with shining boots (she hated that), she soon realised, was holding her back, big time. She'd disappeared from her barracks in Colchester three years ago and had not officially been spotted since. She was an AWOL soldier as well as a missing person, and none of the people tasked with finding her since she'd gone to ground had been able to do so yet.

Spike imagined that one or two locks might need picking before Dave Hunter met his nemesis. She knew pretty much every trick of the trade, and she was well equipped for this. The living room had a timber door (that she assumed led to the stairwell), and a close look at this revealed what she expected to see: a pin-tumbler lock. Easy.

Spike took her bump key from the little aluminium trick box in her rucksack and got to work. She did everything as quiet as a mouse in reaction to the eerie quiet that now came from below. The bashing and crashing had stopped, which meant that someone had won the fight. She didn't care who – she just knew there would be no melee to mask her arrival, so she would have to move in total silence from now on.

A bump key was essentially a modified cylinder key. The teeth – or cuts – were ground down evenly, and the shoulder was filed to roughly the same height and replaced with two small rubber grommets. The modified key could slide into any pin-tumbler lock, and its filed-down ridges would simply rest underneath the bottom set of pins.

The person wishing to gain unlawful entry would then turn the key – or try to. With the key still semi-turned, the illegal entrant then only had to tap – or bump – the exposed, circular end of the key with a cigarette lighter or something of similar size and density and, low and behold, the key would turn – usually. Sometimes it would take two or three attempts.

Spike didn't use a cigarette lighter – smoking was a mug's game to her – and she twisted the key with the thumb and forefinger of her left hand. At this stage, the key didn't turn, but when she thumped her abductor muscle with the heel of her right hand, it did.

At the top of the stairs, she saw that someone had put down a thick carpet so that she could make her way downstairs nice and quietly.

Chapter 29

The obvious thing would be to go for the head, thought Dave. Cave his skull in. That'll teach him.

But Dave didn't do this. Not because he wanted to treat these people with any degree of humanity – they hadn't shown much of that – but because the latest intruder was pointing his shortened shotgun barrel in the direction of Mick Davies. Dave needed to get the gun pointed away from Mick and better still, out of its owner's hands. Gripping his own shotgun like a baseball bat, Dave reared up behind the man who was preparing to put Mick to sleep forever.

Dave brought his shotgun up like an axe and swung its stock down on the 14" barrel of Walsall's identical weapon, hearing the clang of metal hitting metal as well as a final shot fired off in desperation by the man who didn't want to give up his gun.

Dave didn't stop to see if the bullet fired in desperate hope had hit his friend Mick, and he let go of his own weapon feeling this could slow him down. Dave's opponent in this deathmatch hadn't yet released his grip on his lethal Heckler & Koch shotgun, but at least he had some competition now, as Dave too grabbed the barrel and the butt of his weapon.

Let's wrestle for it, fucker ...

In an attempt to gain an advantage, Dave tried to nudge the butt of the rifle into his enemy's face, and perhaps crack his cheekbone or break his nose. It was a nice try, but it didn't work. The two men were a dead match, strength-wise, and Walsall resisted the attempted blow. But Dave had tricked him.

Dave was setting up a distraction so he could headbutt him in the face. Egged on by the satisfying crunch and the sight of blood that followed, Dave repeated the manoeuvre two, three, four times, shaking his head backwards and forwards like someone in the mosh pit at a Metallica concert.

Dave sensed victory was his, but he didn't take the fight any less seriously. He bent down and slammed his shoulder into his opponent's midsection, driving him into the wall behind him. Walsall hit the unforgiving surface back-first. His face had been turned to mush by Dave Hunter's forehead, but he still didn't give up his gun. His grip was loosening though, and Dave, using both hands and nearly all of his upper-body strength, attempted to bench-press the weapon from lower-chest height (Dave and Walsall were of equal height) to a position where it was level with both men's throats.

In his mind's eye, Dave saw and heard his late father. The ghostly image of the late Don Hunter was in training gear, bared teeth showing in his sinewy face like an East End Mickey Goldmill.

"Finish him, you cunt," Dad said. *"Do him like he'd do you."*

Dave didn't need to be told twice. He used all the

strength he had and then some as he pushed the lower side of the shotgun barrel against Walsall's throat. After what could have been a minute – time speeds up and slows down like a drummer in a pub when battle is done – Dave saw the other man's hold on the gun start to loosen as both hands began to lose their grip on the cold steel.

Dave knew he was effectively choking the man, and part of him wanted to let go since the battle was surely won. Another part of Dave wondered if his worthy adversary was trying to trick him by playing dead. Another ten seconds went by, and Dave released the potentially lethal hold. Paul Walsall slumped to the floor, perhaps dreaming of world peace.

"You did alright, kid," said Dave, not knowing if he meant himself or the man he had just fought with.

With a heavy heart, Dave went to check on his friend, Mick Davies. He took a short walk over to his friend who had collapsed into a heap on the barroom floor a moment earlier. After a quick inspection, Dave deduced that Mick had been lucky: he had dodged the bullet that worked its way loose while he and the other man grappled.

It concerned Dave that the kick to the face that Mick had received a moment earlier may have done what bullet was intended to do. He bent down and held his right thumb and forefinger against Mick's jugular.

Dave was relieved to feel a steady pulse in his friends 'Gregory' and to see Mick's chest expand and contract at a stable space

"You know what they say," said Dave, as he pulled himself up to his feet. "You can't keep a good man down."

As Dave stepped into the entrance alcove and shut and bolted the outside door (Dave was knackered, and the final gang member would have to wait), it occurred to him that although Mick was alive, it could be some time before he was well again. Back in the bar, Dave looked at his friend again, out cold on the barroom floor and away in a world of playboy bunnies and jelly and ice cream, which was all he'd be eating with that knackered jaw of his.

Lianda had done the right thing in staying in a place of safety while the real action had gone down. Dave knew she was a sensible sort of person and would probably stay there until he came to get her. Which he'd do right away since she would want to know that Mick and he were okay.

Dave grinned as he spun on his feet to begin the walk across the dancefloor to her hideout in his backroom man cave, wondering if the sight of her happy tears would set him off too. Not that he cared.

But he and Lianda never got their bittersweet reunion. Instead, Dave saw the word HATE, tattooed on a small bony fist that connected with his nose and sent him down like a sack of potatoes.

***

Dave didn't know how long he'd been out for, but he was able to work out that he'd been dragged into the middle of the dancefloor. As his senses reawakened, he didn't spend too much time worrying that the small pool of blood he was laying in might have come from a gunshot wound: it was his nose, which hadn't fused since it was broken by that Alley Oop chap some several weeks earlier.

He was stripped to his underwear, and his legs were bound together by his jeans. He felt cold against the wooden dancefloor, but that didn't matter much.

What mattered a lot was that a small yet obviously strong lady with a shaved head and wearing army boots was pointing a machine gun at him. From six feet away. She got up from the wooden chair she'd pulled over from a nearby table to pass the time while he regained consciousness and emerged from a dream involving a girl much prettier than her.

"I guess you own the place," she said.

"Yes, and I'm afraid we're closed. So if you don't mind, fuck off."

Dave's insult earned him a kick to the head, and not the 'that's no way to speak to a lady' kind of a response he hoped for since her total lack of feminine qualities or attributes would have left her wide open for another of Dave's classy insults. But no – she just got up from her chair, walked six feet over to Dave and BAM! She put her boot right under his chin, and for a while afterwards, he didn't know if he was dead or alive.

To somebody who was outside-looking-in, it would surely look strange to see a captive insult their captor in this way. In such a one-sided fight – Dave knew he was fucked now – his only hope was to attempt to pacify his enemy. Was it wise to try to reverse the roles against such desperate odds?

The answer to the last question was undoubtedly no. But Dave remembered the man who had said we should always face the curtain with a bow, and this made perfect sense to him now that he was as good as dead. Or so he thought.

“I haven’t been told to kill you,” said the little skinhead hovering over him, “but I’m gonna do it anyway. And before I do that, I’m gonna put on a little show involving your lady friend. You might even enjoy it.”

Dave managed to move his jaw enough to speak.

“I thought armed robbers wore balaclavas … Do you save yours for when you go on dates?”

This was a bridge too far for Spike. She took Dave by his feet and started to drag him towards the chair she’d been sitting on when he came to a moment ago.

“Alright, alright,” he said. “I’ll do you a deal: let me go, and I’ll suck your cock first.”

Dave doubted Spike understood him since his words came out sounding like he’d just had a mouthful of fillings.

Dave knew what was coming, and sure enough, Spike rolled him onto his front and lifted his head up by his hair. Then she forced his open, slack-jawed mouth over the edge of the chair so that his top and bottom row of teeth were biting the overside and the underside of the chair. Dave knew this was going to be worse than death. He couldn't see Spike from his downwards-facing position, but his mind's eye could, and in it, her expression was chillingly indifferent as she raised her foot to do the despicable deed.

Bang!

Dave heard a gunshot even though he'd heard enough of those for one day – he'd had enough of them for a lifetime. The next thing he heard was the sound of Spike hitting the floor.

Dave had to force his jaws to open to set himself free from the chair. He pushed/pulled his knees up to his chest while he untied and then removed his improvised leg restraints. Then he looked over his shoulder, and before he collapsed from severe exhaustion and the two nasty blows to the head he'd received, he saw Lianda, pale with shock and holding the revolver that he kept in the safe underneath his office desk.

Chapter 30

Lianda didn't like what she'd done. Dave could see it by the way she was frozen to the spot, her blank expression similar to that of the woman she'd just killed.

"Come here," Dave said, putting his arms around her. "You did that for me. She'd have done the same thing to you." He cradled her against his chest, and she eventually returned the gesture by wrapping her arms around his shoulder. They shared a moment's silence that said more than words ever could.

Don't waste time here ... Danny's fucked, remember

"Give that thing to me," he said.

She passed it to his right hand before kissing him softly on the forehead.

He hated himself for pulling away, but he imagined she understood.

"Danny's in trouble," he said. "I've got to find him. Look after Mick for me, okay?"

"Okay," she said, quieter than a whisper.

This was followed by an uncomfortable silence as Dave retrieved his shoes, trousers and shirts from the dance floor. He dressed himself hurriedly, keeping an eye on Lianda, concerned about her level of shock.

He acknowledged that she, like Mick, was temporarily out of the game. Saving Danny was now his job and his job alone.

If Danny could still be saved ...

Dave heard a series of thumps on the outside door. Oh shit, he thought. Then the thumping gave way to what sounded like a series of heavy kicks.

"That thing's gonna come off its frame," he said.

He came away from Lianda and prepared to battle their next visitor. He didn't need to guess who it was.

***

The series of kicks that Alley Oop launched against the thick wooden double-door did little to help him gain entry.

In fact, this was mere foreplay while he built himself up to the main event.

Without stopping for breath, he took six steps back from the sturdy wooden panels, then charged like a bull who could understand the jeers of a cocky young matador. CRUNCH! Alley was sure he heard something splinter, and it wasn't his right shoulder blade – even though there was a chance that could give way long before the hinges or locking mechanism did.

He couldn't think about that now, and this time he took eight steps back before gritting his teeth and charging forwards again. BANG! This time he bounced off the inch-thick wooden pane and collapsed in a heap. Panting, he pulled himself up to his feet and thought about the long line of 'Charlie' that the Cleavers would reward him with if he saved the day.

He took a dozen steps back, and, with eyes that glistened with tears, he took another run-up.

It didn't work, but afterwards he noticed a gap of about two millimetres between the door frame and the hinges and some splinters and some dust on the doormat.

You can do it, chief!

Alley Oop didn't think about why he was doing this, or what he would do when he got into the building. Instead, he focused his mind squarely on his next cocaine high, that magical buzz that made an ordinary man feel like he could wrestle a lion and then get a whole netball team pregnant – and break down a pair of oak doors (he could have done with some of it now, actually).

There was none available, so he would have to summon up the warrior spirit of his own accord. Not a problem, he thought as he made a final lunge towards the door. CRACK! Both panels were reduced to splinters upon his final impact, and the wrecked door broke loose with an awful sound and crash-landed inside the building. Alley Oop landed face down, carried by his own momentum.

Alley jumped to his feet in a bid to assess the situation and take control. Right in front of him lay the body of one of the chaps he'd met the other night but whose name he couldn't remember. He was sparked-out, but Alley saw his chest moving in and out, which he took as a sign that the mission wasn't a complete washout.

He saw Spike, lying in a pool of her own blood: Alley Oop was no expert, but her head was still intact, so he assumed she'd been shot in the stomach. She was still gripping her machine gun, even though she was too dead to fire it.

Alley Oop also noticed that one of Dave's friends, the tubby one he'd seen the first time he came to the club, was unconscious about six feet away from him. He was breathing, and Alley Oop was relieved to see this.

Then Dave Hunter walked into view, pointing a revolver at Alley Oop's face. Mr Hunter was almost within arms reach, and Alley Oop knew he wouldn't miss from there.

"You're barred," Dave said.

"I knew we shouldn't have trusted that stupid fat oaf."

Samuel Cleaver spoke while pacing the floor of the office he shared with his brother Alex. Like ice to his brother's fire, Alex was trying to keep his cool.

He managed to stay seated, but he had to fight the urge to look at the grandfather clock at the far end of the room and will its hands to slow down. He gave in and had a look. It was 11:00 pm. Something had gone wrong.

"Will you stop that?" said Alex.

"Stop what?"

"Stop pacing up and down. You're making me nervous."

Samuel turned away from the window that offered an expansive view of Kensington High Street and went back to his desk, opposite his brother. "I can't help it," he said as he measured a line of white powder out for himself. “It’s *his* fault.”

Simple denial. Like any substance user who hovered over the line between recreation and addiction, Samuel Cleaver kept his excuses at the ready at all times along with his stash.

This was the problem with addicts. They put a wall up around themselves and dared their nearest and dearest to try to knock it down, sending a clear message that doing so would cause rifts in their relationship. The non-addict, being less reckless and hot-headed, usually wanted to avoid this, so they were forced to sit back and watch the problem grow.

Alex Cleaver knew that he would soon have to talk to his brother about his problem, even though Alex had the occasional line himself and Samuel would certainly use this against him. He could broach the subject lightly, though.

“His fault, eh?” said Alex. “Was it Alley Oop that got you started on that stuff, was it?”

"You what?" said Samuel, turning to face his brother after finishing his line with a delirious snort.

"How is putting that stuff up your nose going to help us deal with the situation in hand?" said Alex.

"Listen," said Sam. "*This stuff* keeps me switched on and alert, okay? *This stuff* tunes me in and turns me on, alright?" Samuel took a cellophane packet of the evil white powder and held it up for his brother to see. He had more to say about it, too.

"This stuff keeps me young, fit and strong, yeah? Vital, effervescent … *This stuff* makes me immo –"

"That stuff," said Alex, "makes you paranoid. It distracts you from what you're supposed to be doing, and if you're not careful, it's going to mean the end of the Cleaver brothers."

It seemed to work, and for a while, both of the brothers fell silent. Alex, who had risen to his feet when he said the bit about breaking up the partnership, sat back down into his leather swivel chair. Sam followed suit and returned to his chair to consider his and his brother's predicament with a cool head, and for the next two minutes, neither of them spoke.

It was Alex who broke the silence. “What do you think’s happened?” he said.

“Alley Oop’s fucked up,” said Sam. He was sure of it, as was his twin brother.

“I think you’re right,” said Alex. “The question is, how badly?”

Alley Oop’s ears weren’t burning as he stared down the barrel of a single-action revolver that he didn’t know had once belonged to the late Ted Maskell. Alley Oop didn’t think he was being talked about right at that very moment, in a dimly lit office above a rather quaint boutique estate agents in West London. If he’d been able to answer Alex Cleaver’s question, the one about how badly he had messed up, then Alley Oop would have had no choice but to tell his boss that the answer was: very badly. He had fucked up very badly indeed. It wasn't all his fault, but his days of working for the Cleavers were over.

There was a question that he was capable of answering now, and if he didn't, then Alley Oop had the feeling that the man who asked it might give him a third eye. Dave Hunter stroked the trigger of the revolver and asked Alley Oop the million-dollar question.

"Where's Danny?"

Alley Oop knew he had to keep schtum since this was his last chance to be the man he'd always wanted to be.

"W-w-why should I t-t-t-tell you an-an-anything?"

"Because I've got this," said Dave as he teased the trigger with the index finger of his right hand. "And *you've* got nothing."

"I don't care," said Alley Oop. "You're r-r-right – I ain't got n-n-n-nuffin'. You might as well do it."

"You're bluffing," said Dave, who hoped this was true.

Sadly, Dave saw a tear welling up in Alley Oop's left eye. And his right eye. Dave Hunter told himself that this was all part of the bluff.

Don't let him fool you, kid ...

"You're bluffing," Dave repeated firmly. "You're a young man with your whole life ahead of you, and you're as scared of dying as I am. Do you think the people you're working for would take a bullet for you?"

Dave knew he couldn't show sympathy, even though he was fast gaining the impression that he was dealing with an abused and misguided individual. To stiffen his resolve, Dave reminded himself that the fat bastard in front of him had brought death and destruction into his peaceful world for a second time and that once had been quite enough.

Alley Oop stayed silent long enough to indicate that the answer was no – neither Alex nor Samuel Cleaver would lay their lives on the line for him. In fact, it was starting to dawn on Alley Oop that they probably wouldn't do much at all for him – especially now that the mission was a disaster, and he'd messed everything up for them. He was as alone now as he'd ever been, and he felt a tear splash on his cheek.

"Stop wasting my time," said Dave, not letting the big man's sobbing affect him. "Where's Danny?!"

Dave didn't have it in him to shoot a simpleton who had fallen in with the wrong crowd. What he did have was the ability to pistol-whip his big ugly head then put the boot in until he confessed. This seemed reasonable to Dave, and he raised his weapon up to do it. Something stopped him at the last moment.

"I'm right here," said a cut-glass voice that could have only belonged to one person.

Chapter 31

"Blimey," said Dave as Danny hobbled through the doorway. "You look like I feel."

Danny ignored Alley Oop and Dave. He walked the short distance to the bar, through the open hatch and poured himself a stiff drink. He put it down in one, poured another, then tottered back and stood next to Dave, his eyes fixed firmly on Alley Oop.

Dave and Danny stood shoulder to shoulder, but Dave felt like he was no longer in the room. He tried to break the ice, but it didn't work.

"Nice to see you too, Danny," Dave said, keeping his eyes and his gun trained on Alley Oop.

Danny let Dave finish talking, but only just.

"Put the gun down and step aside, please," said Danny, addressing Dave but facing Alley Oop. "We've got some unfinished business."

"Not now, Danny."

Dave was back in charge, and Danny wasn't going to break rank and go jaw to jaw with Alley Oop. He gave him a look that seemed to say 'I'll be seeing you later,' and Alley Oop responded by nodding his head as a way of saying 'Not if I see you first.' The stage was set.

Dave ignored these childish antics – he had bigger fish to fry. To complicate matters, he was starting to pity the brainwashed simpleton before him.

"Face it – you're finished," said Dave. "What were you doing getting mixed up with people like th … Who do you work for, by the way? You might as well tell me – I think my friend here will be only too glad to get it out of you."

Alley Oop did something he thought he would never do. He was about to say goodbye to the high life that the Cleavers had promised him.

"Alex and Samuel C-C-Cleaver," he said. "Two b-b-brothers from L-L-London. They've got a f-f-fancy place out west, near Stamford B-B-bridge."

This was news to Dave, if not quite music to his ears. He told Alley Oop to go on.

"That's good. Talk to me."

"They know all ab-b-bout you and how you k-k-killed that gangster a couple of years back. They want your club, and they thought if they made a name f' themselves, then they c-c-could set up 'round 'ere."

He went quiet for a few seconds, and to keep him talking, Dave asked an important question.

"What do I call you, by the way?"

"Alley Oop," said Alley Oop, and Dave and Danny looked at each other in surprise.

Dave heard light footsteps from the other side of the room, but he didn't look to see who it was. Lianda was carrying the one-third full bucket of water from the corridor that led to Dave's office/man cave. Dave was a musician by trade and could recognise the footsteps of people he knew instantly. She walked past them barefooted, not looking up at Dave, Danny or Alley Oop. She went over to Mick and emptied the bucket of water on his head. He came to shivering, shuddering and cursing.

Dave's expertly-tuned ears had shaped his opinion of Alley Oop. He'd wondered if Alley Oop had switched on the waterworks to try to earn his sympathy, and perhaps make Dave let him off the hook. Shamefully, Dave had also suspected that Alley Oop had faked his stammer. But the tremor Dave could hear in Alley Oop's voice was enough to say it all: Alley Oop was a human being – one who was in a great deal of pain.

Dave was so sure of this that he decided to put his theory to the test.

"Something tells me these Cleaver brothers aren't very nice people."

Alley Oop sniffed and nodded his head, and Dave didn't like what he was about to say and do.

"How do you think they're going to react when they find out you botched the job, eh? How do you think they 're gonna take it when you tell them, in person, that you wrecked all their plans?"

"They won't b-b-be happy, chief."

Dave could see it was working.

"Won't be happy? I think that's an understatement, don't you?"

He didn't give Alley Oop a chance to agree or disagree.

"They'll kill you," said Dave. "Or worse."

Alley Oop's face twisted itself into a quizzical expression as if to save his mouth asking what it was that Dave thought was worse than death.

Dave suspected that Alley Oop was somebody who had been lonely for long periods of his life, and who had rarely felt like he belonged. He couldn't have been more right, and his reasoning informed what he said to Alley Oop next.

“You’ll need to go to ground, go into hiding. You’ll need to leave the area immediately, and you’ll always need to be on the lookout.”

Another tear streaked down Alley Oop’s face, but Dave couldn’t let this change anything

“This means you won’t be able to make friends – ever. You won’t be able to let anyone get close. Think about it. Every time you befriend someone, you’ll be putting them in danger. Do you want to live with that?”

Alley Oop shook his head, and more tears dampened his cheeks. He tried to turn his face away from Dave, as though that would make him stop.

“Look at me!” Dave yelled.

Alley Oop did as he was told, and so did Mick, who was still half-dazed from the kick to the head he’d received. Lianda held Mick’s hand in a way that told him everything was going to be alright, and the bad guys were history.

Dave went dizzy from raising his voice after the beating he'd endured at the hands of Spike and had to take a moment to steady himself and curse himself for being so daft. But it got Alley Oop's attention and primed him for what came next.

"Your only hope is to put these Cleaver brothers away for good. You could go to the police if you want. But you'll soon find that money talks loudest in the city. So, take this, " – Dave handed the revolver across to Alley Oop – "and go and find them before they find you. All you need to do is arrange to meet them somewhere dark and put one in each of their heads."

Alley Oop took the gun and slid it under his tracksuit waistband. He didn't say anything for almost a minute, and when he did speak, it was just a half-hearted thank you – half of which seemed to get caught in his throat.

He walked out into the rain, and Danny asked Dave if he'd lost his mind.

“Don’t worry,” said Dave. “He’ll be back in less than a minute.”

Chapter 32

Dave was right about Alley Oop coming back to the light, but he was wrong about how long it would take him. Alley Oop battled against the elements and his conscience for four minutes before coming back to try and put things right.

By the time Alley Oop re-entered the building, Lianda had been to Sam and Earl's kitchen and fetched three steaks, one for each of the men to hold against their bruised faces in an attempt to stop black holes from swallowing up their eyes.

Mick was up and about, and he'd been brought up to speed by Dave as to what had gone down in his absence. Mick was decent again, for while Dave had briefed him on what had happened during his bout of unconsciousness, Lianda had fetched him a Bobby's Bar t-shirt from behind the bar.

The four of them – Danny, Dave, Mick, and Lianda had waited by the doorway. They shivered as cold, damp air blew in from the the rain-slashed car park.

"You've done the right thing," said Dave as the face of the bulky black figure came into focus in the club's subdued lighting. "You're one of us now, understand?"

Alley Oop nodded and gave the revolver back to Dave, who patted Alley Oop on the shoulder to welcome him into the fold.

Mick was confused by Dave's show of generosity; Danny thought he was either on drugs or his head must have copped a hell of a wallop. Lianda was sure of one thing: Dave Hunter was like no other man alive.

"We'd best get upstairs," said Dave. He waved his pistol in the direction of the stairs, and Alley Oop led the way followed closely by Mick and Lianda.

Danny walked beside Dave. He wanted a word with him.

"Good trick, that, giving Alley Oop a gun with an empty chamber, see if he tries to pull a fast one. I like it."

Dave handed the revolver to Danny, who had a surprise when he felt its weight.

"We'd better gather up the other guns," said Danny.

As well as collecting up the discarded shotguns and machine gun that were now scattered across the barroom floor, Dave had to pry Spike's machine gun from her cold-dead fingers, using a bar towel to stop him leaving his fingerprints on it. She had landed on her back when Lianda had fired the lucky shot that had sped up Spik's eternal damnation, and the gun was strapped to her body. There was no time to respect the dead, and especially when, for all he knew, other armed assailants might be on their way.

So Dave gave the ugly instrument of death a yank and pulled the strap out from underneath Spike. Her body convulsed like that of a trauma patient receiving shocks. It occurred to Dave that Spike was a trauma victim and that no amounts of shocks could revive her. He couldn't afford to think like this now, but because he was human, he did so anyway.

The gun he took from her was a horrible thing. Heavy, over three-feet long, with a small bullet-feed clip attached to the chamber and teeth-like ridges in the frame for extra menace. Dave took no joy from handling such a weapon, and it did nothing to boost his male ego.

As the others had gone on ahead, it had occurred to Dave that Lianda was alone with Alley Oop – apart from Mick. As they parted, he had tapped Mick's shoulder, giving Mick a wink and pointing his finger at him advising/warning him to keep an eye on Lianda – and another one on Alley Oop.

Dave suspected he was being overly cautious, but that didn't change the fact that he would feel much better when he was by Lianda's side again.

While Dave recovered the weapons, Danny tied up the last bad guy while simultaneously monitoring the entrance. The sleeping gunman was wearing combat boots, and Danny pulled the laces free and used them to lash his hands together. Then Danny removed the laceless pair of boots, yanked the big man's tracksuit trousers off and tied them around his ankles. Danny was satisfied that if he came to, then this fallen soldier would be going nowhere.

When he'd checked in behind the bar that night, Danny had left a pair of black suede gloves in a space behind the bar, next to some cloths, a tin of Brasso and two cans of Mr. Sheen. Danny reached behind the bar and fetched the gloves, knowing he would most likely handle the confiscated weaponry. Danny made a mental note to remind Dave to give all the weapons a wipe-down before disposing of them.

"Let's go," said Dave to Danny, who was thinking the same thing.

***

Their adventure wasn't over yet, but there was an air of

relief in the living room upstairs when Danny, Mick, Dave, and Lianda – and to a lesser extent Alley Oop – were reunited once more. Lianda threw her arms around Dave as he entered the flat.

It was by the grace of God that Spike had mastered the art of lock-bumping. Both the door from the flat to the stairs and the door from the stairway to the staffroom behind the bar had working locks; for the time being, they were safe there in Dave's flat.

Mick, who had been resting on Dave's couch with a juicy uncooked steak pressed to his face, got to his feet and shook hands with Danny, who congratulated Mick on his performance so far. Alley Oop, who had been sat on the far end of Dave's three-seated couch, just stared blankly at the TV: there was one person whose trust he still had to gain, and he had no idea how he was going to do it.

Adders waited as patiently as he could. He checked his

watch – again – and saw that it was 11:15 pm. Had something gone wrong? Outside, he could hear the wind and rain against the metal roof of the hangar, and he fought the urge to listen in to nature's ominous warning. He lit a cigar and watched the smoke rise in the white light of the bare bulb that hung over his pride and joy.

But he was kidding himself if he thought he could relax at a time like this; he crunched the cigar beneath his feet. As he did so, it occurred to him that he could be losing his famed composure, and, just as he had fought his inclination to treat the biblical downpour outside as a bad omen, he resisted the temptation to do one last cockpit check. Or at least he tried to.

He gave in and decided he would go through his pre-flight checklist once more in case he'd missed something the last three times.

Or at least he thought he would. His mobile was just about to ring, and the waiting would soon be over.

“Adders, it’s Dave.”

All eyes fell on Dave as he talked to Adders and brought him up to speed.

Dave told Adders that they had come under attack from five armed raiders, all of whom they had apprehended and two of whom were now dead. He also told Adders that a sixth representative of the mysterious London firm had turned up. This one had been unarmed, and quickly gave up the ghost and jumped ship to join forces with Dave and co.

Adders asked Dave if he’d ‘lost his ‘effing mind’ welcoming a stranger into the fold like this. Dave explained that Alley Oop had passed an integrity test involving a loaded pistol, and Adders seemed satisfied with that (he even said ‘very good, 007,’ in a voice he’d not had to work too hard to master).

As the conversation went on, Mick, Lianda, Alley Oop, and Danny all listened intently. Not because they were interested in Dave's version of events – they had been players in the game – but because they wanted to hear whatever solution Adders came up with.

The last piece of information that Dave relayed to Adders was that there were five good guys – if Adders was willing to accept Dave's advice that Alley Oop was a good guy. Adders wanted to know if one of them was Dave's lovely lady friend and, catching her gaze from across the room, Dave confirmed that Lianda was there too without actually naming her.

Dave heard Adders say 'listen carefully,' and for the next two minutes, he did just that.

Chapter 33

"Listen carefully," said Dave after he hung up the phone that he'd confiscated/stolen from the late Spike (Danny had shown him how to withhold the number). "Adders is sending a chopper. His son's a coastguard pilot, and he's gonna help us out. Mick, Danny?"

"Yes, chief," said Mick and Danny in unison.

"You'll be going up with him. His name's Reese, and he's alright once he takes the plums out his mouth.

"You two are responsible for getting the bad guys – the dead ones *and* the living ones, that is – aboard the chopper. You need to get them out via the back window since we don't want too many people to see. The bodies will need to be prepped before you load them up."

"Prepped?" asked Mick.

"Yes – Adders said you need to gaffer-tape the guns to their backs," Dave said as he strode the length of the living room with all eyes on him. "All the guns will need to be wiped down then re-smudged with their owner's fingerprints. There's plenty of rubber gloves behind the bar downstairs, so for God's sake use protection. You don't want to meet up with this lot inside, believe me. You might want to wear pinnies an' all."

His audience chuckled, which on a normal day would have seemed like a strange thing to do whilst there was a stack of carbon-length weapons up in the living room, next to the TV, waiting to be disposed of. But this wasn't a normal day.

"Now this is the bit I don't like," said Dave. "Adders says you'll need to cut their arms free before we load them onto the helicopter. As a precaution, feed the ones who aren't dead at least half a pint of Brandy – use that funnel I've got behind the bar for mixing pipe-cleaning fluids. That should keep them comatose. Oh, and once they're ready to go, you can pour yourselves a small one – if there's time," Dave said, giving Mick and Danny a wink.

"Message received and understood," said Danny, while Mick nodded at Dave and got to his feet."

"Lianda – give them your key to the flat."

She handed her copy of the key to Mick, who led the way after Dave passed on one more important message.

"From the moment that helicopter touches the ground, Adders' boy is in charge: you do what he says until he tells you to stand down, okay?"

"Gotcha," said Mick as he opened the door to the flat and headed down the stairs, mentally preparing himself for the grim challenge ahead with Danny right behind him.

Dave turned to Alley Oop.

"I've got a job for you an' all."

"Eh? What k-k-kind of a job."

"We're gonna put these Cleaver brothers out of business – for good."

"Are y-y-you sure, that's a g-g-good idea, ch-ch-chief."

"Have we got a choice?" said Dave.

Alley Oop's silence spoke volumes, and this gave Lianda the chance to ask an important question.

"Dave … What do I get to do in all this?"

She was standing across the room to Dave, and he walked over to her and made sure he was looking her in the eye for what he was about to say. He put out his hands, and she took them in hers. They were soft and warm, but Dave Hunter's blood froze at the thought that this could be the last time their hands touched.

"We're gonna get you somewhere safe. Adders is waiting for you in his plane right now. All you've got to do is get to him. We went there before, remember?"

She nodded and looked down from Dave, and in a way, he was glad they were no longer eye to eye since the last part of the message was by far the worst.

"You've got to go alone. I'm so sorry."

She sniffed, and a lonesome tear slid down her

cheek, followed by one on the other side.

"You can do this, but you've got to be strong. There's no time to waste," Dave said as he broke their hold and patted her right arm, taking care not to make eye contact again as this was no time for long goodbyes.

Reese Addington (or 'Adders junior') of Her Majesty's Coastguard took his usual seat behind his bank of sonar and radar screens that to a layman would resemble the dashboard from the Delorean in *Back the Future*. It was meat and drink to Adders junior, though, and as he sipped cheap coffee from a styrofoam cup, he could tell from just a cursory glance at his dashboard that all was well out there. As it had been five minutes ago, and five minutes before that.

This was his third cup of coffee since Dad made the call about an hour ago, in which Adders senior had suggested that he knew something that would be of interest to Adders junior, and that Adders junior would be flying tonight.

Reese would have preferred it if Adders senior had been more precise about the details of the mission, who, what, where, how and why, etc., but he suspected this was a ploy to keep him on his toes. Was this an off-the-books operation that would require improvisation and more thinking outside the box than the usual capsized dinghy pick-up-and-rescue mission? Probably, Reese decided,

He was neither wrong or right. Yes, his father had hinted that the operation was to be carried out covertly, but the truth was that Dad was almost as in the dark as he was.

But Reese couldn't have been more right to suspect that this had something to do with a young upstart called Dave Hunter. Adders junior didn't approve of Dad's friendship with the musician-turned-publican (via a brief dash of fame as a fighter of crime and a hero of the people), but this wouldn't stop him doing whatever was necessary.

Reese wasn't the only pilot on duty that night, in the

newly-built, state-of-the-art chopper station, near The Cliffs Pavilion, and he wondered if this could lead to problems. The chair next to his was occupied by another coastguard pilot called Phillip Pelfrey. Would he play ball? Reese decided he wouldn't give his colleague a choice in the matter since Pelfrey had recently visited his place of work off-duty. Pelfrey had had a young lady with him, and this piece of crumpet inevitably turned to putty in Pelfrey's hands after he took her up on a private ride in his beloved chopper.

Adders junior decided the cup of coffee he'd just poured would be his last of the night – until Dad's mission was over, anyway. Then his mobile phone rang, and when he checked the screen, he saw the word 'Dad' flashing up.

Time to get this rotor-tailed bird up where she belongs ...

Chapter 34

Dave, Lianda, Mick, Danny, and to a lesser extent, Alley Oop were splitting up so that they might live to enjoy each other's company for a long time yet. Every one of them knew that by avoiding a long goodbye, they stood a better chance of experiencing a reunion at the end of this gruelling ordeal.

Splitting into two groups wasn't much of a problem. Danny and Mick made a start on the bad guys while Dave, Lianda, and Alley Oop prepared to make their way into the night. Dave helped himself to Spike's rucksack, figuring he could use it to see if anyone was waiting for them outside. Her bag was heavy, and Dave knew she hadn't been using it to carry sandwiches.

Dave made for the exit with Ally Oop and Lianda close behind him. Dave reckoned he would see if anyone was behind the glazed doors, but he wasn't taking chances.

He dropped to a crouching position for the last half-dozen steps up to it and tapped one of the remaining glass panes with his knuckles before darting back behind the alcove wall.

Nothing happened. But Dave was open to the idea that someone might be one step ahead of him. Yes, a drug gang hothead may have fired in reaction to this, but a pro – someone like Spike, for example – could be playing the same game he was. So Dave planned to carry out two more safety checks before he – or more importantly, Lianda – went potentially into the line of fire.

"Take this," he said to Alley Oop, who was crouched between him and Lianda on the outwards-facing right-hand side of the alcove, 'this' being Spike's kitbag. "Unlock the door, and throw it outside."

Alley unbolted the door, top first, bottom-half last and, wanting to prove his worth, took the holdall and did as Dave said. Again no shots were fired. Dave was now ninety-five percent sure that the coast was clear, so they were almost ready to go to the next phase of their assault on the Cleaver brothers – almost.

"Go outside and take three steps away from the door," said Dave, and he certainly wasn't talking to Lianda. "When you hear us come up behind you, turn right and walk around to the front of the building."

"What if they open fire?"

"Then you'll die like a hero. Now go," Dave said, prodding Alley Oop in the back with the revolver as he said it.

***

Danny locked the French doors. Then Mick and he moved a dozen tables over to the doorway, piling them up to blockade the entrance. They would be unarmed once they had taped the confiscated firearms to their owners' bodies, and they couldn't risk being taken unawares.

Now Danny and Mick faced the bothersome business

of forcing brandy down the necks of all the bad guys minus the dead ones.

The third intruder lay unconscious on the barroom floor, and Danny took him by the shoulders and dragged him to the centre of the dancefloor. Then, Mick and Danny went back to the man cave and pulled the other two in and lined them up next to their friend. Danny suggested starting with the man they had incapacitated first since it seemed logical that he would come around first.

Danny held the funnel, Mick held the bottle, but it was a disaster. The man who was known as Max Cane to his friends and family regained consciousness when the first drop of brandy touched his tonsils as the result of a gag reflex. With Mick's weight on his chest, Max Cane thrashed around like a crocodile beneath Mick's knees. He refused to take his medicine even with Danny's knees clamping his head still, and Danny eventually gave up and used the butt of one of the discarded shotguns to send him to sleep again.

They had a quick team-talk and decided to abandon the idea of plying their guests with booze. They made another plan.

Danny and Mick roused their victims one at a time using buckets of water before sending them back to the land of slumber the same way Danny did to Max Cane. Brutal but effective.

Satisfied that their guests wouldn't be bothering them again, the next thing Danny and Mick did was give each of the firearms a wipe-down. First, with warm soapy water, then with white vinegar. One by one, the three surviving bad guys had their fingers pressed against the surfaces of a gun each by a rubber glove-wearing Mick.

Like any live music venue in the land, there was a discarded reel of gaffer tape on the stage, and Danny used this to attach the guns to their owners. He looped the adhesive tape six times left-shoulder to right-hip on each man, and six times in the opposite configuration.

Then, aware that time was marching on, Danny sent Mick to get the man he'd nicknamed 'Death'. Two minutes later, Mick wheeled Death out on the chair he was still handcuffed to. Danny, having cuffed Death in the first place, had the key to undo the cuffs. He used it to free Death's arms from their back stack position, and Death's arms flopped downwards. Danny tipped the chair forward, and Death's body left its seat and fell to the floor beside his four chums.

For Mick, now standing at the foot of the five horizontally laid out bad guys – two dead, three unconscious – there was something unsettling about this makeshift mortuary. It was more gothic than grizzly, even though he had no sympathy for any of the people at his feet. He was relieved that Death had fallen face-first, for he had observed his haunted facial expression twice tonight, and that was more than enough.

"Right," said Danny. "Cut their hands free."

Danny took out a pair of scissors seemingly from nowhere and gave them to Mick. Mick got to work hacking through the lengths of shoelaces that the three living men's hands were tied with. They were catering scissors with four-inch stainless steel blades, and Mick guessed Danny had nipped to the kitchen while he had gone to fetch the man that they knew as Death.

After three minutes of hacking, all of the prisoners' hands were free, and they were ready to be transported.

With the first phase of their task completed, Danny experienced a diabolical thirst and remembered Dave's final instruction.

"Get me a brandy, eh?" said Danny.

Mick went to the bar to fetch the tipple (Max Cane hadn't been given the good stuff). He'd noticed that Danny had been hobbling and trying to put as little weight as possible on either of his feet, and while he poured the brandy, Mick made a mental note of his sensei's injuries and vowed to come down hard on his weak-spot at their next training session.

Mick took Danny's drink over to him, sure that this sympathetic gesture would lull Danny into a false sense of security next time they sparred. They clinked their glasses, but before they could sip their alcoholic rewards, both men heard a low rumble to their west: their taxi was here, and playtime was over.

"Let's go," said Danny, before downing his shot and tossing the glass over his shoulder.

Chapter 35

Adders junior didn't mess about when his father's call came through. Directly his father outlined the predicament facing his friend, Dave Hunter – it was him after all – Adders junior told his colleague Phillip Pelfrey that they had a job to do, and both men began the familiar routine.

Their Sikorsky S-92 was, in fact, one of two of the same models, and this one had had all necessary checks and adjustments carried out before it was flown from its permanent base at the local airport earlier that day. Reese and Phillip Pelfrey knew this because they had prepared this chopper for flight themselves before they brought it here at the start of their shift. Several passers-by had watched the changing of the guards, where one S-92 was flown away from the rooftop helipad and relieved of its duty, and this doppelganger took up the new position. And, while Adders and Phillip Pelfrey had enjoyed putting on a show for the public then, now they both hoped nobody would see since this mission was strictly off the books: it never happened.

Indeed Adders junior wondered if it would have made more sense to have somebody (Dave's missus, perhaps?) make a phony distress call to the local coastguard watch desk. They were chancing it big time by flying off on their own personal errand, and Adders junior knew that if anything went wrong, then his – and Pelfrey's – heads would roll.

Adders got out of his chair hastily, and this was enough to catch Pelfrey's attention and let him know something was up. Then Adders junior pointed upwards and then spun his right index finger in a lasso motion. "A friend of mine's in trouble," was all Adders needed to say for now, and both men darted into the prefab lighthouse that was the core of their state of the art facility.

Anyone who has worked in the emergency services knows the unwritten rule. Those precious few seconds before you step into the breach are where men take a deep breath and obtain a level of focus that accountants and estate agents simply can't access. Adders junior knew that this would help him now since as long as he and Pelfrey were observing the two-second rule, there was no chance Pelfrey could bother him with questions along the lines of 'how,' and 'why'.

Exactly two seconds later, they emerged from the lighthouse onto the second floor. With their footsteps still echoing inside the tower, both men became aware of the sterile smell of the locker room and changing area. Both men also felt a chill, as the temperature was significantly lower in this glass-fronted section of the building. Pelfrey headed for his locker but was stopped in his tracks by Reese Addington. "No need," said Adders junior.

Nothing more was said. There was no need for any radios since they wouldn't need to talk to ground at any time, so there was no need for the helmet that Pelfrey was about to retrieve from his locker. One of the functions of the hard plastic orange helmets these two wore to work was to support their radio mouthpieces. The other was to protect pilots' heads, and Adders junior and Pelfrey had agreed some time ago that, if one of these birds went down, then protecting yourself from a minor concussion was frankly small beer.

Speaking of birds going down, it occurred to Adders junior that he may not have to remind Pelfrey that Pelfrey himself had recently used their helicopter to woo a young lady. Adders junior guessed this could be because it had been a quiet summer. Apart from a few misadventures, one of which rather amusingly involved a skinny-dipping couple (the lads remembered the two suicide attempts less fondly), the two pilots and their beloved seven-ton bird had spent most of the season grounded.

"We may as well go as we are," said Adders junior, meaning that as well as skipping their radio equipment and leaving their protective headgear behind, they may as well leave their high-vis jackets and their insulating rubber bodysuits behind as well. “At least this will be over nice and quickly,” he said.

Adders was in the lead – in effect, it was his mission – and he made his way first onto the rooftop walkway, then up the outside ladder to the roof, taking care not to let his feet slip on the slick metal steps. His body temperature dropped as he was lashed by wind and rain.

As well as the two-second silence rule that all quick responders adhere to, there was another unwritten rule that men like Adders and Pelfrey followed religiously that related to rank. Her Majesty’s Coastguard was a rank-structured organisation, and Adders junior and Phillip Pelfrey wore the same stripes. But in some instances – this one, for example – somebody had to take charge, and it usually came down to who received the call. Adders junior had taken the call, and so he was in charge of the mission. “Get in the back and prepare three parachutes,” he said to

Pelfrey, who did as he was told.

Alley Oop didn't waste time in carrying out Dave's instructions. He pulled the door open and took three steps out into the dark, rainy night. He barely seemed to notice the rain splashing on his face, which may have been to do with the fact that he was a tough cookie. Most likely, though, it was because he was concerned about being shot. As far as he knew, there were four other people in the job – five if Alley Oop included the mysterious nameless chap he'd had spoken to on the phone a few weeks back and who he assumed must have met an unfortunate end.

Alley Oop's fears of being gunned down didn't materialise. He stood still in what could have been a fifth sniper's line of sight for five seconds before deciding he was safe. He turned and walked along the west face of the building then around to the front, street-facing portion of the building.

Dave and Lianda couldn't see this from their position, still inside the building, crouching by the exit, but they decided as though by telepathy that it was time for them to move. Dave took Lianda's hand and led the way …

A part of him didn't believe he made it out in one piece. It had occurred to him that Alley Oop may have tricked them and somehow managed to get a signal to another gunman waiting outside. He decided that if that were the case, then he'd be ribbons by now: he must be safe. This didn't stop him feeling massively exposed as he and Lianda walked around to the front of the building. They wouldn't gun him down in full view of the street, would they? On a Saturday night and in full public view?

They made it, and they saw the blob-like silhouette of Alley Oop standing under a streetlight, kicking the curb and looking a bit bored. Alley Oop was standing beside a 1995 Mini that, thanks to the rain, was getting its first wash in quite some time. This was Lianda's car.

Dave used his left-hand to tap Alley's shoulder to congratulate his good work. Then he let go of Lianda's hand.

"Well? Off you go, then," he said.

Even though Lianda already had her car key at the ready, swishing away with five other keys and a small monkey toy, she expected a bit more of a farewell than this. But she was wrong, and Dave turned away from her and started briefing Alley Oop on the next stage of his plan

Dejected but resolute, Lianda walked out into the road and around to the driver's side of her car. She started the engine, put on the lights, and made a u-turn in the road before beginning the short drive to the airport. She didn't wave as she passed the two men, one of whom she loved.

"Right," said Dave. "Where's your motor?

Alley Oop told him it was outside Danny's flat, and the two crossed the road to begin the five-minute walk up the hill towards Danny's flat on nearby Charlbury Crescent.

The first minute passed without either man speaking a word and, Alley Oop, having been taught to know his place over the years, let Dave decide when it was time to talk again.

“These Cleaver brothers,” said Dave. “They sound like a right pair of cunts.”

For the time it took them to walk past the first forty doors of Royal Terrace, Alley Oop mumbled through his rather sad life story. As Dave had expected, it featured childhood abandonment, orphanages, bullying in borstal, police harassment, and brutality as well as periods of sleeping underneath railway bridges. Fighting featured heavily, and though Dave was able to turn down the violins in his head that usually arrived to accompany hard-luck tales such as these, he did find he could sympathise with this somewhat gentle giant.

It occurred to Dave that a key theme in Alley Oop’s ramblings was one of loneliness and a sense of wanting to belong. Which is where the Cleavers came into the story.

"They gave me my f-f-first line of c-c-c-cocaine," said Alley Oop as his voice cracked, a sound that Dave noted was becoming quite familiar.

They left Royal Terrace and started along Oxford Drive.

"D-d-don't g-g-get me wrong, D-D-Dave. They're not all b-bad. It's just they …"

Alley Oop stopped partly because he'd run out of things to say but mainly because he saw how foolish he'd been for this time.

"I ain't g-g-got nobody or nuffin'," he said, still walking at a brisk enough pace to match Dave's but eyeing the cobbled street as he went. "Just tell me one thing," said Dave. "Who came up with the name Alley Oop?"

"Oh, that was an old f-f-friend of mine who ran a gym I used to train at. D-D Donald – that was his name. D-D-Donny took me in when I had nowhere to go. He taught me to fight, 'ow t' look afta' meself. I think he might live r-r-ound here, as it goes."

Chapter 36

Tall, athletically slim Reese Addington slid into position in the cockpit of his beloved SA-92 helicopter. As he reached down and flicked the switch to power up the big old bird, he got the same thrill that he usually did from seeing more than a dozen electronic display panels light up the gloom of the cockpit. The needles on seven different gauges jumped into the red before settling down to give steadier, more accurate readings, and Adders junior took a deep breath: it was time to get in the zone.

Better than seeing the chopper's electrics spark into life was hearing the whir of the rotors that would soon build into a full-blooded war cry. How Reese loved this, and the thrill was given an extra tinge by the knowledge that he was chartering a flight illicitly.

Behind him, in the passenger cabin, Phillip Pelfrey was preparing the blimps that would soon be seen descending from the Essex skyline. Pelfrey reached into his overhead compartment and pulled down three weighty rucksack-like containers. Then he paused for thought or would've done had the answer not come to him from the cockpit and the horse's mouth.

"Half-pull them, please, Phillip."

The first thing Pelfrey did was pull the drogue – a rubber ball a bit like the base of a shuttlecock – from the bottom of one of the holdalls. This released the overhead mini-chute, which was connected to the bridle – the next part in the chain. Pelfrey knew what was going on here: the chutes were not going to be used by willing participants.

Ah well ...

Undeterred and like a young Peter Davison delivering a calf, Pelfrey reached into the container and pulled out the ten-foot maze of nylon webbing that connected the mini-chute to its larger cousin.

This one was ready now, Pelfrey thought. He knew that he had primed the chute enough to catch the upward rush of air on the way down to trigger a full deployment and allow a safe landing for whoever who was strapped into it.

Pelfrey was clueless as to who the chutes were for, but it didn't bother him. If anything, this need-to-know basis on which he was being asked to act added to the fun. It had been a slow summer for him as well as Adders junior, who now looked on in wonder as the Southend coastline fell away beneath him.

Adders took his rotor-tailed beast up to five-hundred feet, and for a few seconds, she hovered directly above her base. Satisfied this was as far up as she needed to be, Adders prepared to make the transition from vertical climb to forwards flight. He and Pelfrey both counter-leaned instinctively as their chopper tipped forwards at a ten-degree angle before Adders tilted the cyclic stick gently forwards. They tore along the coastline.

As the crow flies, it was less than a mile to Dave Hunter's place, which would be their first port of call. For this reason, Adders flew at nothing like the top speed that his Sikorsky was capable of as well as not taking her anywhere close to maximum altitude. This still gave Adders a thrill since he knew he could switch on the hover-position beam and see a gulf in the swell of the sea below, like a big bad Moses of the sky.

Adders junior may not have flown at full speed, but he set the SA-92's white strobes to maximum to cut through the heavy rain and the southerly fog that was rolling across the estuary from the direction of Kent. With these babies set to full power (equivalent to eight thousand candles each), it could have been daylight out there.

It was only thirty seconds before the brick-shaped flat roof of Dave Hunter's American-style bar and grill reared into view. At the precise moment that Reese Addington realised he was close enough to read the painted sign bearing the name of the establishment, an unpleasant thought entered his head and the feeling of invincibility that usually came from being in charge of an airborne vessel all but disappeared.

Dave Hunter had messed with people that you shouldn't mess with (again), and Reese knew that hardened criminals sometimes used guns to make their point. If they fired at his rotors, it would be game over. He decided it was time to bring her down – hopefully, before someone else did.

Dave had impressed himself by not showing his surprise after the revelation a few minutes ago that Alley Oop had known his father, the late Don Hunter. In the little time that Dave had had to think about it, it all made sense. His parents had lived apart for some time in the early 90s, and Don Hunter had moved back to the East End while his relationship with Dave's mother had become strained enough for them to live apart for two years on a semi-casual on-and-off basis.

Not that this was enough to convince Dave of Alley Oop's claims to have been taken in and mentored by the late Don Hunter. What made Alley Oop's claims believable was that his stories brought Dave's memories of his dad back to life since they rang so very true.

It would be like Dad, Dave thought, to pity the underdog. So too would it have been like Don Hunter to use tough love to help someone who'd had a bad break to stand on their own two feet, stick up for themselves, and empower them to move on.

Dave had gone jaw to jaw with Alley Oop the first time they'd met, about three weeks ago. Dave had been on the receiving end of some hammer-blows that night, and this was all the proof he needed that Alley Oop had indeed been trained by the late Don Hunter, the best there ever was and the epitome of the old-school cockney sparrer.

"There she is," said Alley Oop, pointing across the street to the old Ford with the grimy paintwork that he'd half-inched earlier.

“Go start her up,” said Dave. “I’m gonna make sure we haven’t been followed.”

Alley Oop crossed the road to carry out Dave’s instruction, while Dave waited on the spot, avoiding the glow of a nearby street light.

Dave had put a denim jacket on before leaving the club. To the untrained eye, it could have looked like he was hugging himself to keep warm and keep his hands out of the cold night air. But he was concealing two pistols.

Dave heard the ‘93-plated Ford sputter to life, with a cough from the exhaust and a wiggle of the rear suspension. Alley Oop performed a U-turn in the illegally sourced vehicle and stopped for Dave to get in.

“I guess it’s b-back to HQ for m-m-me, then?” said Alley Oop.

“Almost,” said Dave. “We’ve got one more thing to do before we can hit the road.”

Chapter 37

Dave and Alley Oop both knew they were risking it by going back to the club like this. Not as much as they would be when they came to execute the plan that Dave explained while Alley Oop drove them there, but it was risky nonetheless. Alley Oop parked the stolen Ford Escort outside the club, in roughly the same place where the group had split up minutes earlier as Lianda had made her way to the airport. With the engine still running, the two talked briefly.

"Right," said Dave. "You know what to do, right?"

"Yes, ch-ch … Chief," said Alley Oop, grateful for his second chance but still fearing the worst.

"There's one more thing," said Dave. "You're gonna need this."

Dave passed the revolver across to Alley Oop, who took it reluctantly.

"I d-d-d-don't l-l-like those f-f-fings," he said.

“Me neither,” said Dave. “And if this goes to plan, we’ll never see one again.”

Half-way through this sentence, Alley Oop’s brow became unfurrowed, and the corners of his mouth turned upwards, and Dave could tell this was in response to his use of the word ‘we’.

“See you in Chelsea,” said Dave. “You can do this.”

Dave patted his new friend on the shoulder and got out of the car. His motorbike – his beloved Kawasaki hyperbike, no less – was parked about six spaces back, and for what good it might do, he hunched down as he moved towards it in an attempt to use the stationary vehicles he passed for cover.

He arrived in one piece and straddled his greasy machine. As he lined up the three sixes on his helmet lock and prepared to lead the way, something caught his attention: a bass-heavy rumble accompanied by a high-pitched whistle at about the same volume.

Run ... Get to the chopper!

Thank God, Dave thought, and as he started his engine, something profound crossed his mind: just as his late father had taken Alley Oop in and given him a chance to prove himself, he – Dave – like father like son – had done the same thing.

"No fool like an old fool," he muttered as he swung out onto the esplanade.

Mick dragged each of the five bodies up to the opened window, leaving them dangling half in and half out across the bottom pane. Danny – who had already climbed through the eight-foot sash window– dragged each of the bodies the rest of the way and left them splayed across a German-style beer table.

By the time Danny and Mick had removed each of the bodies from inside the club, their helicopter had found its position above the sea-facing beer garden and was preparing to land. Danny looked awestruck at the big-winged beast of the sky and put one hand over his head to hold his beloved Tommy Cooper fez down. Mick put his hand up to shield his eyes as the helicopter's front and rear lights seemed to flip downwards whilst Adders junior prepared to take her down.

Flanked by luminous sheets of rain, Mick and Danny watched the Sikorsky land, their heads gradually tipping from 170 degrees and back to their normal angle. The chopper landed 50 feet in front of them, and after her front and rear end levelled out, the side door slid backwards, and a young man jumped out.

He jogged the short distance between them, not attempting to shield his face from the cold downpour or the disc-shaped sheet of spray caused by the rain against the rotor blades.

"You're Danny, right?" he said, holding out his hand.

"The very same," said Danny, accepting the offer of a handshake. "This is Mick – don't shake his hand. There's no time."

"Right," said the man whose name Danny and Mick neither knew nor wanted to know.

"Reese told me everything," Pelfrey said. You've got five bodies – two dead, three subdued, shall we say," said Pelfrey, eyeing the prize.

"That's right," said Danny, ignoring the possibility that one or more of the others may have died thanks to the treatment they'd received in captivity.

"We're gonna take care of the dead ones first," said Pelfrey. "That means they go on last. Let's get to work, men."

They got to work. Danny, Mick, and Pelfrey took a snoozing bad guy each, following the lead of Danny, who hooked his arms around the shoulders of one of them and dragged him over to the resting chopper. He hopped aboard while Mick and Pelfrey fed the motionless bodies to him one by one, and he dragged them across to the far side of the cabin. Then Mick and Pelfrey brought the bodies of the two dead guys over, and Danny dragged them up one at a time and dumped them on top of their former colleagues. Pelfrey leaned into the cabin, his hands held either side of his face like a megaphone to compete with the roar of the twin-engine and the whirring of the blades, and gave Danny one last instruction.

"You're going in the cockpit with Reese," he said, before pointing at Mick and saying, "he's gonna help me out back."

Danny did what he was told, for he knew that there no time to waste.

Seeing the sea rescue helicopter tearing along the estuary, getting ready to swoop down behind the club and save the day had lifted Dave's spirits a little. His heart would have soared, however, if he had heard the sputter of Adders senior's Cessna, and been able to look up to see it criss-cross the flight path of his son, Reese Addington before heading towards the horizon. This way, Dave would know that Lianda was safe, and he could concentrate on nailing these small-time Cleaver brothers without having to worry about whether or not she had made it to the airport in one piece.

Before visions of her mangled car being found by members of the local constabulary entered his head, Dave realised he couldn't think like this. He shouldn't be out on a bike in weather like this, with the rain falling hard and the wind building steadily, but he couldn't afford to overthink that either.

After a mile, he and Alley Oop turned right and begun an uphill climb heading inland. The rainfall here became less of a problem, even though a stream of excess water followed the path of least resistance and headed downwards in the opposite direction.

They travelled another mile north before they joined the westbound A127, which Dave knew would soon take them past Basildon and on towards Grays, Thurrock. Grays, Thurrock was the home of the infamous Seawall Inn, where Dave, along with Mick Davies, suffered one of the worst beatings of his career after trying to take on three-generations of at least one Irish traveller family.

Preferring not to remember that now, Dave did some thinking. They were taking a straight route. After grazing the outskirts of Thurrock, they would pick up the A13 and follow all the signs for Central London. After about an hour in which his overhead view would become a continuous blur of sodium lights, and his side views a mix of orange streetlight and no-name fast food joints, they would approach the splendour of Chelsea and Kensington.

He'd hoped Lianda would have called by then or at least sent him a text message. But there was no guarantee of this happening, so for now, he would just have to put faith in the idea that whoever or whatever had helped him just when he'd needed it before would come through for him one more time and would extend the hand of friendship to Lianda too.

He told himself – and almost managed to believe it – that this was superstitious mumbo jumbo, and that he was tired and freaked out by the night's events. Instead, he turned his head to more practical considerations – like the distance he still had to travel.

Dave figured he could be in Kensington in about an hour and twenty minutes. On his Ninja, he could cane it and be there in less than half that time, of course, but there would be no point. For his plan to work – a good deal of which he'd explained to Alley Oop in the stolen car, not long ago – he'd need Alley's help. There was also the fact that he couldn't risk attracting the attention of the law when both he and Alley Oop were carrying guns: that could really mess up his plans.

So Dave travelled at about half of his ideal speed in an emergency. He and Alley weren't travelling nose-to-tail, but they weren't far from it, and Dave could see maybe three feet of slick black tarmac between him and Alley Oop's rear tyres.

Chapter 38

Danny strapped himself in next to Adders junior, the pilot and therefore the man in charge of the mission. They wasted little time on small talk, and neither did Pelfrey and Mick Davies, who took their seats opposite one another in the passenger cabin. With five bodies, bloodied, and in various states of disrepair, the scene in the back of the chopper reminded Mick of the Vietnam war movies he'd watched as a kid. There was a subtle difference, of course. The pilots and army medics who took part in these missions had the best interests of the downed soldiers on board at heart – you couldn't say that about this lot.

Adders junior took the SA-92 up to two-thousand feet – twice the altitude that he and Pelfrey had flown in at – and swung her nose in the direction of the sea. As the helicopter pitched forward towards the estuary inlet, Adders junior decided to bring Danny up to speed. As if he needed to.

"This baby can travel five-hundred miles on a full tank – give or take a bit," said Adders junior. "That's more than enough to get us out over the channel."

"We're not gonna drop them over France, are we?" said Danny.

"Not quite," said Adders junior. "Not quite."

There was a momentary pause while Adders finalised the plans in his mind.

"Since we're going to give them a sea burial – well, the dead ones, anyway – it seems appropriate that we do it outside of national waters. You know … Tradition and all that!"

Danny, who already imagined that Death and his rather un-ladylike mistress were on their way to a watery grave, grinned at what Adders junior had just told him.

"And what about the other three? You know they're still alive, right?"

"Yeap," said Adders junior, who had been over the

situation before Danny and Mick came aboard. "I've thought about what we can do with them, too."

"Go on," said Danny.

"I think the answer may be closer to home."

***

In the passenger compartment of the chopper, Mick Davies and Phillip Pelfrey were likewise making plans.

"It's simple. We're gonna chuck the duds over the side. We'll know when Reese is ready. He'll get the speed right down until we're basically prepared to tread air, then we'll open the hatch and… SPLASH!"

Mick didn't know what to say, so Pelfrey picked up where he had just left off.

"It'll be goodnight from him … And goodnight from him," said Pelfrey nodding in the direction of the lifeless bodies that lined the wet, corrugated metal floor of the cabin.

Mick, not wanting to seem like a country boy who

thought Lexden and Stanway was the edge of the world, didn't know what to say, so he kept quiet. Until his curiosity got the better him.

"What about the other three?" he said.

"Well, we're gonna suffocate them all first – best way to avoid a messy death, I say. Then, we're gonna cut off their fingertips, smash their teeth out with the hammer we'd normally use to open the glass fire extinguisher cabinet before we bury them in the woods somewhere."

As these words left his lips, the body of the lady with HATE tattooed on both her knuckles convulsed as rigor mortis began to set in: she seemed to wriggle on the spot for a time, and Mick would have jumped out had the cabin door been open. Pelfrey laughed, and Mick didn't.

On into the night, Dave's journey continued as his new sidekick led the way. As well as the bigger towns you saw when you ventured north-west from Southend – Basildon,

Rayleigh, Benfleet, etc., – Dave saw a host of strange yet familiar village and small town names on roadside postings as he went by them. Fobbing, Horndon-on-the-Hill, Orsett … In Dave's mind, the people of small English settlements such as these lived in permanent darkness, such was the mind's eye's habit of giving gothic qualities to places you only passed at night.

The A30 rushed by and became the A13, and Dave and Alley Oop left North Stifford for dust and crossed the M25, leaving Essex and/or civilisation behind. Thanks to the relatively low speed they were doing, Dave could hear all manner of unearthly sounds from the road below the motorway bridge that connected the two toughest places in England (Essex having a slight lead, natch). He heard tyres screech and engines roar, as well as the occasional cry of brakes and the odd car horn echoing along the slick carriageway beneath him.

After a few more miles, they were past Purfleet and

in London's glorious East End, and though they kept to the same road, the view was different over there. You got the odd former Victorian workhouse, now converted into swanky city pads, but for the most part, it was an unbroken stream of fast-food outlets, taxi firms, tower blocks, bookmakers, and sadly, Dave thought, not an awful lot of traditional East End boozers. The miles clocked up, and the districts and boroughs flew by. Dagenham and Barking, Romford and Ilford, and Aveley and Rainham came and went quickly.

Dave knew he had to put Lianda out of his mind for the good of them both. He was doing a remarkable job of this too – until they passed City Airport. Dave saw a red tail-light blinking and hoped and prayed she'd made it to Southend Airport and that Adders had taken her somewhere far away from the bloody mess they were in.

Eventually, the ratio of fast food establishments to residential properties evened out. As if by magic, this happened just as the balance between grimy terraced homes and agreeable new-build properties marketed at young professionals tipped in favour of the latter. Dave started to miss the East End instantly, or would have done had this change of scenery not served to notify him that he and Alley Oop were getting closer to the Cleaver brothers.

When the A13 became the A1203, it occurred to Dave that they were virtually knocking on the door of the Cleaver's office.

Less than an hour and twenty minutes after they left Southend, Dave and Alley Oop found themselves passing the Royal Albert Hall, and even though Dave knew this was no time for distractions, his inner child got the better of him, and he took an awestruck peek at this rather grand old shrine. One day, son, one day.

Then the two men were driving along the bottom edge of Hyde Park – Kensington High Street. If Alley Oop's description was even half accurate, then they were less than a mile from Cleaver HQ. Yet they passed the quaint boutique estate agency that masked the running of the Cleaver's empire and drove and rode another mile before stopping in a loading bay. Dave smiled underneath his helmet as he pulled up beside Alley Oop.

Still straddling his bike, Dave leaned down next to the driver's side window, and Alley Oop wound his window down.

"Do you want to go over it one more time?" said Dave.

Chapter 39

Adders turned his chopper around and pointed her towards Calais. As the crow flies, it would be half-an-hour until they saw the eerie glow of portlights flickering in the distance, and though this seemed like a long time, two of them – Mick Davies and Phillip Pelfrey – had work to do.

"We'd better get these three strapped in," said Pelfrey. "They'll be coming around soon, and I reckon we'll have an easier time fixing the chutes on with them like this," he said to Mick.

"You got it, boss," said Mick, and the two of them got to work.

Pelfrey scooped the first sleeping bad guy up from the floor of the cabin and dumped him face down on the rear seat, knees on the floor, arms slack by his side. The sandy-haired villain – real name Max Cane – could have been a medieval thief, captured and put in the stocks awaiting jeers and pelting from incensed villagers. But a spot of public humiliation would have been kinder than the punishment that Mick and Phillip Pelfrey were planning.

Mick did the same thing with the other two retired criminals. He scooped them up and set them down next to their friend. All three of them were in a row ready for Pelfrey, who set about getting the first one into a parachute.

Mick watched as Pelfrey put Max Cane's limp left arm under the left shoulder strap of the semi-deployed chute and the right arm under the other. Mick docked himself a point for not bringing the improvised hand restraints that he and Danny had not long ago removed, but it hardly mattered; Pelfrey whipped his tie off and lashed Max Cane's hands together. Max Cane was compliant, what with him being unconscious, but his hands flopped around nonetheless.

Pelfrey soon had him secured, though; he wouldn't break free, and there was no danger of his parachute coming off in mid-fall either.

Mick and Pelfrey gave the other baddies their chutes and secured their hands. The second part of this, lashing their hands together, wasn't a problem. Mick, noticing that the sleeping bad guys looked like naughty schoolboys waiting for six of the best, took off his belt and fixed Paul Walsall's together hands together securely. Pelfrey did the same thing with Karim Haswell, before telling Mick to stand down for a moment.

Mick sat down on the empty front seat, relieved to finally take a breather. He looked out his window and saw that they were approaching the sea.

"I knew this would happen," said Samuel Cleaver, pacing the office that overlooked Kensington High Street. "That silly cunt Alley Oop has fucked up."

"Will you pack that in," said Alex while trying not to believe what his brother was saying.

"Will I pack *what* in?" said Sam, turning to face his

brother and stopping in his tracks.

"Pacing up and down like that – you're winding us both up. And stop being so gloomy, would you? This isn't over yet."

Sam ignored his twin brother's second request and focused on the first, perhaps sensing where this was going.

"It's just *him*," said Samuel. "Alley Oop – he gives me the edge."

"And working with Alley Oop is the only thing that does this to you, right?"

"Fuck off," said Sam, turning away from his brother, who sometimes forgot they were equal partners.

"You're upset about something," said Alex. "You've visited the lavatory four times in the last –"

Alex looked down at his watch …

"– hour and twenty minutes. So yes. I can tell you're nervous."

Samuel ignored – or was too strung out on cocaine to

notice – his brother's sarcasm. Instead, he peered out the window, impatiently scanning the street for vehicles slowing down near the entrance to their premises.

"If he's fucked up …"

"Let me guess," said Alex.

"I'm gonna give him a third eye in that big, empty head of his."

"Yes, I can see how that would solve all our problems. Very good. Have another line of coke. On second thoughts …"

This time the sarcasm didn't go over Samuel Cleaver's head despite the dangerous amount of class A substance whizzing around his system. He spun around and drew his beloved .44 magnum and caught his brother's gaze.

Sam didn't point the weapon at his brother, but Alex still didn't like his brother taking it out at times of anger – or when he was high as a kite.

"Put that away, please," said Alex.

Samuel did as he was told.

Without knowing it, Alex had taken to reacting to his brother's acting like a child by talking to him like one. The tactic worked this time, but this didn't stop Alex wondering if this would always be the case; his brother's behaviour was becoming a problem.

Feeling scolded, Samuel slid his gun back into the holster. Then he turned and faced the dark empty street, wondering if he'd overstepped the mark.

After two minutes of awkward silence, Sam's mobile rang, and he got it out from his jacket faster than he'd just drawn his gun. Rather than answering it straight away, he read the number of the person calling.

"It's him," he said.

***

About one minute after he hung up on Alley Oop, Sam Cleaver saw a car slow to a halt in the street outside. He put his phone back in its case and made for the stairs with his brother not far behind him.

Samuel Cleaver led the way out into the street, but he and Alex stood side-to-side to greet the returning Alley Oop. Alley Oop got out from the car and wandered over to meet the two brothers, and neither of them failed to notice he had a smile and a spring in his step: the boy did good at last.

"I g-g-got him … Right here in the boot. Like I said … He d-d-done a runner … But I cawt 'im in the end. I said I wouldn't mess up, didn't I?"

He gave Alex the keys, and the two brothers shared a look of pleasant surprise.

Samuel stood back to let Alex open the boot and greet their other guest. Alex turned the key and lifted the boot hatch to find an out-cold Dave Hunter in the boot of the Ford Escort, curled up and facing downwards. Sam stepped forward to the lip of the boot and crouched down to look in as well, and he would have congratulated Alley Oop on his good work, but for one thing: Dave Hunter's hands weren't tied. His left hand was over his head as if he'd attempted to shield one of the blows that had put him where he was now.

His right arm was underneath his body and, therefore, out of sight.

Just as Samuel began to smell a rat, their captive woke from his pretend slumber.

"Boo!" he said as he rolled onto his right-hand side, and drew the semi-automatic pistol he'd had in his other hand the whole time and pointed it at the space between Alex Cleaver's nose.

Alex froze, but Samuel retreated two steps back when Dave Hunter sprung to life. This gave Sam the chance he needed; he drew his .44 from the holster beneath his long leather jacket, smoothly rather than quickly, and went to aim it at Dave Hunter, an easy target in the boot of a car. But it didn't work out for him …

Before Sam could take aim at Dave, Alley Oop drew

a gun. Alley was a step ahead of him, tickling his ear with the revolver that Dave gave him back in Southend. "Drop it you cunt," said Alley Oop firmly.

Samuel Cleaver dropped his gun, hoping it would discharge a round when it hit the floor. He'd been outsmarted by Alley Oop, and he was prepared to risk shooting himself in the foot to get revenge.

It didn't come to pass, and no shots rang out in the Kensington night.

Alley Oop decided it was time to take revenge for all the cruel pranks the brothers had played on him, including the phony trust-building exercise that had nearly broken his back. Dave had told Alley Oop they would need to subdue the two brothers as they prepared them for the final stage of their revenge, so Alley did what he did next with a clear conscience.

BANG! He struck Sam Cleaver's head with the butt of the revolver that had belonged to the late Ted Maskell;

Samuel Cleaver tumbled like a house of cards as did Alex Cleaver when Alley Oop gave him the same treatment.

"Good work," said Dave as he climbed from the back of the vehicle and treated his back to a little stretch. "Good work."

Alley Oop noticed Dave was smiling – something he hadn't seen much in his life – and he went to give his new best mate a hug.

Dave accepted the gesture, but only briefly: there was work to do, and this was the kind of place where the sight of guns and people bundling people into car boots would most likely raise a few eyebrows.

"Let's load up and be lively about it."

Chapter 40

Mick knew this wasn't a sightseeing expedition, but it hadn't stopped him from gazing at Canterbury Cathedral out of his side of the cabin not long after he and Pelfrey finished attaching parachutes to the three bad guys. He'd been there on a school trip many years ago and been semi-impressed by the attention to detail structurally and aesthetically. But it was a thing of gothic wonder when it decorated the night skyline below, its outline framed by the modern miracle of light pollution.

As they'd passed over it, Mick had wondered if one of those spooky old spires might catch them and bring them down, but they hadn't. Instead, they'd got on with their business of grazing the sky and watching over the city. All was well.

They'd soon left the Kent coastline behind and started crossing the English channel.

Mick and Pelfrey had sat in silence for fifteen

minutes now. For Mick, boredom was lurking. Then he noticed that the portlights on the French side of the channel were shining brighter than the ones back home.

“Any moment now,” said Pelfrey, who noticed their speed and altitude coming down before Mick.

Now they were hovering at 5,000 feet. It was still noisy in the cabin, but nothing like it had been a moment ago travelling at full speed. Before Adders junior brought her to a virtual stop barely a mile west of Calais, Pelfrey reached down and dragged the male corpse – Death – up from the cabin floor. Pelfrey left the body in a floor-seating position, his back against the sliding cabin door. Then, with both hands on an overhead handrail, he kicked the release bar.

The door slid open and shot sideways-backward as if it had fallen off or suddenly ceased to be. ‘Death’ likewise disappeared in an instant; he rocketed out of the cabin and somersaulted his way down to the crashing sea below.

With him taken care of, Pelfrey decided it was time for the other one to go to the great gig in the sea.

"We're gonna change direction any second," said Pelfrey, raising his voice to compete with the noisy rotors and the whistle of the cold sea wind. "Lay across the other three, and I'm gonna lay across you. No funny business, yeah?"

Mick did what he was told, having silently mouthed the most offensive word in the English language. The three paratroopers were face down and heavily bound, and Mick didn't have to worry that one of them might regain consciousness and try to chew his face off, but he still covered his face with his forearms. Pelfrey lay with his back to the scrum of bodies beneath him, pushing both hands against the overhead handrail to secure all five of them in place.

At first, Adders junior counter-banked left, tipping the heavy side of the helicopter over by twenty degrees. The chopper entered its turn, and for fifteen seconds, everyone in the cabin was squeezed together like sardines. Mick had to fight for his breath, such was the force with which Pelfrey pushed down on him at this angle.

As the chopper moved past its ‘nine o’clock’ phase, Pelfrey’s bodyweight returned to normal. This wasn’t at all comfortable for Mick, but the worst was yet to come.

It was when the Sikorsky hit 180° that gravity became a problem. Rather than crushing the five-man crew, it threatened to tip them out the cabin. Luckily, the rake-like Pelfrey was deceptively strong and managed to pin the others down for the time it took for the chopper to complete its turn.

Spike, however, slid out of the cabin to haunt the sea below – perhaps. There was a chance she might wash up to shore, but she didn’t matter: she was Johnny frog’s problem now.

With the chopper now facing in the direction of

home, Adders junior slowed it to a static hover just long enough for Phillip Pelfrey to lean outside the cabin the pull the heavy sliding door shut. There was no need to get a signal to the pilot since it slammed hard enough that the shudder went through to the cockpit. Adders junior tipped the beast of the sky's nose once more, and she pushed forwards, heading for home and approaching maximum speed.

The Cleaver brothers were both six-foot-one and of medium to slim build. Therefore packing both of them into the boot of a Ford Escort proved impossible: one of them would have to travel in the passenger footwell.

Since Sam had pulled the gun, he deserved to travel in the least comfort; he went in the boot, and it was a tight enough fit with just him. They bundled him there in a hurry, and Alex got the rear seat foot space after Alley Oop deprived him of his belt and fastened his wrists.

Before Dave could close the boot, there was something he wanted to see for himself.

He went around to the rear of the Escort, leaned down and rifled Sam Cleaver's jackets – and found enough cocaine on him to keep Joe Walsh smiling for a week if it was still the 1970s. "Perfect," said Dave, leaving Samuel in possession of the incriminating substance and pushing the boot shut.

The gun that Sam had dropped at Alley Oop's request was now under the car, out of sight but not out of mind; Alley had steered it there with his foot after he'd decked both of the Cleavers.

Dave had wanted Sam Cleaver to be found in possession of a firearm, too, but since he had room to move about in the boot, Dave thought it was too big a risk. Instead, he told Alley to put Samuel Cleaver's finger-printed weapon in the glove box – a compromise.

Before they'd set out for London, Dave had

explained to Alley Oop that though driving more than forty miles with two wounded captives onboard was risky, it was necessary to take the Cleavers away from their hometown for the final phase of the operation. He knew from experience that gang bosses usually had police officers from their patch on the payroll as well as various other public officials. It had to be Essex.

Dave had also told Alley Oop that they would have to stop somewhere on the journey home to wipe his and Alley Oop's prints from the stolen car, even though he suspected that the orphaned Alley Oop's prints wouldn't find a match.

As Dave straddled his Ninja once more, it occurred to him that his mobile hadn't rung yet, but he told himself not to lose faith.

Sometimes faith was all you had.

Chapter 41

The journey back across the English channel felt like fifteen minutes to Mick, and that was precisely how long it took. The outward journey had seemed quicker, but Mick reasoned with himself that it had only seemed this way and that this flexing of his sense of time was down to excitement and adrenaline.

He gave up trying to rest his eyelids and instead peered out the window for the rest of the journey, even though he could see nothing but gloom out there in this murky no man's land.

But Kent soon crept into view, and Mick grinned as he thought of Chas 'n' Dave.

Dahn t' Margate ...

As well as having given up any hope of resting his eyes, Mick had likewise given up on striking up a conversation with this Pelfrey chap. Instead, Mick and Pelfrey sat on opposite sides of the dimly-lit cabin, safe in the knowledge that their journey would be over soon.

It was Pelfrey who broke the silence when it occurred to him that they were almost flying over Southend again without their pilot changing speed or altitude. "What's he up to?" he said, not expecting Mick to know the answer. But he got one anyway.

"I think I know," said Mick.

HM Prison Guard Kevin 'Lanky' Ellefson had good reason to be miserable. Since leaving the armed forces, he'd failed his police entrance exam three times, scoring lower on his third attempt than on his first. So with his mortgage to meet and a heavy heart, 'Lanky' Ellefson had applied to HM Prison Services: his application was successful.

At first, it seemed like an okay gig. Ellefson got to wear a uniform and call his boss sir, which suited a man from a military background. More importantly, he would get to raise his voice and bang a few heads together – great!

Or so he'd thought.

Sadly, he'd been sent to work at Chelmsford prison, which wasn't as notorious as San Quentin or HMS Parkhurst. Most of the lags here were white-collar criminals or – bloody hell – young offenders. Ellefson knew that the guards in maximum security prisons referred to places like this as 'Center Parcs' or 'Butlins,' and called the wardens here 'dinner ladies,' and he would have done the same had the heavy boot been on the other foot.

Wondering what he'd done to deserve a life as tame and as dull as his, Ellefson trudged wearily around the perimeter of the dimly-lit rectangular yard hoping he'd catch some little herbert trying to clear the wall.

"Yeah, right," he whispered. "They're too busy crying out for their mums."

He knew that this prison break fantasy of his – in which naturally he'd need to save the day and give some jumped-up detainee a bloody good shoe-ing – came from the fact that he'd just heard the distant sputtering of a helicopter which he reasonably assumed was the local air ambulance.

"You lucky bastard," he said, his words aimed at the person who flies a helicopter for a living.

He thought and said this almost every time the hospital helicopter passed overhead – which it often did since Chelmsford prison was close to both a busy hospital and the A12. Usually, the chopper hurtled by at such a rate that you could blink and miss it, and Ellefson loved the machine-gun-like sound of its rotors.

Tonight was different. Ellefson saw the helicopter fly across the prison yard at far less than its usual speed. He estimated – roughly – that it was travelling at less than half the rate it usually did. Strange, he thought.

He thought it was stranger still when the helicopter's pilot made an overhead turn before coming back thirty seconds later, moving more slowly than before. The chopper stopped moving forwards and hovered right above the place where the inmates played kiss chase and hide and seek most lunchtimes: this wasn't going to be a standard night shift, Ellefson thought.

Ellefson unclipped his service-issue binoculars from his belt and held them up to his eyes, tilting his head upwards to take a good look at what might not be the Essex Air Ambulance after all. Please, God, let it be a breakout attempt.

"Give them guns, rocket launchers … Anything, just make it exciting," he said.

As he said this, a powerful searchlight shone down, searing his eyes and putting him in mind of the kind of silly alien abduction movies that always seemed to be on television when he tried to skive off in the dirty, miniscule warden's room during a nightshift.

WHOOSH!

Ellefson heard a rush of air like the sound of a flock of pheasants taking flight. Now shielding his eyes from the powerful search beam, he saw a disc-shaped silhouette falling towards him. So this wasn't a breakout, then.

Someone was being parachuted *into* the prison.

Ellefson didn't remember the chief screw saying they had new arrivals coming. So he could only assume that this was the act of a real-life super-hero, an anonymous cape and mask-wearing vigilante who perhaps wore his pants over his trousers.

Lucky bastard ...

Ellefson watched as the parachute and the body that was strapped in descended. The new inmate seemed to gather speed once he was inside the perimeter wall, as though the Earth's gravitational force had doubled its pull just as the limp body (had he been drugged?) prepared to complete its fall. The poor chap landed feet first, and his body seemed to crumple to the ground, becoming buried in a messy heap of wires and nylon sheeting.

Karim Haswell landed only a few metres from where

Ellefson stood; Ellefson sprinted over and sifted frantically through the mess of wire and fabric before getting a look at the man underneath. Male, non-caucasian, approximately thirty years of age, machine gun taped to his back.

Ellefson didn't waste time saluting the mysterious crime-fighter of the sky or mouthing the words "thank you" at him. Instead, he spun the mystery guest onto his front before putting a knee either side of the gaffer-taped rifle on his back, using his body weight to pin the unconscious criminal to the concrete floor of the exercise yard.

Ellefson looked up to see what was coming next. WHOOSH! Another disc-shaped silhouette descending towards Chelmsford prison (but later to be taken to a more robust facility Ellefson reflected). This chap – like the last one – had a rocky landing despite a smooth journey down.

But unlike the last surprise guest, this one must have been semi-conscious, and he landed close enough to Ellefson for him to hear him moan.

Ellefson knew he couldn't keep this a secret any longer. If one of them was armed, then there was a good chance the second one was; he didn't want to die in his place of work even though his professional life sometimes felt like a slow death. The button on his radio made the usual *kssscch* sound.

"Mayday, mayday!" he said.

He heard another *kssscch* before being told to go ahead just as he heard another parachute open.

"It's raining men – bad ones," he said to the lady in the communications room. "I need people down here *now*."

While the final villain glided to Earth, Ellefson watched in amazement as the mystery chopper tipped its nose before rocketing forwards in a south-easterly direction. Ellefson rose to his feet and turned to watch the blinking tail light fade in the distance, and the craft and its occupants were gone like a bat out of hell. Ellefson rose to his feet, and this time he raised his hand in a salute.

Chapter 42

Welcome to Chelmsford – Birthplace of British Radio

So read the sign that Dave saw as he left the Northbound A12 at junction 15 and cruised along Three Mile Hill towards the heart of the city. Dave didn't know why the region's association with broadcasting was still celebrated since Marconi's work was seldom put to good use these days.

Dave had switched his car radio on a couple of years back – but not for long. He soon turned it off as he felt violated by the poor choice of records and the strange regional inflections of the people who announced them. He'd been on his way to a gig in Luton at the time and had decided that spending the rest of the journey in silence was better than potentially becoming brainwashed by the 'artists' who were bothering the charts back then. There was that troubled young chap Robbie Williams (Dave didn't think he sounded well at all), a shrill-voiced young lady called

Rhianna and a girl group who got fifteen seconds into their song before Dave decided he couldn't take it anymore and put him and them out of their misery.

Dave shook his head at the memory before telling himself to stay focused on the task at hand here.

Dave was now leading with Alley Oop a steady distance behind him, and he ploughed on until Three Mile Hill became London Road. To his right was Hylands Park, and Dave mourned the death of the British cultural experience once again. Every year, tens of thousands of Essex boys and girls flocked here in the dying days of summer to listen to off-key singers and guitarists whose playing was rudimentary at best. The one year Dave had attended *V-Festival* it wasn't just the summer sun that had seemed to be dying.

After a mile, he and Alley Oop changed course; now, they were travelling in a north-easterly direction, having left the road that ran parallel to the eastern edge of Hylands

Park. Now they were on Princes Road, and Dave and Alley Oop were one step closer to their destination. And Dave saw something he didn't like the look of.

Not long before they reached the Army and Navy roundabout (and Dave told himself in advance not to grieve over the death of the infamous live music venue that once overlooked this particular landmark), Dave saw what he first thought to be a freak electrical storm over the Springfield district of Chelmsford. But he knew this couldn't be since sheet lightning didn't flash as rapidly or for as long as this. The flashes of light were regular, and from this distance, they seemed to bathe the rooftops below in an icy blue-white glow.

As Dave pulled to a halt at the Army and Navy roundabout, it occurred to him that great minds really did sometimes think alike. Earlier that night (although strictly speaking it was morning now), Dave had explained to Alley Oop that they were heading for the Chelmsford suburb of

Springfield because it was home to Essex Police headquarters. Police HQ was off a small through-road between two A-roads that pared off like scissors around the police headquarters and the surrounding neighbourhood.

Dave had instructed Alley Oop that when the police HQ came into sight, he would need to slow down and drop back while Dave would go one-hundred yards ahead and pull up with the engine ticking over. Alley Oop must then steer his stolen Ford Escort down the small side street that leads to the police headquarters. When he came level with the nick, all Alley Oop had to do was park somewhere in the grounds of Police HQ (preferably in a space reserved for the chief constable), then leg it and jump on the back of Dave's Ninja.

Dave and Alley Oop were confident that their plan would work, and officers of the law would eventually discover the two London drug dealers in the back – and find the gun and the drugs. The two men would be arrested and identified, leading to a thorough search of all properties connected to them. Best of all, the investigation that would take place as a result of Dave and Alley Oop's actions would be carried out by officers of Essex Police and not the 'Met,' some of whom were probably on the Cleavers payroll.

So far, Dave's plan had worked well. Samuel and Alex Cleaver were secured in the back of the Escort in the boot and the passenger footwell, respectively. As a safety measure, Dave had prepared a warning for whichever officer/s of the law found the vehicle. He had torn the back page out of the car's service handbook, using the blank side to outline the dangers at hand:

DEAR COPS. BAD GUYS ON BOARD.

PLEASE ARREST PROMPTLY.

GUN IN GLOVE COMPARTMENT.

Dave had instructed Alley Oop to leave this on the

dashboard or under a windscreen wiper and was confident that Alley Oop would remember to do it.

So yes. It was going well. At least it had been until Dave, and Alley Oop left the Army and Navy roundabout, and changed to a more north-easterly direction and started to close in on Essex Police HQ.

As Dave chugged along the two-mile stretch of bypass that would lead him and Alley Oop to their drop-off point, his heart sank as the flashing white-blue nebula above the streets and houses surrounding the nick got brighter as he got closer. Something big was going down, and he would bet his wheels that Danny and Mick were involved.

Dave suspected that nearly every officer on duty in Chelmsford, Essex, that night was in the area, dealing with whatever was going down. In the near-distance, Essex Police Headquarters could have been hosting a Pink Floyd concert thanks to all the squad cars flashing their blues, and this wasn't all.

About a mile in front, Dave could see three stationary sets of blue lights. Thanks to a little twist in the road, he could tell that the vehicles were staggered one in front of the other. A roadblock. Great.

More worryingly, Dave saw three trucks sitting idle in a layby on the opposite side of the road. Each one had a tarp-covered flatbed at the rear. He couldn't tell the colour thanks to the dark, but Dave strongly suspected these vehicles had green paint on the outside and hot-headed reservists inside.

Oh, for fuck's sake ...

If the mile-long road was blocked off this end, then it would be at the other end too, Dave reckoned. In fact, every road in the area would be blocked, what with the police on high alert and the cop shop being just across the street from the local prison. The final stage of Dave's plan would need scrapping, and there was something else for him to worry about now: the police – or the army – would probably be stopping vehicles in the area.

Alley Oop was driving a car – a stolen one – with two kidnapped passengers. One had cocaine about his person, both of them had head injuries, and a gun belonging to one of them was in the glovebox.

Dave told himself that it was alright and that Alley Oop wasn't the kind of person who would talk to the cops. Yes, Dave thought, Alley Oop would claim he'd never met me if he gets nicked, and we could meet for a pint and a catch-up when he gets out of prison.

Dave liked the sound of this, but just as he was about to do his Homer impression (*Mmmm ... Beer!*) it occurred to him that he too would be in prison. Because he had a gun tucked away in his jacket.

Play it cool, and you might get away with it.

Just as Dave started to wish he was drunk, an unmarked van with flashing blues appeared behind them and overtook them. The police van left them for dust, but it didn't travel at speed for long. Soon, ahead in the near distance, Dave saw the police van's brake lights, and it came to a halt parallel with the middle one of the three stationary police cars that were sealing his entrance. He saw the reversing lights of the car at the back of the three-vehicle roadblock flick on, and whoever was at the wheel took it back by approximately the vehicle's own length. The black Ford Transit likewise rolled back a little way before turning into the road Dave had hoped to go down.

By the time Dave and Alley Oop were approaching the entrance to Sandford Road – where Dave had hoped to go himself – the police car at the back had filled the gap it just created to let the Transit through. Dave knew the road was closed, but this didn't mean an over-zealous young constable was going to miss his chance to boss a civvy around.

A chap whose uniform probably still looked new walked to the front of the temporary blockade and started windmilling his right arm like Pete Townshend to ram home the message that Dave and Alley Oop had to drive on.

Dave would need a new plan. Fast.

Chapter 43

Alley Oop didn't like what he saw. All his life, he'd had nothing but bad experiences involving the police, and now just as he thought he'd be on his way back to Southend-on-sea with his new friend Dave Hunter, there was old bill everywhere. Alley Oop's chest felt tight, and he'd broken out in a cold sweat. In an attempt to calm himself, he thought about how his new mate would handle this, and the only answer he could find was to act naturally.

Alley Oop kept his eyes on the road ahead and took care not to look in the direction of the copper who was waving them on. The chances of making eye contact for long enough to give much away were slim, driving at forty miles per hour and when the only light inside the vehicle came from the dashboard, but Alley wasn't about to chance it.

Some say ignorance is bliss, and in Alley Oop's case, this was probably true. For had it crossed his mind that the 1.3-litre car that he was driving was stolen and would have been reported as such, his brain would have suffered an overload. The resulting panic attack might have caused him to crash or stall the stolen vehicle.

So with his mind untroubled by this thought, Alley Oop followed Dave Hunter along the bypass, keeping a safer-than-necessary distance behind Dave on account of the heavy police presence. He saw Dave slow for a roundabout and indicate to turn left, and Alley Oop did the same.

They left the roundabout at the first exit and travelled back in the direction they had come from. The road they were on and the one they'd just left were like the legs on a set of compasses, and the roundabout was the circular hinge from which they sprung. Alley Oop was confident that Dave knew his patch well and had a plan.

They travelled along Springfield Road for about a mile before encountering another roadblock at the top of the road they'd tried to access on the way in. Alley Oop saw more stationary police cars and flashing blue lights and experienced the same shortness of breath and clammy skin he'd had a moment ago, only this time his discomfort didn't pass as soon as an officer signalled them to keep moving.

There was a prison on Alley Oop's left, and he remembered the last time he'd been driven along here.

He saw the grey, grimy fifteen-foot wall around the yard, and his hands started shaking as he did his best to grip the wheel. He forced himself to breathe deeply, and he couldn't help but notice that the prison floodlights were on – something he'd never seen the whole time he'd been there as a young offender.

He'd been out in the yard after dark twice during his six-month stay – both times he'd been fighting with other inmates, and had had to be moved to a temporary place of seclusion while the dust settled. In recent years he'd imagined he was being shown the dark, high-walled Victorian courtyard to put him off making a break for freedom, now that the nonces knew that he could be trouble. He'd never felt as alone as he did out there in that dark open space, and by comparison, it made his cell feel appealing.

Alley Oop was as grateful to leave HMP Chelmsford behind him now as he'd been ten years ago. He took deep breaths and didn't look in the mirror until he'd made a right-turn about half a mile further along, right behind Dave. With all thoughts of policemen and prison behind him, Alley Oop found his breathing had returned to a more steady rhythm. He saw a roadside retail park, which, being from the city, made him feel at home out here in the sticks. Halfords, McDonald's, Pizza Hut – this place had it all.

Alley Oop figured that Dave was headed towards the city centre, although the signs which told drivers this meant precious little to him; Alley Oop went on instinct, and usually, this worked for him.

Dave and Alley Oop drove for another quarter-mile or so before Alley Oop saw Dave take his left-hand off its handlebar and point his finger left, jabbing it three times in that direction. The road broke off into two lanes, and Dave stayed in the lane to either turn right or continue straight on. Alley Oop was confused, but only for a while. He soon saw a lantern with an electric light in it. There was a steel handrail running parallel to the ground along a concrete walkway, and this told Alley Oop everything he needed to know: it was the local cop shop.

Just as Alley Oop realised there were two police stations in Chelmsford, he noticed the traffic light turning red as did the brake lights on the car ahead of him and, no doubt, the two in front of that. Dave, who was in the next lane, was now level with the traffic lights, and Alley Oop decided that his new mate was going to pull up somewhere over the junction and wait for him to do the deed.

Alley Oop knew it was time to act. He checked his mirrors and saw a line of a dozen or more cars waiting to turn the same way. There would be witnesses, but this was a chance he had to take. When the lights turned green, Alley Oop rolled up to the junction before spinning the wheel to his left and turning sharply in that direction.

After about a hundred yards, Alley Oop saw a set of steps that led to a flat stone concourse between the nick and the neighbouring Crown Court. Without signalling to the driver behind him, Alley Oop turned the steering wheel left-hand down and felt twenty-four bumps as the car climbed a dozen steps up to the stone concourse. Once the vehicle was on the flat surface, Alley straightened her up and eased her forwards by one-and-a-half times its own length before putting her in reverse, this time turning the wheel hard right.

He straightened the wheel just before he completed the quarter turn and reversed until his rear bumper was almost touching the east-facing wall of the courthouse – and his front end was facing the nick. He unclipped his seatbelt and put the car into first gear, and before he started to roll, he put Dave's note on the passenger seat.

Alley Oop reckoned the distance to the double doors of the nick was about the length of a football pitch. By the time he was outside the penalty area, he was doing 20mph. Alley got her in third and reached the half-way line doing forty. He didn't want to get close enough to trouble the away team's defence, and he was sure as shit that he wasn't going to violate the offside rule – at least not while he was still in the vehicle. But he wanted the Cleavers to feel the impact, so he hung in long enough to see the speedometer hit forty-five before he pulled the door catch and lunged out of the driver's seat.

He landed on his right shoulder and rolled twice before landing in a heap. He heard a near-deafening sound that wasn't a boom nor a clang nor a crunch. Instinctively Alley pushed his head against the floor and threw his arms over his head. His right arm didn't move when his brain told it to due to his heavy-landing a second earlier. Alley Oop winced as he heard the two heavy metal doors wrench themselves from their fixings in the brick wall of the nick. He expected to hear glass smashing as well, but the glass portions of the ruined doors survived the first impact, the thick vertical stainless steel door handles fulfilling the remit of their design and working as shock absorbers.

But when the ruined door frame hit the floor, the glass gave way and made a right old din, and Alley covered one ear with his left hand and pressed his right ear into his knackered shoulder on the same side.

Alley Oop knew there was no time to waste. He got to his feet. His broken right shoulder seared with white-hot pain, and instinct made him cradle his knackered arm against himself with his good hand. His right hand flopped uselessly against his left side and slid underneath his open jacket. Knowing it was time to run, he used the elbow of his left arm to hold his right arm in place, freeing up one hand in case he fell as he ran.

Alley Oop hadn't been aware that he had attracted

quite an audience as he'd performed the dangerous manoeuvre in the stolen Ford Escort, whose owner would now be less than thrilled to be reunited with. On the other side of the road, a line of six cars had stopped as their drivers and passengers wanted to see what had just gone down. Worse, three men had got out of a black BMW with shiny alloys and tinted windows, planning to inspect the scene.

The biggest of the three men took the lead and climbed the steps up to the concourse, with his two buddies right behind him.

" 'Fuck you doin' bro?" said the concerned citizen with a bad attitude and some expensive threads.

"Don't you know that's a *po-lice* sta …"

It took Alley Oop three seconds to work out why the have-a-go-hero lost his bottle.

Alley Oop had tucked his knackered arm underneath his jacket, and his elbow pointed in the direction of the man who stood between him and a smooth getaway. Alley Oop wasted no time in taking advantage of this.

" 'Fink yer a fakkin' 'ero, do ya?" said Alley, glaring at the chap who only a few seconds earlier had planned to save the day.

"Whoa … Cool it, man," said the man with the medallion, as he held out his right arm to stop his two friends in their tracks and put up his right hand to persuade Alley Oop not to pop one in him.

Alley closed up the space of about twenty yards between him and the three-man justice squad at a speed that was too slow to be called a run but a good deal faster than walking.

"Get outta my way, and forget what I fuckin' look like, yeah?" he told the leader of the pack, who broke off from his friends to let Alley Oop pass.

In time, he would probably carry out the second part of Alley Oop's instruction – not that Alley was thinking about that right now. He ran across the busy road where he narrowly avoided being squashed by a bus and deafened by a dozen car horns then ran about a hundred yards up to the junction with Victoria Street. He turned left and kept on running, scanning around for a stationary green sports bike amongst the Saturday night revellers and taxi lights.

Chapter 44

Dave felt a hefty pat on his left shoulder, and a second later, the bike's suspension dipped as Alley Oop mounted the rear portion of the saddle.

Dave had left his Kawasaki ticking over in neutral while he waited for Alley Oop to do what he had to do. Now that Alley Oop was on board with his mission accomplished, Dave wasted no time in joining the flow of traffic that was moving west along Chelmsford's Victoria Road.

As he swung out into the road, the driver of the local night bus sounded his horn at Dave, who would have done the same thing had it been the other way round. They were in a 30 zone, and Dave estimated there couldn't have been more than four car spaces between him and the mostly empty coach when Dave had made the dangerous manoeuvre.

Dave cursed the driver not for his rudeness but for drawing attention to him and Alley Oop at a time when they needed to keep their heads down.

Dave stuck rigidly to the permitted 30mph. There was a bend in the road coming up – Dave knew the area well – followed by a pair of mini-roundabouts, so he would take it steady – for now.

Dave heard an alarm blaring in the near distance, a bit like a fire bell only a semi-tone lower. Good, he thought. Someone in the nick has activated the alarm they usually save for when someone in custody kicks off, perhaps strung out on booze, coke, smack, or maybe all three. The sooner the cops find the Cleavers, the better, he thought. And this, combined with the other crisis down the road, will tie up every officer in the area tonight – brilliant.

Unless they seal off the whole city, he thought. And stop any vehicles coming in or out. And find my revolver ...

But this unpleasant thought wasn't enough to make Dave Hunter change his plans or his speed. He soon came to the bend in the road and followed it at just under 30mph, and he and Alley Oop were now moving south-west. To Dave, this was a step in the right direction.

After another hundred yards, they came to one of two mini-roundabouts. Dave turned left at the first traffic island, and they headed east before taking the six o'clock exit at the next roundabout and beginning the journey south.

They were on Victoria Road South, with County Hall looking down at them from the left side of the carriageway. The speed limit here was 40mph, and Dave took the calculated risk of sticking to this speed since he would have to change direction again in less than one mile. Dave checked his mirrors as he had done every four seconds since Alley Oop plowed the stolen car into the police station foyer minutes earlier.

They came to another, more prominent roundabout, and Dave took the second exit. As he saw Victoria Road South become Parkway, he saw a line of police cars approaching from the opposite direction. There were six of them in total, lights flashing and not sticking around to take in the scenery or check whether or not Alley Oop was wearing a crash helmet.

Dave spent a second – but no more – wondering what on earth Danny (Dave knew it was something to do with him) and co. had done to make the police draft reinforcements in from as far afield as Basildon or Southend. Dave took a liking to the idea that his hometown would be largely fuzz-free by the time he returned there.

He'd done over one hundred miles on his beloved Kwacker tonight, never using more than a fraction of its capability. This is how Dave imagined the late Jimi Hendrix must have felt during his mismatched stint with the Ike and Tina Revue, even though Dave Hunter knew, deep down, that a bit of discipline could have done the young James Marshall some good. Nevertheless, Dave felt like his, and his motorcycle's instincts were being reigned in somewhat.

Soon do something about that ...

But not right away, though. Motorists were allowed to travel along Chelmsford's Parkway at 40mph. There was already another bloody roundabout in sight, and so Dave didn't even take his Japanese beast up to this speed. He pulled up to the Army and Navy roundabout and waited for three tarp-covered Leyland trucks to pass. The military vehicles took the exit to Dave's left, guiding them towards the action.

While he waited for the trucks to pass, Dave took a chance to mourn the cultural death of his country. This wasn't the time, but he did it anyway.

Dave eyed the monument to tackiness that now stood on the sight of a bulldozed music venue where a bunch of young Mancunian upstarts dressed in mod clothing and in thrall to Beatlemania had cut their teeth before taking the world by storm. Now it was an Italian-American themed restaurant where Dave was sure you wouldn't find Billy Joel in a corner, scribbling ideas down on a napkin having observed the patrons enough to imagine their hopes, dream, and fears.

And that, thought Dave, was where it was all going wrong these days ...

***

This was no time to pause for reflection, and Dave knew it. Luckily, he had just the thing to pull himself away from his melancholy interlude.

A two-and-a-half-mile stretch of mostly straight road would take Dave up to the A130 – the road home. Now to give it some welly.

"Hold tight, kid," Dave said as he snapped the throttle back.

Going from 0-60 in three seconds was like getting your end away: you never grew tired of it, you had to give it a break occasionally, and you always wanted a repeat prescription. Dave felt the familiar rush of wind resistance as his tyres spun. He suspected the faint smell of burning rubber that drifted through the air inlets in his helmet was a figment of his imagination, but he savored it nonetheless. Like dominoes, Dave and Alley Oop found themselves repositioned ten degrees backward.

Dave, having been taught off-the-books by brash, hot-headed American 'Tornado Jones,' knew not to react too much to this feeling of having stepped out in a hurricane. Don't stiffen up, try not to alter your shape or your saddle posture, and don't try to clamp your legs together.

Dave had understood all of this at the time, and he understood it now, although the same could not be said for Alley Oop, who used his left, non-broken arm to hug Dave's mid-section like a boa constrictor. Dave tried to tell Alley Oop that he wasn't in prison yet, but this was no use when the bike's engine exceeded sixty decibels.

Barely a minute later, Dave found himself slowing down for another(!) roundabout. There had been a brief cloudburst while Dave had had his head down doing eighty, and he noticed steam rising up from beneath him. As always, this made him think of Chuck Berry.

'Rainwater blowin' all under my hood/ (I) knew that was doin' my motor good.'

Underneath his tinted visor, Dave smiled even though there was still one piece missing in the jigsaw: his missus.

Despite the ungodly hour, there were was some scattered traffic on the road, and Dave had to stop to let several vehicles clear the roundabout before he took the third exit onto the A130. Time to chew up the miles between here and home. Dave repeated his 0-60 trick, and his Kwacker tore across the slick tarmac, leaving a cloud of fine spray behind him. Dave hit sixty and kept right on going: he was just getting started.

At sixty, Alley Oop man-hugged Dave again; at eighty, he tightened his grip using strength he didn't know he had, and when they hit ninety-five, Alley Oop cried out for the mother he'd never known.

One-hundred. One-hundred-and-five. One-hundred-and-seventeen ... This was the last figure Dave read. Now it was man and machine, working together with one common goal in mind: survival.

Electric guitar enthusiasts will know that Marshall amplifiers are built and designed to sound their best at high volumes. The one time they didn't sound loud was when the volume was turned all the way to eleven. Likewise, the Kawasaki ZX12 R's sweet spot, where it was engineered to deliver peak performance, was when it was being ridden way above the speed limit, as this one was right now. The higher the numbers on the speedo got, the rounder and more satisfying the sound of the engine became.

It was still loud, though – especially in the small hours of Sunday morning.

As usual, Dave noticed that the broken white lines in

the road had merged into a continuous whole, and the staggered clusters of light from the row of cats' eyes that ran parallel to them had formed a sparkly trail. The sodium lights over the carriageway had probably done the same, although they were now outside Dave's increasingly narrow periphery; tunnel vision was just a throttle turn away, and Alley Oop (sans crash helmet!) was now hanging on for dear life. Then it happened.

For Dave Hunter, everything except the stretch of road in front of him ceased to exist. His hawk-like eyes saw sections of the highway disappear beneath him faster than his brain could process. He was doing two-hundred miles an hour, heading south and heading for home.

Chapter 45

Back at the club, it seemed Mick and Danny had been busy. Dave and a visibly shaken Alley Oop had to wait for Danny to open up and let them in after Dave tapped out the 'Smoke on The Water' riff three times on one of the surviving frosted panes in the French doors. It took Danny just over a minute to unstack the improvised barricade of tables and chairs.

"David," said Danny with a half-smile as he made eye contact with his old friend. "*You,*" he said with a grimace as he acknowledged Alley Oop.

First things first, Dave thought.

"Has Lianda called?"

Danny took a piece of paper out from his pocket with a number he'd scribbled down when Lianda had called to say she was in a lovely four-star hotel in Whitstable and saw his friend's eyes glisten.

"You soppy old thing," said Danny. "Get inside."

As Dave stepped over the threshold, he saw Mick Davies hard at work with an electric planer, giving the dance floor a smoothing over no doubt in preparation for a new coat of varnish. Dave could smell timber and emulsion, and he turned to see that someone (probably not Danny) had given half of the south-facing wall a fresh coat of paint.

With Dave and Alley Oop inside Danny set about rebuilding the blockade across the entrance. But he left one small table and three chairs which, his fortress rebuilt, he set out for Dave and Alley Oop to join him for an update/debrief.

Dave went first and explained how they had dealt with the Cleaver brothers. He told Danny how they had planted the two brothers with a gun and class-A drugs before bringing them, signed sealed and delivered to the police who would be getting ready to tear up the Cleavers' homes and business premises as they spoke.

Then it was Danny's turn, and for the next five

minutes, he filled Dave in on what had gone down since the group had split into three. He told him about the impromptu helicopter ride across the English channel, in which they had dumped two bodies just off the coast of Calais. Then Danny explained that Adders junior had turned the helicopter around and gone back to Essex, where they had parachuted the surviving bad guys into Chelmsford prison. Dave decided this would explain the presence of the police and the territorial army. He was impressed, and he told Danny this.

"Good work, Danny. Good work. I see you've got this place in order, too," he said, tilting his head in the direction of the refurbished sections of his club.

"It wasn't easy," said Danny.

"The first thing we had to do was conduct a thorough sweep of the club for bullets or casings. Mick said that other than the two shots your good lady fired, a total of five shots were fired by our uninvited guests this evening. We've found four slugs and five shells that I've hidden safely. The two bullets Lianda fired are now off the coast of France, buried in the body of the frightful thing she killed. This means there's one shot unaccounted for which we'll need to find before the police get here. And believe me, David, they will be here. A job like this has got you written all over it.

"As for this place, well, as you can see, Mick's hard at it priming the dance floor for a dark coat of varnish. Some of the blood from your lady's first kill congealed rather too thickly and had started to stain. We also had to move the body over to the window to load her-slash-it into the helicopter. This meant more blood on the dance floor, and blood on the wall as we pulled her through the open window frame. That's why I had to go into Winston's janitor cupboard to fetch a paintbrush and some thick emulsion and get to work; otherwise, I'd have got him to do it," he said, pointing to a hard-at-work Mick on the club's dancefloor.

Dave took some time to digest everything Danny had

told him before deciding he was satisfied that, one stray bullet withstanding, there was nothing in the club that could suggest a link between him and the events of the evening.

There was no way he'd let Lianda go to a women's prison, and if need be, he would say that he had killed the machine-gun-toting lesbian himself. Then he'd go to jail and perhaps meet up with one or two or (or fifty or sixty) of the gangsters or crooked policemen he'd helped put there two years earlier.

It was the injustice that bothered him the most. By putting the Cleavers and several of their henchmen out of business, Dave Hunter had done society a favour. Therefore he was damned if he would be punished for it – not that there was much chance of that after Mick and Danny's makeover.

"Good work," he said with his hand outstretched towards Danny, who returned the gesture and shook Dave's hand.

"Nice one – now, you two."

Danny and Alley Oop looked at each other silently. Early on in their acquaintance, Danny had humiliated and abused Alley Oop until Alley Oop had got the upper hand and broken several of Danny's toes and given him a damn good thrashing as payback.

"Do it," Dave said.

"You're mad," said Danny.

"Yes," said Dave. "But we know that anyway. Shake hands – both of you."

Dave had grown to like Alley Oop. Throughout their adventure, he had shown courage and integrity – the two qualities that Dave Hunter valued most. There was also the fact that Winston, the elderly janitor, was old, drunk, and unreliable. He was good company, mind.

But Winston had to go. And with their mission not over yet, Dave knew this was the time to strengthen the strong bond within the team. It had to be now.

Alley Oop stood up and put out his hand first. Danny, realising he was second-in-command now that Dave was back in town, followed suit and shook hands with the man who had called him a 'poofter' several times in the last few hours.

Dave smiled from ear to ear, as did Danny and Alley Oop. Danny and Alley sat down again before the three men leaned into the table for a group hug. Mick turned his planer off and came over to join in, leaning over the three of them to take part in the ultra-manly embrace.

After the group finished their celebratory cuddle, Dave was the first to get to his feet.

"Right then, chaps," he said. "Back to work."

"No," said Danny, also standing up. "We'll take care of that – you've got a call to make."

***

"What took you so long?"

It was cheeky of Lianda to ask Dave this when it

took her six rings to answer, but he figured that this could have something to do with it being almost three in the morning.

"I was going to ask you the same thing," said Dave.

"You know good things come to those who wait, mister Hunter," she said.

"I know, sweetie. I know. Hey – we're preparing a homecoming makeover for you."

"That is sweet of you, David," she said, and he could see her eyes sparkle as she said it.

"Well, I say we're giving the place a makeover – we're cleaning up all the …"

He was going to say they were cleaning up the blood of the butch lady Lianda had shot dead just hours ago but remembered not to despite his weariness. On a night when he and his friends had cheated death, it would be a shame to lose it all due to a crosswire or high-tech police eavesdropping.

"So you're gonna get the bus first thing tomorrow, yeah?"

"First thing, yes."

"Get plenty of beauty sleep for me now, eh?"

"Will do, promise. Now is there something you need to say to me, Dave?"

Lianda must have had a sixth sense, for just as she expected, Danny, Mick, and Alley Oop had wandered over to Dave as the conversation drew to a close and formed a half-circle around him. He didn't care at all.

"I love you. I love you more than anything in this world or the next one."

The other three chaps gave a hearty cheer, and the last thing Dave heard was Lianda say something similar before putting the phone back on her bedside table and getting some rest for her man.

"Very funny, you cunts," said Dave, wiping his eyes. "Now back to work, all of you. Except for you."

'You,' turned out to be Alley Oop. Dave, who'd been sat at the bar to call his missus, pulled out another bar stool for his new friend. They had a lot to talk about.

Chapter 46

There could be no doubting that the Don Hunter who had trained Alley Oop to fight was Dave's late father. The name alone was enough, and Alley Oop remembered Don Hunter saying that he was from Southend-on-Sea. If that wasn't proof enough, Dave also remembered how he'd fought – or attempted to fight – with Alley Oop early on in their acquaintance, how Alley Oop had decked him twice, both times with just one punch. Oh yes, Alley Oop had learned from the best.

Alley Oop told Dave he remembered Don Hunter saying he had moved back to the East End about ten years ago.

It was, in fact, 13 years ago that Dave's parents had undergone a trial separation in which Don Hunter had moved back to his old East London stomping ground for three years. In this time, Don Hunter had bought a gym, and though time and a diabolical thirst had been against him, he'd got back into training young fighters with a vengeance – including, it seemed, a young Alley Oop.

This was around the time that Dave had flown the nest, but he remembered his dad calling him to say he was coming back to Southend around the time that Dave was getting ready to turn twenty-one. Dave remembered thinking he had his won life to live by then and wasn't particularly bothered by what his old man got up to.

" 'E took care of me, your old man did. He showed me how to hold my fists up, how to look after m-m-meself," said Alley Oop.

That sounds like the old man, Dave thought.

"He let me help out around the gym, like. I used to spar with all his up and coming fighters. Just when they thought they were up there with the big boys, he'd send 'em to do a few rounds 'gainst me. He used to take me down the pub with him after a session, too."

That sounds like him an' all ...

"He taught me right from wrong, and how not to suffer fools."

"Hmmm," said Dave. "You didn't quite listen to that part, did you?"

"No, Dave," said Alley Oop, hanging his head in shame.

Dave slapped Alley Oop hard across the cheek.

"You don't bow down to people," he said. "Not even me, got it?"

"Yeah, sure. It's just that all I ever wanted was to fit in. With your old man out of the picture … I was … Lost, I guess."

"Yeah, well, not anymore," said Dave. "You've got us."

"Th-th … Thanks," was all Alley Oop could say, and though Dave saw tears welling up in Alley Oop's cow-like eyes, he resisted the temptation to break off the tough-love stance.

"They also gave me powder. You know … C-c-c … Cocaine," said Alley Oop, and if he thought revealing a drug problem would elicit sympathy from the hardest man in Essex, then he was sorely mistaken.

"Fuck that stuff," said Dave after he delivered another slap around Alley Oop's big chops.

"I'm sorry," said Dave, realising he shouldn't have hit him. "But believe me when I say there will be none of that shit on these premises. If I catch you using that stuff, you'll be back on the streets. Got it?"

"Yeah, I got it, chief," said Alley Oop. "It's just that that p-p-powder makes me feel … What is it? Inv-v-v-vincible."

This was the wrong thing to say, and Dave very nearly slapped him again before deciding upon a more diplomatic route.

"It's a lie, and we're gonna make sure the days of you putting that stuff up yer snout are long gone. It's just gonna take a bit of time," Dave said.

"You're gonna get me some help?"

"No," said Dave. "We're going to help you."

Neither man knew that Danny was listening carefully between brush strokes of the plum-coloured emulsion; they didn't see him grinning demonically at the thought that he would play a part in Alley Oop's rehabilitation either.

"In time," said Dave, "you'll realise that strength doesn't come from what's up your nose –"

Dave paused to lean down and snort an imaginary line of cocaine off his bar.

" – any more than strength comes from what's in your hand," he said as pointed a finger-and-thumb pistol as Alley Oop's head and fired an imaginary shot. Dave didn't blow smoke from the barrel of his imaginary revolver or tuck it under his belt. This was serious.

"No?" said Alley Oop.

"No," said Dave. "It comes from in *here,"* he said as

he used the same finger he'd just used to imitate a pistol shot to poke Alley Oop in the chest.

Silence fell, and Dave took it upon himself to do something about it.

"Let's have a drink, eh?"

He turned round in his stool and repeated the question, this time aiming it at Danny and Mick, who put down their tools by way of an answer.

***

Dave insisted that a drink meant *a* drink.

He used this chance to congratulate Mick on two jobs well done, and Danny clinked his glass against Alley Oop's perhaps to indicate a thawing off of his early frostiness towards him.

Then it was back to work, and this time it was all hands on deck. Dave found two spare brushes – one for him to coat the blood-splattered wall alongside Danny, and another for Alley Oop to help Mick spread a thick layer of

Sikkens across the equally crimson-stained dance floor.

It was another hour before they lads could rest again – all of them bar Dave that, is.

Dave remembered that the THIRD intruder the previous evening had destroyed an eighteen-inch picture frame that contained a blow-up of one of his favourite pictures, one of Dave Hunter, Don Hunter, Snail's Pace Slim, and a wired-looking Wilko Johnson.

Without explaining what he was doing, Dave nipped behind the bar then through the door marked STAFF ONLY and up into the flat, emerging two minutes later with a torch, and a power drill fitted with a 3.5-millimetre titanium blade and a flashlight. He pulled a chair up and shone his torch into the bullet hole where his favourite picture used to stand. Sure enough, he saw a glimmer of light reflecting back at him, and he knew he'd found the last piece of incriminating evidence. He pressed the trigger of his power drill to check the battery was cooked before giving the torch to Alley Oop, who pulled up a chair and shone some light on the subject.

With near surgical precision, Dave plunged the titanium drill bit into the lodged bullet, before easing the drill backwards with even greater accuracy. The 12-gauge slug came out, and Dave held it at arm's length like a wartime doctor who'd just amputated a gangrenous toe. Then he steadied the chuck with his right hand and spun it counter-clockwise with his left, and the drill bit, and the attached bullet fell to the ground.

"Now go get rid of it," he said to Alley Oop.

"Sure, chief. That's everything, right?"

"Almost," said Dave. "I need you to get rid of this an' all."

Dave took the revolver he had used for personal protection (and that once belonged to the late Ted Maskell) out from his jacket and handed it to Alley Oop.

"Lose this, and the bullets, and the bullet bag outside, and we're home and dry, kid – I want you back here in half-an-hour."

Alley Oop didn't waste a second. He put the old revolver under his jacket as well as the last of the bullets and made his way to the door. Mick and Danny helped him move the tables and chairs, and a minute later, he was gone, out into the night one last time.

Neither Danny, Mick or Dave felt it was right to celebrate properly while their friend was still risking his neck, but they had a drink nonetheless. They had a pint and a chaser each, and Dave's chaser went down the hole in one.

"That is downright sinful," he said as he exhaled luxuriously afterwards.

Danny and Mick took their chasers down with equal swiftness, but the three of them took their pints at a much steadier rate. Nobody said anything – they just hoped and prayed for Alley Oops safe return to base. Which came just as the clock over the bar prepared to mark twenty-five minutes since his departure. In an attempt to imitate Dave's coded arrival announcement from earlier, he banged a clumsy rhythm on what was left of the French doors and Mick, Danny, and Dave knew who it was.

They didn't even ask the puffing and panting Alley Oop what he had done with the illegal items. They just took it in turn to pat him on the back and, with the furniture re-stacked, they all agreed that it was time to get the party poppers.

***

They started on pints. This was a special occasion, and so only Estuary lager would do. Alley Oop managed four, Mick six and Danny nine.

Dave, on the other hand, only managed two. He needed to keep a clear head and managed to take advantage of the growing pile of empties at the bar and general bonhomie to trick his friends into thinking he was along for the ride.

As well as keeping a clear head, Dave was trying to

work out the answer to a question that may have had the power to bug him until the end of time: how had Lianda managed to open the man cave safe?

It didn't take him long to work it out, mind. Dave's safe – in which he'd kept Ted Maskell's gun – required a five-digit combination to open it. Dave, wanting a combination he could remember easily, used the title of the classic Rolling Stones album 12 x 5. He'd recently left a dog-eared, vinyl copy of this one out on his man cave desk. Lianda must have worked out – here are great minds thinking alike – that Dave had used 1 and 0 to make up for x, what with 1 and 0 forming the number 10 in conventional numbering and x meaning ten in the Roman numeric equivalent.

She's a clever girl, Dave thought as he supped his pint.

About an hour in, and as the pints flowed, Mick fetched the battered old acoustic that lived in the back corner of the stage. As he tuned it by ear, Dave leant over the bar and fumbled around for the tambourine that had somehow found a home on top of his glasswasher. He passed the instrument over to Alley Oop, wanting the newbie to join in, but suspecting he may not know the words to the songs they liked to sing.

The hits piled up. Bon Jovi's 'Wanted Dead Or Alive'. The Stones' 'It's All Over Now', The Mc Coys' 'Hang on Sloopy.' And of course, George Thorogood's 'Alley Oop,' much to the surprise of their newest recruit.

As the group drank, sang, strummed and bashed, Dave noticed that Alley Oop had a certain amount of natural rhythm, and it occurred to him that he may have also found a new roadie/minder/guest percussionist for their band. Running the bar took up most of their time these days, but they still had gigs as far afield as Wales and the north of England to play before the year was out. Dave smiled and raised his glass to what could be the start of something.

After the booze got the better of all of them – all but one, that is – they switched to the kind of dirty sing-alongs favoured by sozzled rugby teams. 'Friggin' in the Riggin,' 'Living Next Door to Alice,' and of course the old Eton boating team favourite 'We're All Queers Together.' Then they moved on to shorts.

Dave walked behind the bar and fetched the bottle of Jim Beam and four shot glasses. The others were now several sheets to the wind, and though he took one shot for good measure, he discreetly tossed all his refills on the floor, confident that his friends were too busy toasting to notice.

As Dave had expected, it took about an hour for his friends to reach unconsciousness and slump on his bar. Mick was the last one to go, and he passed out, mumbling something about having bacon and eggs for breakfast. As Mick gave up the ghost, Dave noticed the first rays of sun peeking through the blinds over the dance floor window. It was 6:30 am, and Dave had two-and-a-half-hours to kill and one more thing to do.

Chapter 47

Sorting out the bar took up ten minutes of the two-and-a-half hours Dave had to kill. He cleared up all the empty and half-empty glasses, wiped down the bar and replaced the empty bottle of Jim Beam. He spent another ten minutes putting away the paint tins and brushes and bundling up the tarpaulin sheet that Danny used to avoid cross-contamination between his and Mick's jobs.

Then Dave went out for a run, which took up thirty minutes, and the following shave, shower, and rummaging around bollock-naked for a new set of clothes killed another twenty. He realised he was feeling peckish, so he decided to find a café that would do him a good breakfast. What he was about to do was as scary as it was exhilarating, and he needed a full stomach.

He walked West along the promenade for about twenty minutes, passing Cliff Gardens until he found a café he liked the look of. He chose a table facing out to sea, which was possible thanks to the proprietor opening the patio doors to give his only customer a coastal view. Dave watched fascinated as two brave surfers tried to catch a wave out there in the pale grey dawn.

Mad bastards, he thought.

The owner brought Dave the full English he'd ordered, but Dave found he didn't really fancy it at first. He was apprehensive, and his stomach was turning. He took a few bites but decided it wasn't going to happen. He called the owner over and said something about having had a heavy night last night, and the overweight proprietor shrugged his shoulders and took Dave's breakfast away and ate it himself.

There was a Sunday paper on Dave's table, and he found that drinking coffee and reading an interview with Sir Mick Jagger passed the time and settled his nerves a little.

The fresh sea air did Dave a world of good, and he killed another twenty minutes drinking coffee, reading, and doing his best to relax before he pushed himself to his feet.

Outside, it was grey and rather cold, but there were some gaps in the murky cloud cover. Since his was going to be an important day in the life of David Ian Hunter, he decided to take in places that held good memories for him.

He walked a little way inland and caught a glimpse of the excellent Cliffs Pavilion, where every great performer in the land – minus him, damn it – had once played. One day, he thought.

He stood a hundred yards back, and for a second, he could hear the sweet sound of BB King's Lucille ringing in his ears like it was yesterday. Then Dave looked across the street and caught an awestruck glimpse of the new, two-storey coastal rescue facility. Dave saluted the chopper on the roof of the state-of-the-art-complex and hoped Adders junior and his friend had got away with the impressive stunt they'd pulled off last night.

With a spring in his step, he walked a short way up

Westcliff Ave before turning right onto Cambridge Road. Cambridge Road soon became Scratton Road, and after half-a-mile, Dave found himself standing outside The Railway Hotel.

Dave had played here two-hundred times, man and boy. When he started his Sunday afternoon residency here, aged sixteen, he'd been green around the gills and hungry as hell. By the time he'd finished it, he was a seasoned professional but still hungry. On his last night here, a frail, yet sharp as a tack Lee Brilleaux turned up. The two men were pictured shaking hands, and the last time he'd checked the photo was still up behind the bar.

Dave walked on, with at least one more destination in mind before his date with destiny.

A reflective man by nature, Dave Hunter often wondered if he lived in the past too much. Little did he know, he was compelled to take one last look at the past because this was perhaps about to change.

From here, he zig-zagged his way back towards the seafront, cutting through Cliff Gardens and out onto Western Esplanade. He was directly opposite the pier, and although he passed here every day, it seemed to cut a majestic figure on this fine, albeit somewhat pale morning.

He walked past the club and chuckled as he thought of his friends sleeping off their hangovers.

He carried on walking east, and Western Esplanade became Marine Parade. After two minutes, Marine Parade forked into two separate roads, and he took the one to the left. From there, he came upon the bottom of Southchurch Avenue, and decided to rest awhile. He checked his watch. 8:51. Nine minutes to go. He sat down on the wall outside someone's front garden, and he realised his legs were shaking as were his hands.

It could have been the fact that he hadn't eaten properly in over fourteen hours, but Dave didn't buy that. It could have been that his body clock thought it was strange that Saturday had gone by with only a small intake of units of alcohol. But he didn't accept that idea either.

No. For the first time in his life, the man that certain sections of the press had called 'the hardest man in Essex' was scared. Scared, but exhilarated, and he wasn't backing down. He decided he'd have a fag to kill the last few minutes, but as he slapped his left trouser pocket, he found only an empty space. And while he would usually curse at the prospect of leaving home without his Bensons, he reminded himself that *someone* disapproved of him partaking in the weed.

He pushed himself up to his feet and began the last – or first – part of his journey. After he passed the Kursaal, and the Greek restaurant where he and Lianda had celebrated their second anniversary, he saw the wrought-iron sign overhanging the street.

Rechstein & Sons

Jewellers and Pawnbrokers

Est. 1951

***

A bell chimed above the door, announcing the first customer of the day. Dave walked into the Rechstein family's place of business and was greeted by an aging gent who Dave reckoned must have been the head of the family.

Daddy Rechstein was wearing a long black suit jacket over a white shirt, with black trousers and black leather shoes. He was starting to look his age, and though his beard retained some of its natural black, it was greying in places. His first greeting was silent – he just lifted his cowboy-style hat an inch off his head and smiled at Dave, but as he walked out from behind his counter, he spoke.

"I have been open only one minute, and already I have a customer. I think today is going to be a good day. Shalom," he said with a smile.

"Shalom," said Dave, before getting right to the point. "I know exactly what I want to buy."

Dave had checked that the ring he wanted was still in

the window before going into the shop. Now, he walked over to the window display and pointed to the ring, the one that had caught his attention and fired his imagination several weeks ago.

"I can see you are decisive," said the proprietor. His voice was hoarse with age, but he beamed with wisdom.

"Many a young man come in here, and they are often anguished. You, on the other hand, are sure of yourself. This is a good quality, and the lucky lady you are buying the ring for must admire you for this. And she is a lucky lady – I am as sure of that as I am confident that she will have the wisdom to agree to what you are about to ask of her."

"Thanks," said Dave, who gestured to the ring in question.

"Ah yes," said Rechstein, who moved over to the front window with such gentle grace he could have been floating, pulling his robes behind him as he went. He picked up the ring and made his way back to the counter in an equally graceful fashion.

For the second time in his life, Dave used his credit card. Cash was king to Dave Hunter, but he wasn't the kind of person who carried seven-hundred pounds in used notes with him. He took the ring in its box, refusing Rechstein's offer to gift wrap it for him.

"Well," said the old man. "If nobody else comes in today, then you will be my last customer."

"You're closing up?" said Dave.

"Not closing, but retiring. Let's just say I have begun to feel my age. My sons will inherit the business, and they are two fine young men who deserve a chance to thrive on their own."

"Well," said Dave, "I guess this must be a sad day for you then, chief,"

Rechstein's brow furrowed in surprise as Dave said this.

"Not at all," said the old man. "I still have many things to do before I go to the place in the sky. I am not a young man, this I know, but I am open to new experiences, new challenges, and new sensations. Of course, I have my memories, but as I see it, it is all about looking to the future."

Dave Hunter couldn't have agreed more.

DAVE HUNTER MAY RETURN

Printed in Great Britain
by Amazon

64738107R00277